Sarah was too tired to worry about strange night sounds, though she was getting used to them. Things were becoming familiar here. She knew the tree-covered hills that cradled the meadow in their protective arms, the friendly murmuring of the creek, the dependable positions of the stars overhead, the expected way the moon came up over the cliffs across the creek. . . .

Sarah was asleep long before the moon peeped over the cliffs that night. She didn't even turn over until she was awakened suddenly by Ma's scream.

SARAH'S JOURNEY

HOME ON STONEY CREEK

Wanda Luttrell

ChariotVICTOR
◆ P U B L I S H I N G ◆
A DIVISION OF COOK COMMUNICATIONS

Thanks to Sue Reck, my editor, for her help along this journey.

Chariot Books is an imprint of Chariot Victor Publishing,
a division of Cook Communications, Colorado Springs, Colorado 80918
Cook Communications, Paris, Ontario
Kingsway Communications, Eastbourne, England
HOME ON STONEY CREEK
© 1995 by Wanda Luttrell

Cover design by Mary Schluchter
Cover illustration by Bill Farnsworth
Interior illustrations by John Zielinski

First printing, 1995
Printed in the United States of America
00 99 98 97 96   5 4

Library of Congress Cataloging-in-Publication Data
Luttrell, Wanda
Home on Stoney Creek/by Wanda Luttrell.
p.   cm.
Summary: Eleven-year-old Sarah is upset when her family leaves their home
in Virginia to start a new life in Kentucky at the same time her beloved older
brother goes off to fight with the American rebels against the British.
ISBN 0-7814-0901-2
[1. Frontier and pioneer life—Kentucky—Fiction. 2. Kentucky—Fiction. 3.
Christian life—Fiction.] I. Title.
PZ7.L97954Ho   1994
[Fic]—dc20   93-47084
                                                      CIP
                                                       AC

Contents

For my son,
John Bradley Luttrell,
who makes my journey through life
an adventure.

Sarah sat up in bed and pushed back the feather quilt. She didn't know what had awakened her. The house was so quiet now, she could hear the clock ticking on the mantel in the parlor below.

A quick glance around the familiar room showed nothing out of the ordinary. The moonlight fell coldly through the small window panes, making squares across the polished wooden floor. Sarah shivered. The heat from the rooms below, her long flannel gown, and the thick feather quilt had been enough to keep her warm these late April nights without a fire in the fireplace. It was chilly in the room now, though, and she snuggled back under the covers.

"There's nothing so cozy as a thick, soft feather bed under a quilt stuffed with goose feathers," she murmured drowsily.

Suddenly, the thought that never again would she sleep in this bed, in this room, in this house, made her sit straight up once more. When daylight came, they were leaving this beloved Virginia farm for the unknown wilds of Kentucky. Sarah's heart sank to the bottom of her stomach and lay there like a lump of cold oatmeal.

"Nate, you've not got the sense God gave a goose!" Pa's shouted words came straight out of the fireplace.

Nate was home!

"Shhh! You'll wake the children, Hiram!" Sarah heard Ma warn. Then the voices became a soft rumble, like the honeybees inside the beehives, and she couldn't understand the words.

Sarah couldn't wait to see Nate! But why was Pa so angry with him? Her oldest brother was the one Ma and Pa seemed to think could do no wrong. Nate worked hard. He was neat, Ma often said, frowning at Sarah's blotted and squiggly letters. He went to church without complaining about the hard benches or the long sermons. He went to the well and the woodpile without being asked, Pa pointed out to Luke as he sat whittling on the last piece of wood from the wood box.

"Nathan's so good, I expect him to sprout wings and fly off to heaven any minute!" Luke had muttered once. But Sarah believed Nate was all the things Ma and Pa said he was. And he was a good brother. He didn't tease her about her freckles and her green cat's eyes, like Luke did, and he didn't pull her long brown braids. Little Jamie was fun to play with, but Nate always knew just what to say to make her feel better when one of the kittens died or when she had a falling out with her best friend, Martha.

I reckon I love Nate better than anybody in the whole colony of Virginia! Sarah thought as she eased out of the feather bed. She tried not to rustle the corn shuck mattress underneath or creak the tall wooden bedstead.

She tiptoed over to the black, empty fireplace and crouched down on the hearth. She placed her ear close to the opening to catch the words as they floated right up the chimney from the room below.

". . . not a square mile in all England without its own representative in Parliament to help make the laws they live under!" Nate was saying. "But the American colonies are not allowed to send even one representative to Parliament, no matter how much we pay in taxes."

"Maybe we need to send somebody to talk to King George. . . ." Pa began.

"King George dances to Parliament's tune like a puppet on a string," Nate answered bitterly. "The king's soldiers accuse us of crimes we haven't committed so they can take away our possessions. Colonists are ordered to house and feed the redcoats, and aren't paid for it, even though they treat us little better than dogs in the streets. Now Parliament says the Catholic religion is the only religion to be allowed in the western lands, and . . ."

"Surely you're mistaken, Nate!" Pa gasped. "Freedom to worship God in our own way was one of the reasons we came to America."

"I'm not mistaken, Pa. Parliament plans to set up a new group of colonies west of the mountains who will do exactly as they say. Then they will have the eastern colonies right where they want us. I tell you, before long we won't be allowed to breathe without permission from the king's governor, and then we'll have to pay a tax on it!"

Sarah giggled before she could stop herself.

"That sounds like more nonsense from that ragtaggle bunch of rebels you've befriended," Pa said. "I wouldn't have sold off my best forty acres to send you to school in Williamsburg if I'd thought you'd be hobnobbing with ignoramuses! A handful of ragged colonists can't whip the strongest, best-trained army in the world! England will put down this upstart rebellion in a matter of days, and those who took part in it will be shot or hanged for treason!"

Treason! Sarah felt the ugly word shiver down her spine.

"Pa," Nate said quietly, "I believe with all my heart that God is leading these colonies to independence. If God be for us, the size of England's army won't make any more difference than did the size of the giant Goliath when God helped little David hit him between the eyes with a rock."

Sarah strained to hear Pa's answer to Nate's bold statement, but there didn't seem to be any. Finally, Nate said, "I believe God is leading me to join the fight for the

12

freedom of the American colonies."

"Oh, Nathan, no!" Ma gasped.

"Son, wait!" Pa's voice was pleading. Sarah had never heard Pa plead with anybody. "Come to Kentucky with us. We can make a new life there, a good life free of all this turmoil."

"I tell you, we will never be free until we cut ourselves loose from England," Nate insisted. "It may be that I will get to that new place in Kentucky someday. But, whatever happens, God go with you."

"And with you," Ma answered with a catch in her voice.

Sarah listened to her brother's footsteps crossing the floor and to the quiet but final closing of the door behind him. Suddenly she was running—down the back stairs, out the kitchen door, down the path to the road—holding her nightgown out of the way of her flying bare feet.

"Nate! Nate!" she called. "Wait! Please wait for me!"

Nate leaned his gun against the fence and waited by the gate. Then he swung her up in his strong arms. "I wanted to say good-bye, little sister," he said, "but I didn't want to wake you up in the middle of the night when you've got such a long journey ahead of you tomorrow."

"I don't want to go to Kentucky!" Sarah cried. "And I don't want you to go to war! Nate, you might be killed!" Tears flooded her eyes and spilled down her cheeks.

"There's a fresh new wind of freedom blowing through these colonies, Sarah," he said, wiping her tears away with his hand. "And, as surely as Moses heard God's voice in the burning bush, I hear Him calling me in that wind to take my place in the fight for freedom."

"Then let me go with you!" she begged. "I want to stay in Virginia. I want to feel that new wind on my face."

Nate laughed and hugged her close, then set her down on her feet.

"That's God's wind, Sarah, and it will reach every corner of this land, even into Kentucky. It has a special call from God for everyone. Someday it will call your name. . . ."

She threw her arms around her brother's waist. "I can't leave this place, Nate!" she said desperately. "I've lived here all my life, in this same house for eleven years!"

"I was born here too, and lived here nearly seventeen years. But God has a purpose for each of us, Sarah, and sometimes it takes us far from home."

"But surely God's purpose for me is something better than to go to that heathen wilderness Pa's so set on taking us to!"

Nate ruffled her hair where it had pulled loose from her braids. "Your purpose right now, little sister, is to obey your mother and father. But someday, God willing, I will come for you. I don't want you to grow up ignorant in the backwoods. Aunt Charity has a tutor for her girls. I'm sure she would be glad to have you join them. You'd love Williamsburg, Sarah!"

"I love you, Nate," she whispered past the lump in her throat.

"And I love you, sweet little sister. Be a good girl, and remember, I will come for you when I can."

Nate picked up his gun, walked through the gate, shut it behind him, and strode quickly down the road. At the bend, he turned and waved. Sarah waved back, and let the tears run unheeded down her cheeks and drop off her chin. Then Nate walked into the deep shadows under the trees and was swallowed by the blackness.

Sarah's bare feet and the hem of her skirt were wet with dew from the long meadow grass, and she could barely see for the tears that filled her eyes. They ran down her face, and fell onto the gray-striped fur of the cat she held tightly in her arms.

Instinctively, her feet followed the cold, damp path through the woods, along the shortcut she always took to Martha's house. Any other time, she would have stopped to pick a bouquet of dainty bluebells, purple sweet Williams, and little yellow and white flowers that grew along the path. Today, they only reminded her that this was the last time she would see them beckoning from every sun-dappled spot. This was the last time she would walk this path to her best friend's house.

She brushed away the tears and wiped her face on Tiger's soft fur, recalling that dreadful evening a year ago when Daniel Boone and his friends had stopped by the farm and convinced Pa he should follow them to Kentucky. "We never got to the bluegrass region when you went with us before," Mr. Boone had said, as he drew Pa a rough map. "It's a rich, rolling land—a paradise on earth!"

Sarah had her doubts about that, but ever since that terrible night, Pa had talked about little else. She had prayed that Pa would change his mind, but God had not answered her prayers, she thought bitterly. Pa had sold their farm. They were going to Kentucky, and there was nothing she could do about it.

Her brother was as excited about it as Pa was, acting more like a four year old than a fourteen year old. Luke didn't care where he lived, so long as he had his carving knife in his pocket and his big black-and-tan hound dog at his heels. Pa was letting Luke take Hunter. Sarah understood that the dog would help keep the cow and calf and the two pigs from straying off the trail, and he could warn them of prowling Indians or wild animals at night. She was glad they were taking Hunter. It just didn't seem fair that she had to leave Tiger behind.

Sarah sank down on a fallen log at the edge of the woods, put the cat across her lap, and stroked his fur. Tiger closed his eyes and began to purr contentedly, unaware that Pa had said his legs were too short and he was too old to keep up on the long, hard journey to Kentucky, not realizing that Sarah was delivering him to his new family.

She held up the big cat so she could look into his ringed yellow-green eyes, and he stared back at her with solemn dignity. She put her head against his. "Oh, Tiger," she choked, "I wish I could take you with me!"

"He will have a good home with the Hutchinsons," Ma

16

had tried to comfort her. And Sarah knew she was right. It was just that ever since she had found him snuggled up against the old mother cat, before he even had his eyes open, Tiger had been her special pet. She just couldn't bear to give him up. And she knew Tiger didn't want a new home any more than she did. She had taken him over to Martha's twice already, and he had come back home.

Lovingly, she traced a streak of sunlight across the cat's gray fur. Suddenly she jumped up. The sun was climbing. She had sat here too long! Ma had cautioned her to hurry. Pa wanted to get an early start before the sun got too hot, and he would be angry if she dallied.

Sarah hurried down the path and burst out of the woods in front of the Hutchinson's sprawling white house.

I can't stand to say good-bye to Martha and *Tiger!* Sarah thought desperately. Then she blinked away the tears and swallowed the lump in her throat. It would be best to get it over with as quickly as possible, she decided, and knocked at the kitchen door.

Martha opened the door and looked out. Her brown eyes grew wide as she saw Sarah and Tiger. Then she burst into tears.

Sarah handed Martha the cat, hugged them both, and, a sob catching in her throat, fled back down the path to the woods. She couldn't resist looking back, though, just before the path went into the trees.

Martha stood on her doorstep, holding Tiger. She waved a lonesome little wave, and Sarah waved back. Tiger struggled to get down. Sarah plunged blindly down the path, her sobs muffled by the thick silence of the woods.

"Come on, slowpoke!" Luke yelled when he saw her coming across the meadow behind the house. "Pa's got everything loaded on Bess and Willie—even the chickens and the geese!"

Sarah stopped and wiped her eyes with the hem of her skirt. She wasn't in the mood to hear Luke call her a crybaby.

"Hurry up, Sary girl!" Pa called as she came around the house. "We're leaving, soon as I get this load secured under these deerskins."

Pa couldn't load one more thing on either of those horses! Sarah thought, looking at the crates, kettles, and odd-shaped bundles piled on the horses' broad backs. She could see the spindles from Ma's spinning wheel sticking out from one bundle, and Pa's ax handle poking up from another.

"I've got to get Samantha and my shoes!" she called back. She ran into the house, pulled on her stockings and shoes, grabbed her rag doll by one arm, and ran out again.

Sarah stopped halfway down the stepping stones to the front gate, and looked back at the dear little brick house with its neat flower-bordered paths, saying a silent good-bye. She felt tears stinging her eyes again and turned away, only to catch Ma blinking away tears of her own.

Ma had tried to make it sound like a good thing, this leaving home. "The farm land here is getting as scarce as hen's teeth, and ours is about worn out," she had said. "We can claim hundreds of acres of rich land in Kentucky just by clearing the trees and building a cabin."

Now, as Ma quickly bent to rearrange a pile of things lying on her gray woolen shawl, Sarah suspected that Ma didn't want to go any more than she did, that her cheerful words as she gave Aunt Charity her flowered china and Aunt Rose her harpsichord were all a pretense.

As Ma tied the corners of the shawl so that it formed a pack, Sarah glimpsed several small cloth bundles that held garden seeds, and under them the clock from the parlor mantel, wrapped in Ma's white Sunday shawl.

"Make sure my feather quilts are covered by those deerskins, Hiram," Ma called. "If it rains, we'll be glad of dry covers!"

Pa tucked in the corner of a quilt, then gathered the family together for a sending-off prayer.

"Oh, Lord," Pa began, "as you led the Israelites through the wilderness to their promised land, lead us safely to ours. We ask it in the name of our Savior, Amen."

Sarah bowed her head, but she didn't pray. She had prayed that they would not leave home, and they were going anyway.

"Let's go!" Pa yelled, slapping the reins across old Willie's back.

"Giddap!" Luke called to old Bess.

"Please carry Jamie a while, Sarah," Ma said. "I'll take him when you get tired." She picked up the shawl bundle and started down the trail behind Pa and Luke.

Jamie gave Sarah a grin that showed his six teeth, and held up his little arms. Sarah picked him up and settled him astraddle one hip. Her baby brother was getting heavy now that he was a year and a half old, but she knew his legs were too short to keep up . . . just like Tiger's. If only he would come yelling, "Meow! Meow!" as he always did when he thought she was going somewhere without him. If only she could pick him up, like Jamie, and carry him with her!

Sarah threw one last look back at the brick house nestled among its green fields and orchards, with the barns and outbuildings behind it. Again, she blinked away tears, and she started reluctantly down the trail behind Ma.

"Hossie! Hossie! Gid'up!" Jamie cried happily, enjoying his ride on Sarah's hip.

Sarah knew the baby did not understand that they were leaving their home and would not be coming back. Would he even remember their cozy house here near Miller's Forks, Virginia? Would any of them ever see it again?

"I will!" she vowed fiercely to herself. "Someday, I'm coming back home!"

By the time the sun was straight overhead, Sarah's legs and feet were sore, and her back and arms ached from carrying either Jamie or Ma's shawl-wrapped bundle. She looked ahead at Pa and Luke leading the horses. Behind her, she could hear the soft, lowing murmur of the cow to her calf and the pigs' grunting complaints, with now and then a squeal as Hunter nipped at their legs to keep them from straying.

Jamie had fallen asleep and was a dead weight against her shoulder. Carefully, she shifted him to the other arm. She sighed. "Ma, I know this road is wide enough for a wagon and not all that rough, either."

Ma smiled at her sympathetically. "I'm tired too, child," she admitted, "but your pa says the wilderness road farther on is barely wide enough for a horse and pack, and taking time to clear it for a wagon would slow us down considerably."

★ Home on Stoney Creek ★

"Here's a spring of water," Pa called back to them. "Della, hand out some of those ham biscuits I saw you packing this morning. We'll eat here and rest a spell."

Ma opened her bundle. She pulled out the white shawl and spread it out for Sarah to lay Jamie on. Then she unwrapped one of the tea cloths and passed around cold brown biscuits with ham hanging out on all sides.

Sarah felt her stomach roll with hunger. She could hardly wait for Pa to ask God's blessing. She ate her biscuit on the way to a big rock she had spotted near the stream. Then, taking off her shoes and stockings, she paddled her hot, tired feet in the icy water of the stream. When Pa said it was time to move on, her feet were nearly numb with cold, and it felt good to pull on her heavy stockings and shoes.

Before long, though, her feet burned again inside her shoes. She forced herself to concentrate on placing one aching leg before the other, mindlessly following Ma, Pa, and Luke, carrying first Jamie, then the shawl.

When the sun began to sink behind the hills in front of them, and Pa finally stopped beside a clear, sparkling creek, Sarah didn't know which she wanted more—rest or food!

Looking back down the trail, Sarah wondered how many miles they had walked since they left the farm that morning. The image of the brick house nestled in its green valley among the hills crept into her mind, but she pushed it away and turned to watch Luke make a circle of stones to hold their campfire.

"Here, Sarah," Ma said, handing her a small bag of corn, "go feed the chickens and geese and give them some water."

"Wa-wa!" Jamie repeated bossily, waving one hand toward the creek as Ma had done.

★ Chapter Three ★

"Fill this kettle with water for your Ma, Luke," Sarah heard Pa order. "Then while supper's cooking, you can feed and water the animals, and I'll cut some boughs for beds. That ground's harder than old Jeb Hawkins's heart!"

Sarah giggled as she poked corn through the slots of the crates, remembering Jeb Hawkins and his threats to horsewhip any "young 'uns" he caught on his farm. He was convinced that every boy and girl in Miller's Forks was after his apples or his melons. A wave of homesickness swept over her, and then Sarah had to laugh at herself. She was even homesick for old Jeb Hawkins!

As she got back to the fire, Sarah could smell Ma's supper. She peeked in the kettle at the chunks of meat and potatoes dancing in the boiling water. Her mouth watered and her empty stomach rolled.

Sarah looked down toward the creek where Luke was hobbling the legs of the horses and the cows with rawhide strips. When they were hobbled, they could graze on the tender grasses that grew near the creek without straying from camp. She was glad the little calf was being left free to kick up her heels and run. She wouldn't go far from her mother.

"Leave the pigs free to forage for food, Luke!" Pa called. "They're not apt to leave the acorns under these oaks for the slim pickings in the pines above us, and the creek will keep them from straying in the other direction."

"Sarah, I need your help. Supper's ready," Ma said.

Sarah took the tin plate Ma handed her and mashed some potatoes and meat for Jamie.

"Bicket?" Jamie begged, wriggling his fingers toward the warm bread Ma had just taken from the fire. "Bicket? Jeddy?"

Sarah broke off a small piece of biscuit, and Jamie opened his mouth wide, like a little bird waiting to be fed. She poked the bread into his mouth. "You'll have to do without jelly tonight, sweets," she apologized, placing the rest of the biscuit in his hand.

Sarah saw Luke reaching for another biscuit. She had lost count of how many he'd had. Quickly, she filled a tin plate with food for herself and piled two biscuits on top before Luke could eat them all. She set the plate down nearby, then washed off Jamie, dressed him in his night shirt, and laid him on a pile of spicy-smelling pine boughs Pa had covered with one of the deerskins. She threw one of the feather quilts over him.

Jamie patted the space beside him. "Seep, Sadie!" he said.

Sarah laughed and dropped a kiss on his bright yellow hair. "Jamie sleep," she said firmly, reaching for her plate. "I'll come to bed after I've had my supper!"

Luke sopped his plate with the last piece of biscuit, popped it into his mouth, and stood up. "That was good!" he said. "I was hungry enough to eat a whole cow fried in gravy!" He stretched, walked over to the second pile of pine branches, and lay down, pulling the other feather quilt over himself. In no time, Sarah heard his deep, even breathing and knew he was sleeping as soundly as their baby brother.

Sarah looked at Ma and Pa sitting by the fire talking. Then she looked at the lumpy pine bough beds Pa had fixed. No matter how uncomfortable the makeshift bed might be, it would feel good just to stretch out and rest. She lay down beside Jamie and pulled the feather quilt around both of them.

24

"Miller's Forks, Virginia, was a nice place to live," she heard Ma say wistfully. "I wonder if we'll ever have neighbors as nice as the Hutchinsons or the Carvers. If we'll have a church to go to with our friends. And if we'll ever be able to shop at a store or go to the blacksmith or the miller again."

"Of course we will!" Pa assured her. "We'll have all those things in Kentucky, Della. Someday. It'll just take a little time, that's all."

Sarah wasn't sleepy now. She lay awake on the lumpy pine boughs, remembering her cozy, comfortable bed under the eaves of the brick house. Would she ever feel at home again anywhere? How long would it be before Nate came for her? How long before she saw Miller's Forks and her dear little house again? A tear slid out of the corner of her eye, rolled down her face, and dripped into her ear. She brushed it away, but another followed.

Desperately, she started to count the stars shining in the deep blue night sky. She spotted Ursa, the big bear; the little dipper; and the Hunter with Sirius, the Dog Star, following at his heels. But seeing the Hunter only reminded her of Luke's dog Hunter, and how Tiger enjoyed teasing the dog. The cat would frisk up a tree, leaving Hunter on the ground having a fit because he couldn't catch him.

Sarah hoped Martha's Pa's hounds wouldn't hurt Tiger. She hoped Martha would scratch him on the white spot under his chin where he liked to be scratched. She wanted Tiger to be happy, but she hoped he would miss her just a little. She surely did miss him!

"Will we be in much danger from Indians, Hiram?" she heard Ma ask.

★ Home on Stoney Creek ★

"Well, there's all kinds of Indians," Pa hedged. "You know, Boone has made friends with some of them."

"But I heard you and Mr. Boone talking that night, Hi," Ma broke in, "after the children and I had gone to bed. You said the Indians don't want settlers coming into Kentucky. They burn their cabins, carry them off as captives, even kill them."

Pa reached for another log and threw it on the fire. As the flames leaped up, Sarah remembered Pa saying a fire scared off wolves and mountain lions. She guessed there was more danger here from wild animals than from Indians who might see the fire and attack.

"Those things have happened in Virginia, too, in isolated places," Pa replied. "There are forts in Kentucky now for protection from the Indians. The men ride around and warn folks to go into the forts when Indian attack is expected."

"Will we settle near one of the forts, Hiram?" Ma asked hopefully.

"I aim on settling near the Kentucky River in the blue-grass region," Pa said. "They say the land there's as rich as one of your custard pies!"

Ma didn't respond to Pa's flattery, and he went on. "Boone's fort is on the river, not too far from where we're headed, but I reckon we'll be a mite closer to James Harrod's settlement. And then Ben Logan has a small new fort about twenty or twenty-five miles this side of Harrodstown."

"How far will we be from Harrodstown?" Ma asked quietly. Sarah wondered if Ma were thinking the same thing she was: How long would it take them to get into the fort if Indians came?

★ Chapter Three ★

"Oh, we'll be just a hop, skip, and jump from the fort. Harrodstown ought to be growing into a real little town," Pa changed the subject. "It's the oldest settlement in Kentucky, all of a year old by now, I reckon," he added with a chuckle.

Ma didn't join in his laughter. "Why don't we just live in one of the forts, Hiram?" she suggested.

"You'd hate being cramped up in one of those pitiful little cabins all crowded up against one another!" Pa said. Sarah saw him reach over and pat Ma on the shoulder. "Don't you worry, Della," he said. "God will take care of us. And we likely won't see an Indian for weeks. . . ."

Hunter's low growl cut off Pa's words. Then the dog began to bark furiously, running first to Luke, then to Pa, then into the woods.

"Whatsa matter, boy?" Luke murmured sleepily, sitting up and rubbing his eyes.

Suddenly, a blood-curdling squeal erupted from the woods behind them. Sarah sat straight up, her heart pounding.

"The pigs!" Pa exclaimed. He grabbed his gun and disappeared into the woods after Hunter. Sarah heard some crashing around, more squeals, some strange grunts, and then, farther up the mountain, one last squeal that ended abruptly.

Jamie sat up and began to cry. Sarah picked him up and hugged him close, listening to someone—or something—crashing through the woods toward them. She threw Ma a frightened glance over Jamie's shoulder.

"That's your Pa coming back," Ma said reassuringly, but Sarah saw her take a stick from the fire and hold it in both hands, the flames glowing bravely in the dark night. She didn't throw it back into the fire until Pa appeared at the edge of the circle of light.

"What was it, Pa?" Sarah asked.

Pa sat back down beside the fire. "It was so black in there I couldn't see my hand before me," he answered, "but I reckon it was a bear. Whatever it was, it was mighty big—big enough to carry off . . ."

". . . one of my pigs!" Ma finished angrily. "I wish I could get my hands on him!"

Pa began to laugh, quietly at first, then aloud. Luke joined him, whooping and rolling on the ground. Sarah saw Ma glaring at them. She didn't see anything funny about it either.

"What's so funny? We've lost a pig, and we only had two!" she reminded them.

"I know," Pa said, trying to stop the laughter that shook his whole body now. "I just keep imagining you ahold of that bear! What would you do with it, Della? A three or four hundred pound bear?"

Ma still glared at him. "Well, I'd . . . I'd . . . make him wish he'd never had a pig for supper!" she said hotly. She turned her back on them, walked over to the last pile of pine boughs, and lay down, pulling the cover all the way over her ears.

Chuckling a little herself, Sarah put Jamie down and lay down beside him. The night air held a distinct chill now, and she snuggled close to his warm little body, tucking the quilt tightly around them both.

Off in the woods, she heard a whippoorwill call. There had been a little brown whippoorwill that sat in the walnut tree under her window back home. "Whip-poor-will! Whip-poor-will!" he would call. Sarah always wondered if his name was Will and he was trying to tell her someone had whipped him. She had thought he was funny. Tonight, however, the whippoorwill sounded lonely and sad, and he reminded her of home.

It had been a long, hard day, and Sarah could feel herself sinking into sleep in spite of her makeshift bed and the night sounds around her. She didn't stir until Ma called her to help fix breakfast.

By the time the first rays of morning sun peeped over the hills behind them, they were on the trail. *Minus one pig!* Sarah thought, as she forced her aching muscles back into the rhythm of keeping up with Pa's long strides. What else would they have to give up before they saw civilization again? Or would they ever again see anything but wilderness?

It was amazing how quickly they settled into the routine of making camp at sunset and moving on at daybreak. Pa was determined to cover as many miles as possible between what he called "rooster crow and whippoorwill call."

They were enjoying good traveling weather, and Pa said they were making good time. For several miles, the strain in the backs of her legs had told Sarah the road was rising.

"See that gap in the mountains up there?" Pa called. "That's the gateway to Kentucky!"

Sarah squinted her eyes and looked up, up, up—to where a slice seemed to have been cut out of the tree-covered mountain. Boone's map showed that the Indian trail they were following led right over the mountain, but as they climbed the steep mountainside, to Sarah it looked as though the gap disappeared.

Finally, late that afternoon, Pa called out, "There she is! Kentucky! Paradise!"

"Hoorah!" Luke shouted.

Sarah hurried to where Luke and Pa stood on a flat ridge, looking down the other side of the mountain. Below them were the rolling, tree-covered hills of the new land. Sarah gazed out over the treetops. She wasn't sure what paradise should look like, but if that was it, she was disappointed. She couldn't see all that much difference from the Virginia side of the mountain.

Sarah caught her breath as a fresh wave of homesickness swept over her. Miller's Forks wasn't paradise, either, but it had been a nice place to live. It was home. Not anymore, though. When they got to their new land, Kentucky would be home.

"No, it won't," Sarah vowed aloud. Right now, as Nate had said, she was a child and had to obey her parents, but someday she would be grown up and could live where she pleased. And Virginia was where she pleased! She reckoned a body never had but one place that really was home.

"I'll just be a visitor in Kentucky until I'm old enough to go back home," she promised herself as she followed Pa and Luke over the gap.

"There's not enough blue in the sky right now to make a boy a pair of breeches!" Pa said as they started down the other side of the mountain. "We'd best find shelter before the rain starts."

As they continued walking, the rain began to fall. In no time, the trail was slippery, and Sarah's heavy skirt and the shawl she had thrown over Jamie and herself were soaked. He laid his head on her shoulder and whimpered softly. She could feel his small body trembling with cold.

★ Chapter Four ★

Pa came back and took Jamie from her. "It's hard to keep your footing in this mud. I'll carry him awhile," he said, wrapping his coat around the baby.

Sarah plodded along behind them, but soon Pa's long strides carried them out of sight around a bend in the trail. She turned to look back at Ma, who looked as miserable as Sarah felt. Her hair straggled down from its usual neat tuck, and her soggy dress was smeared with mud around the hem. Ma smiled wearily and waved Sarah on.

Sarah fastened her eyes on the trail ahead and concentrated on placing one wet, tired foot before the other. By the time she looked up and saw that Pa had stopped the horses and was waiting for her and Ma, Sarah had gone beyond a teeth-chattering chill to a cold numbness that dulled her senses. She had given up hope of ever being warm and dry again.

"We'll camp here for the night," Pa said when she and Ma finally reached hearing distance. "This rock ledge will give us some shelter from the rain."

Sarah's gaze swept over a long, narrow, three-sided room nature had cut into the rock of the mountainside. The rain had filled a nearby spring to overflowing so that it poured off the ledge, down over the open side of the shelter like a silver curtain. Inside, though, the little room looked dry and cozy. Eagerly, Sarah stooped to enter it.

"Wait a minute, Sary," Pa warned. He handed Jamie to her, picked up a stout stick, and began to beat and sweep the dead leaves that had piled up in the shelter during the winter. He turned over every loose rock with his foot, holding the stick ready in one hand.

"Copperheads like the rock ledges, too," he explained. "They're poison, and they know it! They won't run from the devil himself!"

"Sarah never waits around long enough to see if a snake runs from her," Luke teased. "She's too busy running from the snake!"

Sarah shivered. "I don't like snakes, and I don't care who knows it!" She was glad Pa had made sure there weren't any in their shelter.

The little rock room was soon warm and glowing as Pa got a fire going from some dry wood he found under the ledge. Hunter shook the water out of his fur and plopped down beside the fire with a contented grunt. Sarah longed to do the same as she stood trying to warm her hands and Jamie's by the flickering flames.

When Pa and Luke left to take care of the animals, Ma handed Sarah one of the quilts that had been kept dry under the deerskins. "You and Jamie get into your dry

clothes and wrap up in this," she said. "I'll dry your wettest
things here by the fire."

Sarah didn't argue. Even her underwear was soaked!
She wrapped herself up in the quilt with Jamie, and by the
time Luke and Pa came back with a bowl of milk from the
cow, they were both warm and drowsy. Sarah looked down
at Jamie. His blond eyelashes drooped. Before Ma would
finish their supper, he would be asleep.

"Ma!" Sarah called, indicating the drowsy baby with her
eyes. Ma smiled. She crumbled some left-over corn bread
into the warm milk and handed the bowl to Sarah with a
spoon to feed the baby.

I am so hungry, I could eat this myself, Sarah thought,
inhaling the tantalizing smell of Ma's supper cooking. Soon
the hot food would warm her inside as the fire chased away
the chill outside.

Sarah went to sleep easily that night, listening to the
cold rain fall beyond the shelter of their cozy rock house.

W hat's that noise?" Sarah asked as she woke the next morning.

"Boone's map shows a river down there," Pa answered, refolding the drawing and putting it in an inside pocket of his coat. "I reckon we're getting close to . . ." Then he grinned that mischievous grin, and his deep-blue Irish eyes sparkled as he turned to packing their things on the horses. "It'll take us a little out of our way, but I want you all to see something you've never seen the likes of before," he said mysteriously.

The rain had stopped, and as soon as they got all their things packed on the horses, the family set out on the trail once more.

That river must be mighty big to make a noise like that! Sarah thought, as she side-stepped yet another spring that tumbled down the mountainside right across their path. The farther down they went, the louder the roaring grew.

37

★ Home on Stoney Creek ★

As they came out of the forest onto the riverbank, Sarah caught her breath in amazement. In front of them, the water dropped into a wide, deep pool from a ledge higher than the tallest tree on the hills around them. She could feel the spray from its roaring cascade even as she stood on the rocks above it! And the force of the water stirred the pool below into a foamy froth that reminded her of the soapsuds Ma emptied from the washtub when she had finished her washing.

Pa took out Boone's map again and studied it. "We need to cross this river somewhere around here," he said.

Sarah looked at the tons of murky, brownish water racing past them, shooting up in small geysers when it hit outcroppings of rock, swirling into giddy whirlpools before it moved swiftly on downstream. How did Pa think they could cross that angry water?

"Why, not even Bess and Willie could keep their footing in that flood, Hiram!" Ma exclaimed.

"No, we can't cross it here," Pa agreed quickly, "and probably not anywhere else right now. We'll set up camp near here and let the river run down some before we try to make a crossing. Tomorrow's Sunday, anyway. We'll take a day off for worship and rest."

Sarah let out her breath in relief, glad they weren't going to try to cross that raging torrent, and glad for a chance to rest while the river ran down. She wondered how long it would take.

They made camp under a huge white-trunked sycamore tree still in sight of the falls, but Sarah was grateful to find that its roar was not quite as deafening here. At least they could hear each other talk!

Sarah looked around the hills that encircled the little

valley. Dark green cedars pointed straight to the sky, redbuds had tiny pink blossoms all along their gray limbs, and twisted dogwoods scattered clouds of white bloom among the darker trees.

Suddenly, as she watched Ma brush off a rock to use for a table, Sarah could see the snowy white cloth of the supper table back home, with a bouquet of flowers right in the middle, and the pretty china dishes. . . . She choked back threatening tears, snatched a tin mug from the utensil pack, and filled it with redbud branches mixed with a spray of white dogwood blossoms.

"La-de-dah!" Luke teased as she set the bouquet in the middle of the rock, but Ma gave her a special smile Sarah hadn't seen for a long while now.

Pa took one look at the flowers and slapped his hand to his forehead. "I clean forgot about Easter," he said. "We don't rightly know when it is, but tomorrow's as good a time as any to celebrate the resurrection of our Lord."

Sarah exchanged a puzzled glance with Luke. "What made you think of Easter, Pa?" she asked.

"Why, those dogwood flowers," Pa replied. "Haven't I told you the legend of the dogwood tree?"

Sarah shook her head no, and Luke said, "I don't think so, Pa."

"Why, those twisted dogwood trees once stood as tall and straight as any tree in the woods," Pa began in that lilting Irish voice that meant a story was on its way. "Carpenters prized them for their wood and made beautiful things out of them." His voice fell to a whisper. "Then, one terrible Friday, a huge rough cross made of dogwood was used by wicked men to crucify the Son of God!" Pa looked at them so sternly that Sarah felt a quick stab of guilt, even though she wasn't even alive that Friday long ago.

"Of course," Pa went on, "it was all a part of God's plan. Ever since Adam and Eve, man has sinned and willfully separated himself from the Creator. But the Bible says, 'The Father sent the Son to be the Savior of the world.' Jesus was willing to die on the cross so that all who believe He took the punishment for their sins can become a part of God's family.

"But the Roman soldiers and the Jews who asked the Romans to kill Jesus didn't know that," Pa went back to his story. "They simply followed the orders Satan whispered in their ears: 'Get rid of Jesus!' "

Sarah shivered, and goose bumps popped up on her arms. She hugged herself and rubbed them away as Pa continued.

"The dogwood trees, the story goes, felt so ashamed that one of them had been used to kill their Creator that God promised them they would never be used for such a thing again. From that day to this, the dogwoods grow too twisted and stunted to be used for anything. And if you look closely, the petals form the shape of a cross with blood-stained nail holes, to remind the world that the Son of God was nailed to a cross to take away our sins."

Sarah bent and traced the creamy petals with one finger. They were cross-shaped, and at the tip of each petal was a brown-stained hole. Was the dogwood story true? Or was it just more of Pa's Irish blarney, like that blue grass he kept telling them Kentucky had. So far, all the grass Sarah had seen here was as green as the grass back home.

If Pa's story were true, though, and God cared enough about a tree's shame to grant its wish, why hadn't He cared enough to answer her prayers to stay in Virginia? Why had

★ Chapter Five ★

He made her leave her home to come to this forsaken wilderness?

Ma said everybody has trials and tribulations in this life and some kind of a cross to bear. Maybe Kentucky was her cross "for a season," until she could go back home.

"Someday, I'm going back!" Sarah repeated her vow. She lived on Nate's promise that he would come for her. But even if he didn't, somehow, she would find a way!

Pa discovered a shallows a short distance from the falls, and Monday morning found the family preparing to cross the river. Pa packed the usual things on Willie, but he left Bess' broad back free.

"Ride Willie on across, Luke," he ordered. "Della, you, Sary, and the baby get up here on Bess, and I'll lead you across the river, high and dry!"

Sarah held her breath as Bess carried them through the water, her hooves stumbling over stones and sliding on the slick rock of the riverbed. She got them safely across, though. And, except for Pa, who had waded across beside them and was wet nearly to his waist, they were high and dry.

Sarah waited while Ma dismounted, then handed Jamie down to her. She slid down after him. Pa mounted the horse and rode back across the river after the rest of their things. When he had loaded it all on Bess, he made the crossing one last time, then they were back on the trail.

The trail led them across a wide river bottom of level ground, turned north, and left what Boone's map called "the Cumberlands" behind.

"Why is the trail so wide and smooth all of a sudden?" Sarah called to Pa late that evening. "We could take a wagon through here!"

Pa pointed to the packed earth beneath their feet, and Sarah's eyes widened as she saw the thousands of animal tracks embedded in the dried mud. "Buffalo," Pa explained, "on their way to a salt lick, or I miss my guess."

True to Pa's word, soon they came upon the salt lick. Pa pointed out the tracks of deer, elk, and other animals that had come, like the buffalo, to lick the salty banks of a shallow river. He let their cattle and horses have a few licks before he made them move on across the river and up the bank to a spring of fresh water.

"That salt may taste good right now, ladies and gentlemen," Pa said to the animals, "but before long you'll be wanting a drink of fresh water. Just watching you lick it has made me want a drink!" he added, kneeling to drink thirstily from the spring.

As they set up camp, Sarah's eyes kept straying to the salt licks. At dusk, just before the first stars came out, she saw three deer come to lick the riverbank. Later, along the stream, she could see the eyes of smaller animals glowing in the dark, but there were no buffalo. *I would like to see one of those strange creatures*, Sarah thought as she settled down to sleep, *but at least I don't have to worry about buffalo trampling right over my bed!*

Early the next morning, Sarah was awakened by a

terrible snorting and blowing, like a thousand cows or horses had surrounded them during the night. She looked toward the river and gasped. Dozens of shaggy brown beasts had taken over the salt licks.

"It's a herd of buffalo!" Luke yelled excitedly. "Shoot one, Pa!"

Pa laughed. "We'll get us a buffalo when we get where we're going and can salt down the meat and cure the hide, Luke. It would be a sin to waste as much as we'd have to out here."

Sarah looked at the buffalo with their matted and dirty hides. They looked tough, and she was glad they weren't going to have one for breakfast. She was also glad they were on the other side of the river! The creatures were bigger than cows. Their huge heads were topped with wicked-looking horns, but their hips were small. Or maybe they just looked small because their shoulders were so broad and had that big hump.

The buffalo, contentedly licking salt, showed no inclination to cross the river. Sarah was still relieved, however, to see Pa packing their gear, and she was even more relieved when they had traveled out of sight and sound of the strange beasts.

As the trail led them through the foothills of the mountains and across many small streams, Sarah lost all track of the days and nights. They walked and camped, then walked some more. Pa said they had been traveling a little over two weeks.

Finally, they came to a fork in the trail that Boone's map called Hazel Patch. From there, Pa turned onto the narrower western trail that led to Harrodstown.

"We'll be at Logan's fort—Saint Asaph, he calls it—in

two or three days," Pa promised. "Then it's just another day or two to Harrodstown."

"Praise the Lord!" Sarah heard Ma murmur. Sarah knew Ma was as tired of the wilderness as she was, but at least they seemed to have left the mountains behind. Except for an occasional hill, the trail now wound a fairly level course through thick woods. Many of the trees were so big, Sarah couldn't have circled one halfway with both arms.

"There's every kind of tree here there was back in Virginy," Pa said. "I've seen oak, maple, hickory, beech, walnut, poplar, ash, sweet gum, elm—plus some I've never seen before!"

I've seen enough trees to last me for a long time! Sarah thought. She was used to living on a farm where acres of forest separated them from the next farmhouse, but here the tall trees seemed to close in with a silence and a loneliness so thick it made the air heavy and hard to breathe.

Then, just when she felt she couldn't stand being shut up in the woods another minute, they came into a wide meadow of tall, waving grasses. Hunter wasted no time finding a brown cottontail rabbit to chase.

Surely the world must have looked just this way when God created it, wild and fresh and . . . lonely, Sarah decided, feeling the silence close in on her even here in the open meadow.

"Surely this place has never felt the tread of man's foot!" Ma's voice broke into her thoughts. "Why is there cleared land here, Hiram?"

"The Indians burn away the trees and brush to flush out game," Pa explained, "and that gives the grass a chance to grow."

★ **Chapter Six** ★

"This grass is as green as the grass back home, Pa," Sarah challenged. "You said Kentucky had blue grass!"

"Well, we haven't reached the bluegrass yet, Sary," Pa answered smugly with that secret smile that made her wonder if he were playing a joke on her about that blue grass

Oh, well, she thought, *at least Kentucky has some of my favorite wildflowers.* From this one spot at the edge of the meadow, she could see fire pinks, sweet Williams, larkspur, and columbine. And there at the edge of the trees were her special favorites, little yellow and white Dutchmen's breeches, growing among the pretty little violets that formed a carpet underfoot.

Sarah heard the muted roar of a river in the distance. Pa always liked to camp near water. Maybe they would camp near here for the night, and she could pick a bouquet . . .

"A flatboat!" Luke yelled from up ahead. "And it's full of people! And a dog and an ox!" he added.

Sarah began to run, the contents of Ma's shawl bumping against her leg. When she caught up with Ma and Jamie, Luke and Pa, she dropped the shawl on the sand. "Why didn't we float to Kentucky?" she panted. She could have brought Tiger on a boat, although he didn't much like water.

"We didn't have a river right handy!" Pa answered with a laugh.

"I'll bet Hunter and Willie and Bess would like riding along in a boat so easy-like," Luke sighed. Sarah guessed he was tired of walking, too.

"I don't know about that," Ma put in. "That dog looks like he'd feel better on the bank."

"I feel better just knowing other people are coming to

47

Kentucky," Sarah said. "At least we'll have neighbors."

"Child, they may settle a hundred miles from us," Pa said. "Kentucky's a big place. It's likely we won't see another human being from one end of the year to the next, unless a hunter or an Indian drops by."

Sarah shivered. *Hunters, yes. Indians, no thank you!*

"They're coming in to the bank!" Luke yelled.

Sarah watched excitedly as the boat eased to the shore. She scooped up the shawl and ran, stumbling in the deep sand, thinking how good it would be just to see other human beings again.

When she reached the boat, Sarah was disappointed to see there were no girls in the family. Luke and three of the boys were soon acting like old friends. Sarah forgot her disappointment, though, as she tried to hear what Ma and the woman were saying, while listening to Pa and the man and his oldest son at the same time.

"We just got tired of the walking and the packing up," Mr. Whitton was explaining to Pa. "So when we got to this river, we decided to build us a boat and ride the river awhile. I don't know where it's taking us," he added, "but it's got to be somewhere in Kentucky!"

"Those Tories stripped the house, the barn, the smoke-house—just like a swarm of locusts!" Mrs. Whitton was telling Ma. "And then they burned the house. I tell you, we were lucky to get out alive!"

I wonder why the Tories want to remain loyal to King George instead of joining the rest of the colonists in the fight for independence, Sarah thought.

". . . looting and burning and killing. Neighbor fighting neighbor," Mr. Whitton was saying to Pa. "I've never seen the like! We got together what supplies we could, packed up our three youngest and William here, and just lit out."

"There's hardly a woman in Massachusetts who will serve tea anymore, now that we can only buy it from the king's shopkeepers and the tax on it is so high," Mrs. Whitton declared. "Leastways, we won't buy it unless it's smuggled in by our own people."

". . . and if they had caught them, the prison ship was waiting to take them back to England for trial," William Whitton was saying.

"But we're Englishmen!" Pa broke in. "The English Constitution guarantees any Englishman anywhere the right to be tried by his own people!"

William's laugh was short and harsh. "I know that, and you know that," he said bitterly, "but Parliament seems to have forgotten it!"

"Still, dressing up like Indians and dumping three whole shiploads of tea into the harbor was downright sinful!" Ma said. "Such waste!"

"Is it any more wasteful than letting the tea sit rotting in the warehouses?" Mrs. Whitton asked. "Much as I love it, I will never drink another cup of tea until we're free to buy and sell it as we please! I don't intend to give the British one shilling to fight us with."

"That's what I've said, too," Ma agreed, "ever since our Nathan joined the Revolution. God only knows where . . ."

"I've got a boy with the militia somewhere too," Mrs. Whitton broke in. "And William here is aching to join him."

"I say we should have stayed and fought!" William said

angrily. "We drove 'em out of Boston in March. . . ."

"And they drove us out of a few other places," his father answered.

"I'm afraid there's nothing on God's green earth that can lick the British army," Pa put in. "They're the best trained and best supplied army in the world."

"Then they can kill me on the battlefield or hang me for treason when it's over!" William shouted. "But I will not be a British slave, and I'm not too cowardly to fight for my freedom!" He jumped up and stalked off into the woods.

Sarah saw a look of pain cross Mr. Whitton's face. "William thinks I'm running away to keep from fighting," he explained.

Pa nodded. "I fear my Nate feels the same way about me."

Sarah's thoughts whirled as she ate the supper Ma and Mrs. Whitton had fixed together, clucking away like two hens while they worked. Who was right? William's words were so like Nate's the night he left for the war. But Pa couldn't be a coward. Did Nate really think he was?

She wished Nate were here with them, safe from the British, safe . . . but would any of them ever be completely safe again? Sarah finished her supper then got herself and Jamie ready for bed.

Sarah wrapped up with Jamie in the warm feather quilt and threw a glance over her shoulder. It was comforting to see the Whitton's fire just a short distance down the river and to know that another family was camped nearby. But as she listened to the fearful night sounds of the forest, she wondered if she would ever again know the safe, warm feeling she once had known in her cozy room under the eaves.

Our house might not even be there! Sarah thought suddenly. Back on the other side of the mountains, neighbors were fighting each other. Already, their home and Martha's might have been robbed and burned. It wasn't even safe in Miller's Forks anymore! And who knew what lurked out there in the deep, black Kentucky forest.

It was a long time before she fell asleep that night, and when she did, her dreams were troubled. Sarah dreamed she and Martha were hiding from the British in the hayloft, and the Tories set the barn on fire. She dreamed she and Luke were helping Ma and Pa bury all their valuables in the apple orchard when the British came and caught them. She dreamed Tiger was accused of killing a soldier and sent off to England for trial.

When Sarah awoke the next morning, William was gone

and the Whittons were preparing to take their flatboat on down the river without him.

"I knew he would go back sooner or later," Mr. Whitton said sadly. "His heart never was in coming with us. He had it set on fighting the British."

Sarah knew how William felt, at least about not coming to Kentucky.

"I'm sorry," Ma said to Mrs. Whitton.

"Well, it's what he wants," she answered. "He's just like his pa—stubborn as a mule when he sets his head! William and his pa are just looking for freedom in their own ways, and who's to fault either of them for doing what he sees as right?"

Mrs. Whitton was right, Sarah supposed, but she felt sorry for them anyway. It must be a lonely feeling to leave with one fewer son than they had with them the night before.

Sarah watched the Whittons push their boat into the current of the river. She waved a lonely wave as the boat and its passengers were carried rapidly downstream, growing smaller and smaller in the distance. Soon, they were gone.

After the Whittons' boat glided out of sight, the Moores plunged deep into the forest again. They spent the day traveling a narrow trail strewn with the stumps of trees that had been cut to make the path through the forest.

Sarah looked at Ma walking along in front of her. Neither of them looked very elegant. They had shortened their heavy skirts to their shoe tops to make walking easier, and their faces and arms were sunburned brown. The days of walking had toughened them, though, and she had to admit she felt good. She shifted Jamie to the other arm and took a deep breath of the cool evening air.

"Pa, I smell smoke!" Sarah called softly, aware that it could be from an Indian campfire.

"Don't worry!" Pa called back. "I figure it's just the supper fires from Saint Asaph."

"Oh, glory!" Sarah breathed. Were they close to Logan's fort at last? It would be so good to walk into a house again, to feel a floor underfoot, to have four walls around her and a roof overhead!

Sarah put Jamie on her back and began to run. She passed Ma and Luke and caught up with Pa. Still she could see nothing but trees ahead. "How long, Pa?" she asked breathlessly. "How long before we get to the fort?"

Pa reached over and patted her shoulder. "Tired of the wilderness, little girl?" he asked. "Well, I can't say I blame you. We ought to be there in less than half an hour—before nightfall, anyway."

True to Pa's word, it wasn't long till they came into an opening in the forest. There was a wall across the clearing, made out of logs with the bark still on them. It looked like a row of trees without limbs or leaves, standing guard side by side.

One of the gates in the middle of the wall swung open, but Sarah couldn't see anyone. She glanced at Ma, but Ma had stopped to smooth her hair and her bedraggled skirt. Then Ma took Jamie so Sarah could brush her own skirt and try to smooth the hair that had come loose from her braids.

Sarah had to hurry, though, as Ma quickened her usual steady walk to a pace that had Jamie giggling as he jiggled up and down in her arms. Sarah guessed that Ma, too, was eager to be in a civilized place again.

Sarah ran ahead of Ma and Jamie and went into the fort right behind Luke and old Bess. Then she stopped short. This was Saint Asaph? This funny-looking square of hard-packed dirt surrounded by a few ugly little shacks built of rough, unpeeled logs?

"Praise the Lord, folks!" she heard someone shout. "It's not Indians. It's settlers come to join us!"

★ Chapter Eight ★

Then she noticed the people, a dozen or so of them, clustered behind the gate. They surged forward, all talking at once, wanting news from back home and inviting the Moores to supper. That's when Sarah noticed that she and Ma had no reason to worry about how shabby they looked. The people of Saint Asaph didn't look much better. Their clothing was as patched and make-do as their cabins.

"Ben Logan," one of the men introduced himself, holding out his hand to Pa. Then he peered out the gate. "Are you folks alone?" he asked in surprise. "I can't imagine how you got here without being massacred by the Indians! Most settlers travel in groups of twelve to fifteen men with guns for safety these days."

"We've seen some Indian sign," Pa answered, "but most of it was old. We haven't seen one single live Indian!"

"You've something to be thankful for, then," Logan said, pushing the gate shut and securing it with a heavy wooden bar. "Where are you headed? Can we interest you in settling here at Saint Asaph?" he added hopefully.

Pa shook his head. "I aim to stake my claim somewhere along the Kentucky River. Daniel Boone tells me it's prime land. A paradise on earth, he calls it."

"Oh, well, guess we can't compete with paradise," Logan said with a shrug and a grin. "But come have supper with us and spend the night, anyway. Your wife and young ones can go with Mrs. Logan on over to our blockhouse there in the corner. I'll help you and your boy put your stock in our pen out back."

Sarah peered into the one-room cabins they passed as they followed Mrs. Logan to the two-story blockhouse at the end of the row. She was amazed at how small the cabins were, most of them not much bigger than their henhouse

57

back in Virginia! And some of them seemed no more comfortable, with dirt floors and almost no furnishings.

Sarah entered the Logans' log blockhouse and stopped just inside the doorway to look around. The house consisted of one room, four or five times the size of the other cabins, with a squared-off log stairway in the right back corner leading to another room above it. The single room was as big as two of their rooms back home, she figured, and she was relieved to see that it had a wooden floor, though she wouldn't have wanted to walk barefoot on the splintery thing!

The back corner opposite the stairway held a crude wooden bedstead, and the rest of the room was sparsely furnished. There was a massive table surrounded by mismatched chairs, and a tall cupboard that took up most of the front corner near the fireplace.

"How in the world did you get those dishes here without breaking them?" Ma gasped. Sarah knew she must be thinking of her own flowered china—now Aunt Charity's—that looked so much like the set displayed in Mrs. Logan's cupboard.

Mrs. Logan chuckled. "I wrapped them in our spare clothes and packed them between the bed covers. Even so, I lost my meat platter and two saucers. Still, I figure if I'd left them behind, I wouldn't have any of them. This way, I've got most of the set."

"I wish I'd thought of it that way," Ma said wistfully. "All I could think was that they'd get broken on the trip, and I gave them to my sister."

Sarah wished there were something she could do to get Ma's dishes back. She hated to see her look so sad.

"Oh, well," Ma said with a smile, "Charity always had a

hankering for that set of china. It was our mother's. I'm sure she'll enjoy it. Now, what can I do to help with supper?"

Mrs. Logan returned her smile. "We'll have nice things again some day," she said comfortingly. She handed Ma a long wooden dough tray. "You can finish these biscuits. Better throw in some more flour and milk," she added. "We'll need extras."

As Ma mixed and kneaded the dough, Sarah saw their hostess add water to a kettle that was hanging from a crane over the fire. She wondered if they had chosen their place for supper wisely. Watered-down soup or stew wasn't going to satisfy her appetite tonight! But she could smell sweet potatoes baking in the ashes, and Ma was making biscuits. Sarah could hardly wait to get one between her teeth! They had eaten mostly cornbread lately. Biscuits were too much trouble to make at a campsite, Ma had declared after her first attempt.

Sarah's mind wandered back to their first camp. How long had it been since then? She had lost all track of the days. Was it two weeks or three since they had set out from Miller's Forks?

Ma's voice broke into Sarah's thoughts. "Sarah could set the table," she suggested to Mrs. Logan. "How many are you expecting?"

Mrs. Logan laughed. "I never know! Whoever is here and has no family with him will end up with his feet under my table, most likely. Set all the plates, Sarah. If more show up, I'll just add more water to that venison stew, and they can eat in shifts!"

Sarah set Jamie down where he would be out of the way and handed him Samantha. He looked up at her in surprise. "Manfa!" he crowed happily, reaching for the rag doll.

Sarah felt a little ashamed that she hardly ever trusted him with the doll when he loved it so, but he always wanted to pull off her button eyes, or plant smudgy wet kisses on her embroidered face. Sarah wanted Jamie occupied while she handled Mrs. Logan's precious dishes, though. If she dropped one and broke it, she would just die!

Soon Pa, Luke, and Mr. Logan came into the cabin, followed by a half dozen other hungry men. Sarah was sure there wouldn't be enough supper left over for her, Ma, and Mrs. Logan.

There turned out to be plenty, though, and even the watered-down stew tasted very good.

After supper, Luke went off with some boys. Sarah sighed and went back to scraping plates for washing. There had been no girls in the Whitton party, and, so far, she hadn't seen a single girl anywhere near her age in Saint Asaph. She hoped this wasn't always going to be the way of it. Surely there would be girls her age in Harrodstown!

Harrodstown. All her hopes were fixed on that place! Saint Asaph was a brave, pitiful attempt to create a civilization in the wilderness, and maybe someday it would be a real town. But Pa had said Harrodstown was the oldest settlement in Kentucky. Surely it already had real houses; and shops where she and Ma could buy ribbons and buttons, cones of rich brown sugar, and spicy cinnamon sticks; and a smithy where Pa could get nails and horseshoes. And there would be a tavern where he could talk with other men and get news of home, maybe even hear from Nate.

Surely Pa would settle near Harrodstown. They would build their new home close enough to travel there when they needed supplies. They would be close enough to attend Sunday meeting, as they had in Miller's Forks.

"You're more than welcome to stay on here," she heard Mr. Logan say to Pa. She held her breath to hear Pa's answer.

"I thank you kindly," Pa said, "but if we're to get land cleared and crops in the ground this year, we'd best be on our way."

Mr. Logan nodded. "You'll need to be on the trail before sunup then, if you aim to reach Harrodstown before nightfall."

Sarah didn't care how early they had to leave. Visions of the civilized life she knew she would find at Harrodstown beckoned her. They filled her dreams that night as she, Ma, and Jamie slept on their feather quilts before the fireplace.

Sarah thought of Harrodstown all through their hurried breakfast, and all day as they covered the miles between Saint Asaph and the place on which she had pinned her hopes. There would be a girl her age at Harrodstown. There would be music and laughter. There would be all the things they had left behind in Miller's Forks—or most of them anyway.

"There she is!" Pa called out finally, just as the sun sank behind the western horizon. "There's Harrodstown!"

Sarah felt her heart do a flip-flop. She hurried up beside Pa. Yes, there was the clearing up ahead. And there was . . .

Sarah stopped dead still at the edge of the forest. Surely Pa was playing a joke on them! Or he had made a terrible mistake!

That couldn't be Harrodstown! The place was no better than Saint Asaph! A little bigger, maybe, but just as pitiful and make-do with the same log buildings behind the same log stockade.

"Halloo, the fort!" Pa called, and heads appeared above the pointed logs of the stockade. Sarah gasped as the sun glinted off gun barrels pointed straight at them.

"Put the guns away!" Pa shouted. "We're not Indians. We're settlers! The Hiram Moore family from Miller's Forks, Virginia!"

"It's Hiram, Jake!" Sarah heard a man call, as two of the heads disappeared from above the wall.

"Hi, you rascal you!" the voice shouted as the gate of the fort swung open. "Where have you been? Boone thought you'd be here a month ago. We thought sure you'd been scalped!"

"Caleb?" Pa asked. "Is that you? I haven't seen you

since we went on the long hunt with Boone!" He went to meet the man at the gate, and Sarah saw them clasp hands, then slap each other on the back.

Sarah followed Pa through the gate, wanting to cry. This just couldn't be Harrodstown! Where were the houses with real glass windows and chimneys that weren't built of mud and sticks? Where were the neat shops along brick-paved streets? Where were the tall white churches? Surely Pa had led them to the wrong place! Surely this was just another fort along the way!

"Welcome to Harrodstown!" another man said, joining them at the gate.

"Good to see you, Jake!" Pa exclaimed, holding out his hand. "This is my family. We've come to settle along the Kentucky River."

Sarah felt her hopes fall again. They were shattered. Vaguely, she heard the invitations to supper and to spend the night. She heard Pa accept. She followed the Hartley family to their cabin, one in a row of tiny, one-room structures along the side of the stockade.

Sarah stopped just inside the door, noting the cramped space and rough, homemade furniture. Mrs. Hartley was showing Ma a matching ironstone platter and bowl which were printed with a rose-colored English country scene. They sat on the mantel above the fireplace, the only visible evidence that the family had ever known better living conditions.

"I brought them from home," she said proudly, "buried in a sack of cornmeal!"

"I'm so glad you're here!" a voice said in Sarah's ear.

Sarah turned and saw a girl standing beside her. It was too dark now to see what she really looked like, but—

wonder of wonders—she appeared to be about Sarah's age!

"I'm Ann Hartley," she said. "Do you think your pa will settle here? Oh, I do hope so! All the girls here are either married, thinking on getting married, or still in diapers. There were two sisters, one ten and a half and one twelve years old, but their family went back east. Sometimes I think I must be the only eleven-year-old girl in Kentucky! There's plenty of pesky old boys, though! What's your name?" she finished breathlessly.

"Sarah Moore," she answered, Ann's friendly chatter taking her mind off her ruined dreams of Harrodstown.

"Keep the boys out from underfoot, Ann, while I put something together to feed these travelers," Mrs. Hartley ordered briskly.

"I know," Ann said, reaching up on the mantel for a small stone, "we'll play rock school." And in no time, she had four little boys—her three brothers and Jamie—seated on the ground in front of the steps to their cabin, guessing which hand held the concealed rock. As they guessed correctly, she "promoted" them to the next step. When they reached the top, she started them all over at the bottom.

"It works better with a whole flight of stairs," she whispered to Sarah, "but here we have to make do with what we have."

"What can I do to help?" Sarah heard Ma ask, and she saw Mrs. Hartley hand Ma a stack of wooden plates to set the table. Ma had some pewter plates, but Sarah had never seen any wooden ones.

Ann caught her staring curiously at the plates. "Most everything we have here is made of wood, unless we brought it with us," she explained. "Right hand or left?" she said to one of the boys. "We have a potter among us

65

now, though," she continued to Sarah. "He plans to make dishes once he finds a vein of good clay—if it isn't too far from the fort for safety," she added.

Wooden plates, clay plates, Sarah thought. *What difference does it make?* As Ann had said, everything here was make-do.

"Supper's ready!" Mrs. Hartley called, breaking into Sarah's thoughts.

"We've already eaten," Ann said. "I'll put the boys to bed while you eat, then we can talk some more."

You mean, you can talk some more and I can listen, Sarah thought, but she didn't mind Ann's constant chatter. She was enjoying it, really. Ann reminded her of Martha, except Martha didn't have red hair and freckles. If they had more time, she thought as she dug hungrily into a plate of beans and cornbread, she felt sure they could become good friends.

The Hartley children climbed the pole ladder to the loft above, and after supper Luke and Pa went off to spend the night in Boone's blockhouse with some of the other men and boys.

Then Sarah, Ma, and Jamie bedded down in front of the fireplace. As the sound of a gentle rain lulled Sarah to sleep, she realized how grateful she was for the wooden shingles overhead and the glowing fire beside her.

By morning, a determined spring rain had set in, and Pa said they would stay at the fort until the weather cleared. Sarah was delighted at the chance to visit with Ann a little longer.

Before the morning had passed, however, Sarah knew why most pioneer families moved out of the forts and into their own cabins as soon as they could. It was so crowded in the Hartley cabin—with Ma, Jamie, Ann, Mrs. Hartley, and Ann's three little brothers—that Sarah couldn't wait to get outside again.

"You think this is crowded?" Ann laughed. "You should have been here last winter when we had another family— four of them— living with us."

Sarah gave the one-room cabin with its low overhead loft a measuring glance. "Whew!" she exclaimed. "I'm glad I wasn't here in the winter, then!"

Ann laughed again. "Come on," she suggested, "let's go to school. You'll like Mrs. Coomes, the teacher, and we can get away from this cabin for a while. I go to school whenever Ma can spare me."

"Girls go to school here?" Sarah asked in amazement. Only Luke and the other boys had attended school back in Virginia. Ma had taught her to read and write, but she had always envied Luke's history and Latin lessons. And she just knew she could have beaten him in those spelldowns he was always bragging about winning.

"Well, not really. But there certainly are no tutors and no elegant ladies to teach us how to serve tea and curtsy and carry on polite conversation!" Ann said, as she led the way to a very small cabin built off by itself. "And, other than survive, there's not much to do here," she went on. "What books that are here, I've read at least three times each. So I help Mrs. Coomes with the little fellows whenever I can."

Once inside, Sarah found that the schoolroom had a hard-packed dirt floor and backless benches made of rough, splintery logs. There were no writing tables, and one end of the room was taken up by a huge stone fireplace that had a big hole in the back.

"That's so the men and boys can slide logs into the fire without coming into the schoolroom and disturbing lessons," Ann whispered when she saw Sarah's puzzled look. "They thought of everything when they built this school. They even made sure we'd have paper greased with bear fat in the window instead of just an open space."

In spite of the paper window and the fact that she could see right through the cracks between the log walls, Sarah thought the room was dim and stuffy. She didn't say anything, though. Ann seemed quite proud of what they had.

"We're glad to have you visit us, Sarah," Mrs. Coomes said with a welcoming smile. "Would you like to read the children a Bible story?" She held out a New Testament, opened to the Book of Acts.

Sarah took the book and began to read the story of Paul's shipwreck, while Ann corrected the sums the children had worked on wooden paddles using sticks blackened in the fire for pencils.

From what Sarah could see, all Mrs. Coomes had to teach from was the New Testament, a wooden paddle with numerals on it, and another paddle showing the alphabet. It surely was a funny little school, not at all like the neat, one-room school the boys of Miller's Forks attended.

"We didn't have any school at all until Mrs. Coomes came and started this one," Ann said as the two girls made their way back to the Hartley's cabin.

Sarah just smiled at her new friend. She didn't want to say anything to hurt her feelings, but the school had seemed very poor to her—like everything else at the fort, and everything else in Kentucky!

By afternoon, the weather cleared and the sun was

shining as though it had never rained. Pa said they had better travel while they could.

"The Wilderness Trail ends here at the fort," he explained, "and we will be traveling through unmarked territory until we reach the river and can follow it."

Sarah wasn't as sorry to leave Harrodstown as she had thought she would be. She had enjoyed being with Ann, but the crowded cabins and make-shift living had depressed her. At least their cabin would be all theirs. They wouldn't have to share it with everybody who came along and needed a room, except for a visitor or two now and then.

Sarah hoped they would get to their own land soon. She was anxious to have four walls around her and a roof over her head again.

Of course, nothing they could build here would be like home had been, but compared to camping out and packing up and moving on all the time, even a log cabin would seem like a palace!

For two days, Pa led the family along the big river called the Kentucky. Then he left it at the mouth of a deep, green creek, where catfish and perch flitted in the murky depths of quiet pools.

Gradually, the deep water of the creek gave way to swift, rocky shallows that allowed them to walk right up the creek bed instead of fighting their way through the undergrowth along the bank.

Crawfish and minnows darted under the rocks at their approach, and gray water snakes slid quietly into the water. Frogs plunged into the pools in panic, and one old turtle sunning on a sandbar simply went into his shell house and firmly closed the door. Sarah laughed. "I guess that means, 'No visitors welcome!' " she told Jamie.

"Naw! Naw!" a black crow cried loudly from the trees along the shore. Whether he meant, "No, it doesn't mean that," or "No, you're not welcome," Sarah wasn't sure.

"What a pretty little meadow!" Ma's voice broke into Sarah's thoughts. Sarah went to join her where she stood gazing over the right bank of the creek.

The trees overhanging the creek here were just a fringe around an open meadow. The sky overhead was as blue as the cornflowers Sarah saw at the edge of the meadow, with clouds as white and fluffy as the beaten egg whites that had topped Ma's pies back home. Tall grasses grew in the meadow, along with purple bergamot and clumps of yellow and white daisies.

"Madam, would you like to have this meadow?" Pa asked seriously, but Sarah saw that his blue eyes were twinkling.

Ma looked at him questioningly. Then Sarah could tell she was fighting a smile, for the dimple at the corner of her mouth was showing. "Sir, I would love it!" she answered.

Pa bowed low, sweeping his hand toward the meadow. "It is yours," he said, like a king bestowing land on one of his subjects. Ma laughed a clear, happy, young girl's laugh as Pa led old Bess up the creek bank. He began to unload her pack in the tall grass, even though it was only midafternoon and there were several hours of travel left in the sun.

"Do you mean it, Pa?" Sarah cried. "Is this our new land?"

"It's nobody's land but God's," Pa answered, "and I reckon He'd as soon we had it as anybody. All we have to do is claim it, build a cabin on it, and plant crops. Then it will be ours by the laws of the Commonwealth of Virginy, too."

"Oh, Hiram, it's such a likely spot!" Ma said, her eyes shining.

"It is a likely spot," Pa agreed. "There's open land I can break for a garden without having to clear away trees. We're late for planting already, and here we can get seeds into the ground in a few days. There are trees handy for building and for firewood, and there's a spring just under this bank where we can get cold drinking water."

"And we have our own creek where we can go fishing and swimming!" Luke added.

"What's the name of this creek, Pa?" Sarah asked.

"Don't reckon it has one," he answered.

"You and Luke can name our creek whatever you want to," Ma said.

How exciting! Sarah thought. But they had to choose the name carefully. Or maybe this creek already had a name of its own, and nobody knew it yet. *Let's see,* she pondered, *if this creek had a name, what would it be?* Suddenly she knew. "I think its name is Stoney Creek," she said aloud.

"I wonder why!" Luke laughed.

"It has plenty of stones in it," Pa agreed. "We won't have to have one of those mud-and-stick chimneys that catch fire so easy. That's what causes many frontier cabins to burn."

"That and Indians," Luke said. "At the fort, they said the British are paying the Indians for every scalp. . . ."

Pa glanced at Ma and Sarah. Then he gave Luke a long, hard look, but Luke wasn't paying attention. ". . . summer's a good time for Indian raids, they said, because of the weather and the easy liv . . ."

"Go water the horses and hobble them, son," Pa said quietly, "unless you'd rather have a good dose of hickory tea."

Sarah giggled as Luke picked up the reins and started to the creek immediately. She knew Pa meant a hickory limb would be applied to the seat of Luke's breeches if he didn't quit scaring them with that Indian talk.

Pa busied himself building a rock fireplace that was bigger and more permanent-looking than the ones they had used along the trail. Then he disappeared into the woods with his gun. Before long, they heard the gun go off three times.

Sarah held her breath, straining to hear some sound that would assure them Pa was all right, that he hadn't met up with Indians. But no bird call nor animal cry, not even an insect's buzzing, broke the silence that stretched around her.

Sarah looked at Ma, standing over the fire with a long-handled wooden spoon in one hand, her other hand on her chest over her heart. Sarah could feel her own heart beating all the way up in her throat. What was going on out there in that dark, eerie forest?

Ma lay the spoon carefully across the kettle. "Watch the baby, Sarah," she said quietly, starting across the clearing toward the trees.

Just as Ma started out, Pa emerged from the forest, carrying three lifeless gray squirrels by their fluffy tails. Sarah felt her heart thump, then settle back into a steady rhythm.

"Hiram Moore, I thought sure you were killed and scalped!" Ma said weakly. "I never heard a sound before I saw you walking toward us. Where'd you learn to walk so quietly?"

"That's a trick you learn early on a long hunt with Daniel Boone," he said with a grin. "Sometimes, your life depends on who walks the quietest—you or the Indians. Hand me that wooden bowl, Della, and we'll have squirrel for supper!" he added, taking out his knife.

"There's rabbit, raccoon, and deer sign all over the place," he told them as he skinned and cut up the squirrels. "There'll be good hunting here. We won't go hungry for meat."

Sarah heard the meat sizzle as Ma dropped it into the hot grease in the small kettle over the fire. It would be crisp and brown and wild-tasting, and Ma would make brown gravy from the grease and crumbs of meat and a little flour and water. And maybe they would eat it over puffy brown and white biscuits baked in the spider, their three-legged skillet.

"I've got to find something to keep me busy till it's all cooked, or I'm going to starve to death right here in sight and smell of supper," Sarah told herself. She looked around the camp. This wasn't just another camp. They were getting ready to eat their first meal on their new land. That was a special occasion if ever there was one.

Sarah glanced at Jamie. She had to keep an eye on him while Ma cooked, but he was playing happily with Samantha. She ran to the packs Pa had taken from the horses and unpacked the pewter plates and mugs. She wished Ma hadn't given her pretty china dishes to Aunt Charity, but they still had the six silver forks and spoons Grandma had given Ma for her wedding present.

Sarah unwrapped the linen table cloth from around the china teapot. At least Ma had brought that, and it was still all in one piece, except for the chip that had been out of the spout for as long as she could remember.

Sarah looked around for a table. The empty crates the chickens and geese had traveled in would be fine, once she washed them in the creek.

She spread the linen cloth over the clean crates, placed the plates around her make-shift table, and put a spoon, fork, and pewter mug beside each plate. She filled the teapot with water from the creek, put some daisies in it, and set them in the middle of the table. Then she stood back and admired it, thinking how pretty it all looked, and how nice it would be to sit down to supper around a pretty table like civilized folks instead of grabbing a bite to eat around the campfire.

Ma looked up from forking the squirrel meat out of the kettle. She gave Sarah a warm smile. "Come take up the biscuits while I finish the gravy," was all she said, but Sarah knew Ma understood why she had set such a fancy table there in the wilderness.

Ma pulled the spider out of the coals and handed Sarah

a wooden bowl. It was almost like helping Ma with supper in the big kitchen back home. Sarah brushed away thoughts of that cozy kitchen. Even when she was old enough to go back to Virginia, even if the Tories hadn't burned it down, she wouldn't be able to go back to the brick house, for it had been sold.

To fight off the threatening homesickness, Sarah tried to count all the reasons she was glad to be there. In the morning they would not have to pack up and move on. They could eat breakfast, dinner, and supper on that table in this same spot. Every day they could make their meadow more of a home. At least they could make it more of a home than anything they had known since they left Virginia.

"This is nice!" Pa exclaimed when he saw the table with its flowers and the bowls of biscuits and gravy and crisp, brown squirrel. He bowed his head. "Lord, we thank Thee that we got here safe," he began the blessing. Sarah agreed with that with all her heart, but she still couldn't understand why God hadn't let them stay safely in their home in Virginia. She had prayed so hard!

"We've seen our last camp," Pa said later as they bedded down for the night. Sarah stretched out on her springy cedar bed. At least she wouldn't have to hunt a new bed tomorrow night.

The moon had not yet risen, and the few stars that had come out in the dark sky shed little light on the banks of Stoney Creek. The wind whispered through the cedars on the hills around them, and the water made a drowsy, murmuring sound as it made its way over the stones. Sarah could feel her eyelids drooping.

Suddenly a screech owl sent his eerie cry through the night, and Sarah's eyes flew wide open. She couldn't see a thing in the blackness. *Surely you're not afraid of a little old feathery screech owl!* she scolded herself, settling back under the quilt.

Over by the creek a rain crow called its eerie call, and was answered from the woods. All at once, Sarah wondered if those were bird calls. What if they were Indians calling to each other from all around them? She edged closer to Jamie. The creek seemed to murmur a warning now, and the wind in the cedars took on a low moaning.

There was a new wind in this new place, but it certainly wasn't calling Sarah's name. "Rush! Rush!" it seemed to say. "Get away from here!"

Gradually, though, the bird calls moved away, and the murmur of the creek, combined with her tiredness from the day's journey and the excitement of settling on their new land, put Sarah to sleep at last.

Listen to that wild canary sing!" Ma said.

Sarah stood listening to the trills of the canary. It was a pleasant sound, not at all like the cries of the birds she had heard last night, if they were birds. But the bright morning sun turning the meadow grasses to gold, the creek babbling merrily through the stones, and the song of the little yellow bird off somewhere in the woods made her fears of the night before seem foolish. Surely there was nothing to fear in such a place on such a morning!

Right after breakfast, Pa began fitting new wooden handles to his plow. He had taken the handles off of all his tools except the axe to make them easier to carry on the journey to Kentucky.

"As soon as we get some seeds into the ground," he said, "we'll build a cabin on that rise over there, close enough to the creek so water will be handy, but far enough back so high water won't be a danger."

"It's a likely spot," Ma agreed. She was unpacking and settling in like she never intended to move again.

Sarah knew just how Ma felt. Once Pa got that cabin built, she hoped they never had to be uprooted again. Unless, of course, Pa decided to go back home. But she figured she had about as much chance of getting that wish as she did of getting the moon for a play-pretty! She would just have to make the best of living in Kentucky until she was old enough to go back to Virginia on her own.

"I just pray these apple twigs still have life in them," Ma said, standing back to admire the slim, dead-looking sticks she had planted in front of the rise where Pa had said the cabin would be. "I'm going to plant these peach seeds over here to one side," she continued. "Where's Luke? I need him to get me some more water."

"Pa's got him cutting saplings, Ma," Sarah answered. "They're building a pen for the animals until they can build the barn. I'll get the water."

After she had carried the water and helped Ma plant her seeds, Sarah looked across the meadow and saw Pa stop old Willie long enough to wipe the sweat from his face. She ran to the spring, dipped up a fresh bucket of water, and carried it to him, breathing in the warm, rich smell of fresh-turned earth.

Pa smiled at her and thirstily drank the cold water. He splashed some of it over his sunburned face. Then he reached down to pick up a handful of nearly black soil and crumbled it in his fingers. "It's good land, Sary girl," he said, looking down the long, dark rows of plowed ground. "As rich as any I've ever seen." He looked back over the meadow to where Bess and the cow and calf were eating the tall grass. "A likely spot," he repeated, "right in the heart of the bluegrass."

"Where is that blue grass, Pa?" Sarah asked. "This grass is as green as the grass back home!"

Pa's face took on that aggravating secret smile. "Just you wait, Sary," he answered. "Just you wait."

Sarah was tired of this same old joke. "You're not fooling me one bit, Pa," she said. "There's no such thing as blue grass!"

Pa just smiled and pushed the plow under the tough meadow grass to start a new row. "Tell your Ma to get her seeds ready," he said. "This ground will raise corn so tall we'll have to use a ladder to pick it!"

Sarah knew he was joking again, but as she walked back to the camp she realized that raising corn wouldn't be any joking matter out there in the wilderness. Back home if the corn crop failed, they could buy corn from a neighbor. There they must raise enough corn for themselves and their animals or do without. She hoped Pa was right about that corn crop!

"Corn's one thing there's just no waste to," Ma said that afternoon as she and Sarah walked barefoot down the long rows of cool, soft dirt. They dropped kernels of corn and raked dirt over them with their feet. "I can't wait to get some dried shucks to stuff some mattresses, and there's nothing better to kindle a fire with than a dry corncob."

"I want some of the best shucks to make dolls," Sarah put in, "and Luke might want to make another farm out of cobs like he did last winter."

"Luke may think he's too big for play-pretties this year," Ma said, smiling as though she knew better. "But maybe he'll make Jamie some barns and fences and animals," she went on, glancing over at the baby who was playing in the dirt at the garden's edge. "Jamie would like that."

"What I'd like is for summer to hurry so we can have roasting ears," Sarah said, "and fresh fried corn!"

"I want to save some lye water so I can soak some corn and make hominy, too," Ma said. "And your pa and Luke love grits, if we can rig up a way to grind the corn. It doesn't have to be ground too fine for grits," she added, "not like it does for good meal to make cornbread."

Sarah stopped in the middle of covering a hill of corn. "I forgot we don't have a mill," she said. "What will we do for flour and meal, Ma?"

"Oh, your pa will think of something," Ma assured her. "Let's just get these seeds in the ground. This soil ought to raise a garden like we've not seen in a long, long time." She handed Sarah two little rag bundles. "Here, plant these summer squash and pumpkins between the hills of corn while I plant these sweet potatoes."

When they had planted all of Ma's vegetable seeds, Sarah looked back over the neat rows. She could hardly wait for the little green shoots to come through the ground! How good the fresh beans, cabbages, cucumbers, radishes, beets, and peas would taste after the dried foods of winter!

"Gardening is my favorite chore," Ma said as she stuck a stick in the ground to mark the place in the row where she had run out of peas. "It makes me feel close to God, helping Him make good things grow."

During the next few days, Sarah felt sure they had done their share. Pa plowed two more patches of ground, and they all planted corn in one and wheat in the other. Now it was up to God.

"We're planting seed in soil that's never been plowed and planted before," Pa pointed out.

The old, worn-out dirt back home was good enough for me,

★ Chapter Eleven ★

Sarah thought, but she didn't say anything.

"We'll just plant what we need for ourselves this year," Pa went on, "but someday we'll have roads, mills, and markets here just like back in Virginy. Then we'll plant crops to sell."

Sarah knew Pa believed what he said, but she couldn't imagine this place as anything but a lonely wilderness.

"If you all find any Indian arrowheads," Luke called, "I want 'em!"

"I'll keep them myself!" Sarah called back. "You've found five or six already!"

"But I can use 'em to make arrows for hunting, Sarah," he protested. "Girls don't hunt," he added scornfully.

"I could if I wanted to!" Sarah shot back.

"Children!" Ma scolded. "Why are there so many arrowheads buried here just under the grass, Hiram?" she asked.

"I'd guess this meadow was a battleground at some time," Pa answered.

"And there weren't any little Indian girls fighting on it, missy!" Luke said to Sarah.

She made a face at Luke, but she knew most likely he was right. Indian girls probably didn't hunt or fight battles. What was it like to be an Indian girl? Indians didn't live in houses, so there were no floors to polish or windows to wash. She didn't suppose they made quilts, curtains, or rugs, other than those from animal skins. Did they ever stay anywhere long enough to plant and harvest a garden? Were their lives just one long camping trip? And did they grow as tired of packing up and moving on as she had while they were on the trail?

People who knew they would not be around at harvest time did not plant gardens, Sarah thought with a feeling of security as she looked back over the long rows they had planted that day.

"Plant this dill over by the cabbages, Sarah," Ma said. "It'll be good to season pickles. And this sage will be good in cornbread and dressing."

By the time Ma was ready to start supper, they had surrounded the garden with herb and flower seeds saved from last year's garden, and from the borders along the fence and stepping stones back home.

"I like sweet basil," Sarah said, "in green beans and scrambled eggs."

Ma nodded. She straightened up and rubbed her back. "We'll plant the sweet flags up close to where the cabin will be," she said. "They'll come up every year, and I want them handy to grind up for spices. I know my little supply of ginger, cinnamon, and nutmeg won't last forever."

"Did you bring any moss roses, Ma?" Sarah asked. They were her favorite of all Ma's flowers. All through the long, hot summer, every morning the delicate green stems would hold up their bright red, yellow, or rose-colored cups to catch the early morning sunshine around the well box. In the evening, they would fold their petals and nod drowsily in the dew until morning came again. She hoped Ma hadn't forgotten to bring moss roses!

Ma smiled. "You know I like a few moss roses and nasturtiums in my salads," she reminded her. "We'll plant them up by the cabin, too. I want some pretty flowers in our new yard. And I want nasturtium juice handy to spread on poison ivy if—God forbid—one of us should get it."

Sarah remembered that when folks took sick in Miller's Forks, rather than send for old Doc Benson over at the next town, often as not they sent for Ma. She always had a supply of herbs and flowers to make whatever medicine was needed. And if the taste of some of Ma's bitter brews didn't kill a person, the medicine would likely cure him.

"I can't think of the name of that little yellow flower you use to make medicine for fever, Ma. What is it?" Sarah asked.

"Calendula," Ma answered. "I planted some over there by the beans. It's good in soups and stews, too. And, let's see, I planted lavender down there by the radishes. It's the best thing I know to clean out a wound, and I'll need it to keep moths out of our clothes."

"It makes our clothes smell good, too," Sarah added. "And it's so pretty!"

"I put rosemary at the edge of the garden," Ma went on. "I wish I had some right now. I'm plumb out, and that hot sun has given me a headache. I could do with a cup of rosemary tea.

"Well, I need to get supper going anyway. That sinking sun tells me your pa will be wanting to eat before I know it," Ma said with a sigh. "You bring the baby, and I'll go get it started."

Sarah didn't need the sinking sun to tell her it was suppertime! She wished the vegetables they had just planted were grown and ready to eat right now. Sarah was ready for fresh food. But at least there might be deer meat tonight. Pa had killed a deer yesterday morning and hung the dressed meat high in a tree so wild animals couldn't get it.

"Here, Sarah," Ma said, handing her a dozen or so flat seeds. "I clean forgot these gourds. Plant them around here somewhere. If they grow well, we can dry the long-handled ones for dippers, and the round ones will make good bowls."

Sarah dug up a small space near the camp and planted the flat seeds. Later she would make a tripod of poles for the gourd vines to climb.

"They tell me it takes a fool to raise gourds," Pa teased as he and Luke came up from the creek where they had washed up for supper.

"If you ask me," Ma answered tartly, "that's a foolish saying!"

Sarah just smiled. She was too tired to answer Pa's teasing. As soon as she had eaten some of the meat and bread Ma had fixed and Pa had read his chapter from the Bible, she went to bed.

Pa was carving a wooden hoe, and Ma was mending Luke's shirt. Luke was still sitting by the fire, whittling something out of a piece of firewood. They could sit up all night if they wanted to, Sarah thought, but her tired bones felt like they might sink all the way through the cedar boughs into the ground.

Sarah was even too tired to worry about strange night sounds, though she was getting used to them. Things were becoming familiar here. She knew the tree-covered hills that cradled the meadow in their protective arms, the friendly murmuring of the creek, the dependable positions of the stars overhead, the expected way the moon came up over the cliffs across the creek. . . .

Sarah was asleep long before the moon peeped over the cliffs that night. She didn't even turn over until she was awakened suddenly by Ma's scream.

Sarah sat up and looked around wildly. Ma stood by the fire in her long nightgown with Jamie in her arms. Beside her stood a fierce-looking Indian with a knife in one hand and a piece of Ma's cornbread in the other! Sarah could feel her heart pound in her chest. She could see Luke sitting up in bed, his eyes wide and scared-looking, but where was Pa?

"Lord, help us!" she heard Ma breathe. Just then Sarah heard the click of a rifle being cocked to shoot, and Pa stepped out from behind a tree into the firelight. He was pointing his rifle straight at that Indian. Sarah had never been so glad to see anybody in her life!

The Indian took a step backward and held up the hand with the cornbread in it. "Friend!" he said, pointing to himself with the knife. "Little Captain friend Boone!"

"You speak English?" Pa asked in surprise. Sarah noticed that he kept the rifle pointed at the Indian's middle though.

The Indian grunted. "Spik English. Spik French. Spik many Indian tongues." He rattled off a phrase in what seemed to be each of them.

"You're a friend of Boone's, huh?" Pa interrupted the flow of words none of them could understand.

The Indian nodded. "We hunt. We fish. We fight. We friends." The Indian pointed to himself, then to Pa. "Friends," he repeated. Sarah guessed that meant he wanted to be friends with Pa, too.

"If you're looking for friends, why do you sneak up on people in the middle of the night and scare 'em half to death?" Pa growled, but he lowered the rifle, still holding it at his side in one hand.

"Little Captain much hungry. Smell deer meat. Smell bread. Good bread," he said to Ma.

"Why . . . uh . . . thank you," Ma answered in a very small voice.

"Little Captain go long journey for big soldier chief S'washington. Little Captain walk many moons. Walk much fast. No hunt. No fish. Little Captain much hungry!"

"You poor thing!" Sarah heard Ma say. If she knew Ma, she'd be feeding that Indian in a few minutes. Ma never turned down anything sick or hungry.

"Sarah," Ma called, "come take the baby while I heat up some supper for this . . . uh . . . gentleman."

He didn't look much like a gentleman to Sarah, standing there in his fringed, grease-stained buckskin breeches and dark blue soldier's coat with only one brass button left. Sarah guessed this was why he was called "Little Captain." He wore silver earrings, and a round, carved silver disk dangled from a rawhide string around his neck, along with a small rawhide bag. A couple of feathers hung from his black braided hair. Gentleman, indeed! Sarah couldn't help giggling at Ma's term for their mismatched visitor, but when his dark, solemn eyes turned to her, she got up quickly and went to take Jamie.

"Jumpin' Jehosaphat!" she heard Luke breathe as she went past him.

Well, I reckon a body can expect just about anything in the wilderness, Sarah thought as she rocked Jamie back and forth to get him to sleep again. But seeing an Indian, feathers and all, sitting calmly by their campfire in the middle of the night took some getting used to! So did the rank smell of that bag around his neck.

The firelight played over the Indian's face. It looked like it had been carved out of some dark, coppery-colored wood. His eyes were as black as his hair; they were flat black pools that reflected the firelight and showed no hint of what he was thinking.

He didn't seem so big, now that she had recovered enough from her fright to take a good look at him, but he had eaten enough for three men. Now he and Pa sat by the fire talking while Ma cleaned up the remains of his supper. Sarah could tell by the stiff look to Ma's back that she didn't approve of their guest's table manners. She saw Ma shudder when the Indian let out a loud belch.

"Your woman good cook," he said to Pa. Pa grinned impishly at Ma, but he politely said "thank you" to the Indian. Sarah noticed that Ma's back didn't seem quite so stiff after that.

Long after Sarah had laid a sleeping Jamie back down on the pine boughs, she lay listening to Pa and the Indian talk. Ma had gone back to bed, and Sarah thought she was asleep, for she could hear her deep, even breathing. Luke was too far away and it was now too dark to see if he were awake and listening, too. But if she knew Luke, he was as wide awake as she was.

"Then it doesn't bother you for settlers to move into Kentucky?" Pa was asking.

The Indian grunted. "Ken-tuck-ee good hunting ground. Much game. Much fish. Settlers clear land. Kill game. Waste. Indians fight for hunting ground. Redcoat warriors pay good for settlers' scalps."

"Then why are you friends with the settlers?" Pa asked skeptically.

"Little Captain friend Boone," the Indian corrected.

"All right," Pa agreed, "but why didn't you kill us and just take what you wanted tonight?"

"You friend Boone," the Indian answered simply.

90

"How do you know that?" Pa asked.

"Little Captain watch. You travel like Boone. You make camp like Boone. You no waste game. Boone make you map. Little Captain see sign of Boone on map. You friend Boone. You friend Little Captain."

Sarah shivered. That Indian had followed them. He had been close enough to read Daniel Boone's initials on the lower left corner of Pa's map. He could have killed and scalped them at any time, and they hadn't even known he was around! Thank God Daniel Boone and Pa were friends!

"Little Captain no like redcoat warriors," the Indian added.

I'm glad you don't like the British, Sarah told him silently, *or all our scalps might be dangling from your belt!*

"Little Captain not spik with forked tongue. Little Captain give word, word good. Little Captain hunt in Kentuck-ee when feel like it. Little Captain no kill settlers. No take scalps for redcoat warriors. Little Captain work for big chief S'washington. Little Captain wear blue coat." He patted his shabby army coat proudly.

"How does it go for General Washington?" Pa asked.

The Indian raised his hands, palms up, and let them fall. "S'washington brave warrior. But many redcoat warriors come across big waters to fight S'washington. Little Captain go far above big river, O-hi-o. Talk with chiefs. Now go back tell S'washington many Indians fight for redcoat warriors. S'washington no be happy!"

"No, I reckon he won't be," Pa answered. His voice sounded like he was worried. Or maybe he was just tired. It had been a busy week. Sarah was tired herself, and getting awfully sleepy.

★ Home on Stoney Creek ★

"Little Captain no like travel Ken-tuck-ee trails alone," the Indian admitted. "Happy find friends Boone on trail. Many spirits haunt Ken-tuck-ee."

Sarah almost giggled. This fierce-looking Indian, who had nearly scared them all out of their wits, was afraid of ghosts! Sarah felt much older and wiser than the Little Captain. She wasn't afraid of ghosts. She didn't even believe in them. But apparently the Indian did, for he was telling Pa about the spirits that lurked in the wilderness.

"Very long ago people," he said, "white skin people. Like you. Like Boone. Like S'washington. Name Allegewi. Know many things Indians not know. Make writing. Do strange things to dead so bodies no rot and make dust. Have much laws. Make stone wigwams to their god. Make much strong forts by big waters, O-hi-o and Ken-tuck-ee. No fight. Like peace. Like farm."

Sarah wasn't the least bit sleepy now. She had never heard of a "very long ago" white-skinned people living in Kentucky. She thought the settlers at Harrodstown were the first white people to live in this land beyond the mountains.

"Leni-Lenape Indians come from sunset. Find trail to sunrise blocked by Allegewi forts," the Little Captain went on. "Leni-Lenape much angry, but Allegewi forts much strong. Then fierce Iroquois come from far into sunset. Iroquois and Leni-Lenape drive Allegewi to island in O-hi-o waters. Kill all. Now Ken-tuck-ee dark and bloody ground haunted by angry spirits of very long ago people."

In a way, it made Sarah feel better to know that, although the settlers were taking parts of Kentucky away from the Indians, the Indians had first taken it away from other people. And who knew where the Allegewi got it. Kentucky surely was, as the Little Captain put it, "a dark and bloody ground."

★ Chapter Twelve ★

And she, for one, wished she were back in Virginia!

Sarah yawned widely. Were Pa and that Indian going to talk all night? Then another shiver crept down her spine. How did they know they really could trust the Little Captain? Suppose after they went to sleep, he decided to murder them and take their scalps after all?

I'll just have to keep watch, she promised herself. *And if that Indian moves one inch from wherever he beds down, I'll scream loud enough to wake all the dead Allegewis in Kentucky!*

Her eyelids, though, grew heavier and heavier, and her yawns grew wider and wider. One moment she was Sarah Moore watching her pa and the Little Captain sitting by the fire, and the next she was a young Allegewi girl running from a fierce Leni-Lenape warrior. Just as she felt his hands grab her by the hair and heard him laughing as he raised his tomahawk to scalp her, she woke up to find Jamie laughing out loud as he pulled her braids with both chubby hands.

She sat up and rubbed her eyes, glad to be awake and to find she had been dreaming. Ma was starting breakfast in the half-light of early dawn. Pa and Luke were still asleep.

Sarah looked around for the Little Captain, but he was nowhere in sight. For a moment, she wondered if she had dreamed the whole thing. Then she saw the round silver disk swinging from its rawhide string around Ma's neck. The rank-smelling bag was gone, and she didn't know whether the Indian had kept it or Ma had thrown it away. But she knew they really had entertained an Indian visitor in the night, and that he had tried to pay Ma for his supper by giving her his necklace.

There was nothing Sarah liked better than watching Pa add logs to the walls of their cabin. For days he and Luke had cut thick, heavy logs and dragged them to the cabin site with the horses. Then they notched the ends of the logs so they would fit closely together to keep out the cold winter winds. Finally they started stacking the logs to make the cabin walls.

When the four walls reached Pa's waist, the cabin started to look snug and inviting. Sarah could hardly wait for the work to be finished, but it seemed to go so slowly!

Day by day, the walls grew until they were higher than Pa's head. Then he added a loft above, with a pole ladder to reach it. "Your bedroom, son," he said to Luke.

Finally, Pa laid poles across the top logs to hold a roof. He cut wide, flat slabs of wood from one of the bigger trees to make shingles. Then he asked Luke to whittle some wooden pins to hold the shingles on the roof.

When the roof was finished, Pa hung a thick wooden shutter on leather hinges over the small window opening that faced the woods behind the house. He took thicker slabs of wood and made a door to cover the opening in the front of the cabin facing the creek. He fastened the slabs to heavy wooden cross pieces and whittled a door latch with a hole in it.

Ma tied a deerskin string to the latch and pulled it through the hole to the outside. When pulled, the string lifted the latch and let the door swing open.

"When the latchstring is hanging outside, that tells visitors 'walk right in,' " Ma said.

"I wish we had some," Sarah said, thinking how nice it would be if Martha would come to the door, pull that latchstring, and walk into the cabin. And maybe Tiger would be with her. . . .

Luke pulled the string, and the door swung open on its leather hinges.

"Whew! Let me grease those hinges," Ma said. "I can't stand to hear that leather creak every time the door opens or shuts."

"What if a mean old Indian creeps up and pulls that latchstring some night while we're all asleep and . . ." Luke began.

"That latchstring will be pulled inside at night, young man," Ma said firmly, "and that door will be barred with a heavy wooden beam!"

"The Indians won't need the latchstring," Sarah pointed out, "with that big hole in the end of the cabin. Is that for another door, Pa?"

Pa chuckled. "If you and Luke and your Ma will help me get some rocks up here from the creek, I'll show you what that hole's for," he answered.

"That hole is where my fireplace is going to be," Ma said happily. "Oh, won't it be grand to have a fireplace to cook in again, and a place to hang all my utensils?"

"I'll just be glad to have a roof over me and four thick walls around my bed!" Sarah said.

"Whoa, there Sary! You'll have to do without a bed a while longer," Pa said. "It'll likely be winter before I have time to make furniture."

"I don't care," Sarah insisted. "At least the covers won't be damp from dew and rain."

"Amen to that!" Ma agreed. "Let's get to carrying rock!"

Before Pa quit yelling, "More rock!" they all had rough callouses on their hands. But Pa shaped and fitted those rocks into what Sarah was sure was the finest fireplace and chimney in Kentucky. Then he took the horses and hauled one very large, smooth stone to lay in front of the fireplace as a hearthstone.

Sarah was dreaming how nice it would be to have a hearthstone again when Pa broke into her thoughts.

"Come here, Sary," he said. "I'll show you how to chink the cabin to keep out the wind."

Anything to speed things up, Sarah thought as she watched Pa wedge chips of wood into the cracks between the logs. Then he smeared clay over the chips.

"You've got all summer to get the job done," Pa said, "but before the winter winds begin to howl, I want all the cracks filled." Pa stepped back to admire the sturdy cabin with its stone chimney rising white and strong against the dark logs.

Ma went over to lay her hand on his arm. "It's a comely house, Hi," she said softly.

"It's as cozy as a woodchuck's den," Pa agreed proudly.

It's almost as dark as one too, Sarah thought, but she didn't say anything. Anyway, the light from the fireplace and Ma's tallow candles would make a big difference. The only thing the cabin really lacked now was a floor. "Pa, are we going to have a floor?" Sarah asked as she remembered the dirt floors of some of the cabins at Harrodstown.

Pa grinned. "I'm not that ornery, Sary," he said. "And even if I was, your Ma wouldn't let me get by without putting a floor in that cabin."

"Well, a wood floor will make it warmer, and a whole lot cleaner!" Ma said firmly.

"See what I mean?" Pa asked, laughing.

Pa laid log floor joists across the dirt inside the cabin. The joists would hold the floor up off the ground so it wouldn't rot. Over the joists, he laid split yellow poplar logs

★ Chapter Thirteen ★

with the flat side up, and pegged them with some of Luke's wooden pins.

"We can't go barefoot on that!" Sarah said, disappointed at the floor's rough, splintery surface. The floors in their brick house had been as smooth as glass and waxed to a shine she could almost see herself in.

"It's not ever going to be the ballroom at the Governor's Palace," Ma said, "but I think I can improve it some. Luke, go down to the sandbar there by the creek and get me two half buckets of sand."

Luke looked up from his whittling. "Hand me the buckets, Sarah," he ordered.

Sarah turned around, ready to tell him to get them himself, but she was so eager to get the cabin finished and their things inside, she went after the buckets without a word.

"You'll just have to make two trips after the sand," she told him, handing him one empty bucket. "The other bucket's full of fresh drinking water. Unless you want to go to the spring again . . . "

Luke grabbed the bucket. "Oh, no, I won't. I'll just bring one full bucket and save myself a trip, smarty!" He strode off toward the creek, swinging the bucket in his hand by its leather handle.

From where she stood, Sarah could see him scoop up some sand in the bucket and then heap it full with his hands. He straightened up and lifted the handle, but the bucket stayed right where it was on the creek bank. Luke took both hands and tugged at the leather handle, but the bucket seemed to have taken root in the sand.

"Hey, Luke! Where's that sand?" Ma called from inside the cabin.

99

Sarah could see Luke hurriedly scooping sand out of the bucket with both hands. When he had it about half full, he lifted it, but just barely. He staggered up the bank with the bucket, and half dragged it to the cabin. He looked straight ahead as he passed Sarah, who was holding both hands over her mouth to keep Ma from hearing her laughter.

"Dump it on the floor and go get some more," Ma ordered. "And, Sarah, stop that sniggering and come help me scrub this floor!"

Sarah went into the cabin, got down on her knees, and, like Ma, began scrubbing the rough floor with the loose sand. When Luke came back, this time with exactly half a bucket of sand, he dropped to his knees and started scrubbing. Sarah guessed he was tired of camping out, too.

At last Ma stood up and began sweeping the sand out the door. "We'll have to sand it again from time to time," she said, "but every time we do, it will get smoother and whiter. And nothing cleans a floor like sand."

Sarah had to admit the floor was smoother, but it was nothing to compare with their home in Virginia. It probably never would be.

"Well, let's get everything moved inside," Ma said.

Sarah felt her heart turn over. The cabin was finished! "Jamie, you stay right there," she warned, setting him in the sunlight just outside the door. She handed him Samantha to play with, then ran to catch up with Luke. He had grabbed the small iron kettle and the spider and was hurrying toward the cabin. Sarah picked up the feather quilts. Ma had her arms full of clothes and sacks of food.

"It looks kind of bare," Luke commented when they had finished stowing their few possessions neatly inside the cabin.

★ Chapter Thirteen ★

Sarah looked around critically. Luke was right. "It needs rugs and curtains," she said, "and beds and tables and chairs . . ."

"Children," Ma said quietly, "be thankful for what we've got. At least we'll be protected from the weather and the wilderness."

"I've got a big poplar log laid by," Pa said from the doorway. "I'll make a table and some benches as soon as I get the barn done. This winter, I'll make bedsteads and a china cupboard. You'll have nice things again one of these days, Della," he promised.

Ma smiled at him. "We can make do a while longer, Hi. Summer's here, and there's plenty to keep all of us busy. This winter when we're holed up in this cabin, you and Luke can make furniture. But the first thing I want is a loom, so Sarah and I can make rugs and curtains and bed covers. This cabin won't be bare come next spring!" She sashayed around the cabin. "Oh, it's grand having a house again! I don't know how to act! I feel like the Duchess of York or somebody!"

Sarah laughed with the others, but she knew exactly how Ma felt. Not having to sleep under a deerskin was going to be wonderful! And with their clothes and covers hanging from wooden pegs on one wall, and Ma's cooking utensils hanging around the fireplace, the cabin had begun to seem homey in spite of its bareness.

She walked to the door and looked out. The garden, corn, and wheat were green and growing, and with the cabin and animal pen finished and the barn taking shape, their place here on Stoney Creek was beginning to look something like a real farm.

Then a picture of another farm flashed across Sarah's

mind. There was a brick house with stepping stones leading past neat flower and herb borders to its doors, a barn full of sweet-smelling hay, and orchards abloom behind it. But she had been a part of the wilderness for so long now, Miller's Forks seemed like a dream or something pleasant remembered from another life.

I'll never forget it! I'll never be at home anywhere else! Sarah vowed fiercely. *And someday I'm going back!*

"It's easy living in the summertime," Ma said as she stirred the clothes boiling in water and lye soap over the hot fire. "I purely hate to do a washing in the house. It makes such a mess."

"Remember that Saturday night back home, Ma, when you hauled out the wooden tubs for baths, and Luke said he wished he was like a heavy bed cover and had to wait till spring to be washed?" Sarah asked with a giggle, as she looked for a place to spread the rest of the clean clothes to dry. She had filled the clothes poles and still had a basket of wet clothes to go.

"Luke didn't mind taking his bath as much as he minded carrying the water," Ma said, laughing. "I reckon he'd be glad to know that after I shaved off the soap for this morning's washing, there wasn't enough left for him to take a good bath! I think I'll stir up a batch of soap after we eat. . . ." Then she gasped. "Mercy sakes, Sarah, run in and stir that soup! I clean forgot it!"

Sarah ran inside, swung the crane away from the fire, and stirred the vegetable soup bubbling in the small iron kettle. It was just thick enough and smelled so good it made her mouth water. "I think I love Ma's vegetable soup better than anything she makes," Sarah said aloud to the empty room. "Except, maybe, that spice cake with brown sugar icing."

They hadn't had any kind of cake for a long time now, for Ma was saving what little sugar they had left to make wild blackberry jam.

Pa had promised they would have a sugaring off next spring when the maple trees were ready to be tapped, but it was too late this year to make maple sugar. The trees had to be tapped for their sweet sap in February.

Sarah hated to think of doing without anything sweet until next February. Back home, they sometimes had bought cones of brown sugar, and they had raised sorghum to make a thick, dark-brown molasses. Sarah didn't like it nearly so much as maple sugar, but it was welcome on the table when the sugar bowl was empty. They hadn't had any sorghum to plant this year, though.

Surely Ma would find something to take the place of sugar and molasses. She was good at what she called "making something out of nothing." When both their tea and coffee ran out, Ma discovered a tree with pods of seeds that could be boiled to make a slightly bitter drink that tasted something like coffee. Pa said it was "better than nothing, but just barely!"

Sarah stirred the soup one more time. It smelled so good! Maybe she could take just one sip before she went back outside. She glanced out the cabin door. Ma was dumping the soapy water out of the wash kettle. She rinsed it out, hung it back over the fire, and began ladling grease into it to melt for making soap.

Sarah dipped up a spoonful of soup, blew on it, and let it drain from the wooden spoon into her waiting mouth. "Whew!" she breathed. It was hot! But it was delicious! The first soup of the year from fresh garden vegetables was always the best.

"Sarah!" Ma called. "Come finish hanging out the clothes!"

Quickly, Sarah laid the spoon down and swung the kettle back closer to the fire to keep the soup hot. She ran back outside. Where in world was she going to hang that last basket of clothes? She supposed she'd have to spread them on the grass. But where? The taller grass at the edge of the meadow would be better for keeping the wet things off the ground, but . . .

Sarah gasped at the sight that met her eyes. The whole meadow was covered with a beautiful purplish-blue haze. "Ma!" she called. "Look at the meadow! What is it?"

Ma laughed. "You thought your Pa was teasing about that blue grass, didn't you? Well, there it is, Sarah, bluegrass in bloom!"

Sarah couldn't take her eyes off of it. The whole meadow was covered with that bluish color. It was breathtaking! And now she understood: The grass was green, but its blooms were blue!

"Here, I'll help you spread those clothes to dry, and then we'll have some of that soup," Ma said.

Sarah didn't wait for a second invitation! "You go on and dish it up, Ma," she said, spreading clothes on the tall grass as fast as she could. "I'll be right there!"

Before they were through eating, both she and Ma had finished two big bowls of vegetable soup, and even Jamie had cleaned his bowl. Then they went back outside to make soap.

They had been saving wood ashes from the fireplace in a wooden tub that had a small hole near the bottom. When they poured water over the ashes, it trickled through them and out of the hole in a brownish stream of lye water that was saved in another tub below.

Ma took some melted grease from the fire and poured some of the lye water into it. The lye made the mixture boil just like it was still over a hot fire.

"Watch the baby, Sarah," she cautioned. "That lye water will burn the skin right off his bones!"

Sarah held tightly to Jamie's hand as they watched Ma stir the lye mixture with a wooden paddle. Finally it formed a soft, cream-colored soap that would harden into the big cakes they used to wash everything. "It looks a lot like maple sugar," Sarah said, her mind returning to sweetening.

"I wouldn't want to take a taste!" Ma said. "I wouldn't even wash my face in it. But it does get dirty hands and clothes clean."

"And it makes hair soft and shiny," Sarah said.

"I think we've got enough soap to last till next summer," Ma said, setting the lye tub back under the ash tub. "Looks like we're done."

"Whew!" Sarah said, wiping her face on her arm. "I'm worn to a frazzle!"

Ma smiled, smoothing a stray curl into the tuck on the back of her head. "You've been a lot of help, Sarah. I just don't know what I'd do without my girl," she added seriously.

★ Chapter Fourteen ★

Sarah caught her breath, feeling a strange warmth spread through her. Ma seldom said anything like that.

"If you don't need me, Ma," she said, "I think I'll go down by the creek awhile. It's so pretty down there, with wildflowers blooming everywhere. And that creek bank is a regular apothecary shop! There's the orange butterfly weed you use to treat fevers and rheumatism, and those fuzzy mullein leaves you make poultices out of for asthma or the lung fever, and there's wild cherry trees to make cherry bark cough syrup." She knew she was babbling, but Ma's unaccustomed praise had confused and embarrassed her.

Ma picked up the bucket of cream she had saved from the morning's milking and dumped it into the cedar churn.

"Oh, are you starting a churning? I reckon I'd better not go, then," Sarah said. "You'll want me to watch after Jamie." She couldn't keep the disappointment out of her voice.

"Take him with you," Ma suggested. "And see if you can find that old goose's nest while you're down there. I fear a fox or a 'possum will get the goslings when they hatch if we don't keep an eye on them."

"All right, Ma," Sarah promised, taking Jamie by the hand.

"Go keek, Sadie?" he asked happily, toddling along beside her.

Sarah dropped a kiss on his blond hair. He was still small enough to need watching most of the time, and Ma stayed so busy the job fell to her more often than not. She was used to helping, though, and she had more time there. The work was harder and they had fewer tools to help with it, but there were no windows to wash, no furniture to dust, and only the one floor to scrub with sand. Back in Virginia, they had been constantly scrubbing and waxing and polishing.

Luke had more free time there too, with no school and only the one fireplace to keep supplied with wood. Of course, Pa was always having him help build something, but it seemed to her that Luke spent a good bit of time alone on the creek bank, whittling while he waited for the fish to bite. He wouldn't let her go with him. He said she talked too much and scared away the fish.

Well, let him have his old spot on the creek bank! Sarah had discovered a place of her own that Mr. Luke didn't even know was there. From the yard, it looked like just another giant sycamore tree spreading its white limbs over the creek. Even from down on the creekbank, the opening was hardly visible, hidden behind that small cedar bush. Once inside the hollow trunk, though, Sarah could stand upright, and she could stretch both arms wide without touching either side of the secret room inside the heart of the tree.

It was her own special place where she could go to think or to daydream, to plan all the wonderful things she would do when she went back to Virginia. And it was there that she kept the family of stick dolls she had worked so hard to make, along with their wood chip plates and little acorn cups and saucers. She also had made a rock table and chairs and a small fireplace, which Jamie had knocked over one day. He had torn up one of the dolls, too.

Sarah was ashamed to remember how she had yelled at the baby and slapped his little hands. Jamie, of course, had run to Ma, crying. But Ma hadn't scolded her. She understood about the playhouse, maybe because she had been a little girl once herself. Anyway, she kept Jamie at the cabin when Sarah went to the hollow tree after that, and she hadn't let Sarah's secret out to Luke.

Sarah sighed. She couldn't go to the playhouse today with Jamie along. She looked down at him, toddling happily beside her. "Come on, Jamie," she said, "we'll find that old goose's nest, and then we'll go play in the creek."

"Pay keek?" Jamie repeated.

"Ouch!" Sarah yelled as her bare toe hit a sharp rock. She examined the cut under her big toe. It was bleeding freely. Wearing shoes would have protected her feet, but she and Luke always went barefoot from the first day of summer until the first frost. She doubted that she could get her shoes on, anyway, if her feet had grown the way they usually did.

Sarah wondered if the cobbler would come around to make shoes this fall like he had in Virginia. She swished her foot in the creek to wash off the dirt and blood. But there probably wasn't a cobbler in Kentucky. Ma would just have to make them deerskin moccasins like the Indians wore. She had already made Luke some to wear when he went hunting, since they were quieter than his heavy shoes.

Sarah sat Jamie down, and he promptly began to cover his feet and legs with sand. She looked at her cut again. The cold water had slowed the bleeding, but it hadn't stopped. Ma had put a spider's web on a cut on Pa's leg once when he hit it with the ax, and the bleeding had stopped soon afterward. Sarah slowly made her way along the creek, looking for a web. There wasn't a spider's web anywhere in sight, though. "If I wasn't looking for one, I'd run smack into the creepy thing and get it all over my face!" she said aloud.

She bent down to examine her foot again. The bleeding

had finally stopped. *I'd better look for that goose's nest if I'm going to find it before dark,* Sarah thought. There was no telling where that old goose had hidden her eggs.

"Let's go, Jamie," Sarah said. But when she turned to where she had left him in the sand, he wasn't there.

"Jamie!" she called softly. Ma would give her a switching if she found out Sarah had taken her eyes off that baby for a minute. Then cold fear crawled down her spine. What if he had wandered into a bear's den or stumbled over a copperhead or fallen into a deep hole of water? What if he had run into a band of Indians?

"Jamie!" Sarah strained her ears to hear over the gossipy whispering of the creek. If Jamie was nearby, he was probably playing "mousie," a game she had taught him to play when she wanted him to be quiet and not bother her.

Then relief swept over her. Sarah could hear Jamie singing one of his little "happy" songs. All at once, Sarah knew where he was. She tiptoed over to the hollow tree and peered inside.

Jamie sat in the secret room, rocking back and forth, singing his funny little off-key lullaby to a stick doll he held cradled in his arms. His eyes widened when he saw Sarah, and he let the song trail off.

"Sadie mad?" he asked fearfully. "Sadie 'pank Jamie?"

Sarah grabbed him and hugged him, not caring that she was crushing the doll. She even let him keep it when she carried him to the cabin.

"Did you find the nest?" Ma asked as they came through the doorway.

Sarah had to think a minute before she remembered what Ma was talking about. "Not yet, Ma," she answered, "but I'm going back to look right now." She sat Jamie down

★ Chapter Fourteen ★

on the floor and ran out of the cabin before Ma could ask
what she'd been doing down there all that time.

The closest Sarah came to finding those goose eggs,
though, was when the old goose waddled proudly into the
yard several days later with eight fluffy yellow goslings
trailing along behind her.

P_a, let's go fishing tomorrow," Luke said at supper one evening toward the first of August. "We don't have much to do until harvest."

Pa sat there a minute, holding a bowl of green beans and summer squash, staring at Luke. "How do you think your Ma's going to make bread out of whole corn and wheat kernels, son?" he finally asked, passing the bowl to Sarah.

Luke looked puzzled. "But after we take the corn and wheat to the mill, Ma will have cornmeal and flour. . . ." His words trailed off. "Oh," he said. His face turned red as they all laughed.

"That's right," Pa said. "There's not a grist mill anywhere near here. There was one over on Elkhorn Creek, but the Indians burned it."

Sarah looked at Ma. How could she sit there with an unconcerned smile on her face, knowing there was no mill to grind the wheat into flour or the corn into meal? "What are we going to do, Ma?" she asked anxiously.

"It appears to me your pa's fixing to become a miller," Ma answered.

Pa nodded. "I aim to start on our mill first thing in the morning. We've got good water power here to turn the mill wheel and plenty of rock and timber to build any kind of mill we want. It may take the rest of the summer," he added, "but, come harvest time, God willing, we'll have our own mill."

Sarah clapped her hands in delight. "I always loved the dusty, musky smell of the mill at Miller's Forks, and the roar of the wheel as the water poured over it!" she exclaimed.

Before Pa's mill was finished, though, Sarah wished she had never heard of a grist mill. She, Ma, and Luke carried rock until their hands were calloused and their backs ached, and still Pa yelled, "More rock!"

"I think Pa discards more rocks than he uses!" Sarah panted under her load as she passed Luke carrying two buckets.

Luke nodded. "And it sure takes a lot of wet clay to stick 'em together!"

"More clay!" Pa yelled.

Luke rolled his eyes. "I'm glad he's only building the part of the wall that goes down into the water out of rock!" he said fervently as he trudged up the creek to the clay bank.

At night, they were all so tired they dropped onto their pallets on the floor and didn't stir until the rooster's crow announced the sunrise. Pa said later he reckoned that was why none of them realized they had had a midnight visitor until it was too late.

One misty morning when Luke went to turn the cow and

calf out to pasture, he came running back to the cabin. "Pa! Pa!" he panted, falling in the cabin doorway, "a bear's . . ."

Pa grabbed his gun and was out the door and gone before Luke could get his breath. ". . . tracks are all around the barn," he finished saying to Ma and Sarah. Then he turned and ran after Pa.

Pa was just coming back around the barn when Ma and Sarah got there. "Did you see which way he went, Luke?" he asked. "There are tracks in the mud all around the barn, but they don't show up in the grass outside the barn lot."

Sarah thought the tracks looked like they were made by a giant with claws on his toes who danced around the barn barefoot.

"I didn't see the bear, Pa," Luke explained. "You left before I could finish. I was trying to say, 'A bear's tracks are all around the barn. And there are claw marks on the doors.'"

"I see," Pa said, a funny half-smile playing over his mouth as he examined the tracks and claw marks. "He's a big one," he said, "at least a 400 pounder I'd guess, but it looks like our barn stood the test. I don't think he got inside." He swung the big barn doors open. The horses and the cow and calf were all right.

"What was he after, Pa?" Luke asked. "The calf?"

"Maybe. I think it's a mite big for him, though. Black bears are full of curiosity. Full of tricks, too. They can climb a tree like a kitten. Once I came upon a pair of black bears who were standing on their heads and turning somersaults and dancing around like two young 'uns playing." Suddenly Pa stopped talking. He turned and ran outside.

Sarah came up behind Pa at the rail of the pigpen and saw his shoulders slump. "That's what he came after, and that's what he got," he said. "The pig's gone."

"Are we going after him?" Luke asked eagerly.

"It's too late to do the pig any good," Pa answered. "Wonder why that hound of yours didn't bark last night and wake us up? I was so tired from working on that mill, though, I doubt I'd have heard thunder!"

"Here, Hunter! Here, boy!" Luke called. Then he whistled his special whistle that always made the dog come running. But if Hunter heard, he didn't answer. Pa was looking worried now too.

"Hiram!" Ma called. "Hunter's out here behind the cabin. He's hurt!"

Luke ran toward the cabin, with Pa and Sarah right behind him. Sarah caught her breath when she saw the dog. His head had a large gash across the top, one of his long ears was tattered, and his left eye was swollen shut.

"I heard him whining back here," Ma explained. "He was trying to get to Luke when he whistled, but he's too weak to stand up."

Pa leaned over and picked up the dog gently. "He's lost a lot of blood," he said. "Ma, send me some lavender water out to the barn and some bread soaked in milk."

Sarah followed Pa and Luke to the barn, trying to swallow the lump in her throat. Hunter might die, and all because he had been brave enough to tackle that murdering old bear. Ma soon followed with the lavender water and bread.

"He'll be all right," Pa said as he bathed the dog's wounds. "Your ma's lavender water will clean the cuts and help them heal, and the bread will give him strength."

Hunter wasn't eating, though. He just lay on the hay and let Pa doctor him, with only a low whimper of pain

116

when the lavender water stung the cuts. His good eye was glazed and dull-looking.

"Pa," Luke said loudly, "we've got to get that bear!" Then he turned and stumbled out of the barn. Sarah knew he didn't want them to see the tears in his eyes. She felt like bawling herself. No matter what Pa said, Hunter looked like he was dying.

For the next few days, Ma doctored Hunter, and he seemed a little stronger. At least she no longer had to coax him to eat the food she carried to the barn.

Finally the rock work was done, and Pa and Luke cut, hauled, and notched logs for the upper walls of the mill. When a day of rain set in, they both sat in the cabin whittling paddles for the mill wheel.

Sarah had gone back to chinking the cabin, working quickly to make up for the time lost in carrying rock for the mill. "Wish I could just yell, 'More clay!' and somebody would bring it to me," she said wearily as she sank onto her pallet one night, almost a week after the bear had paid them his visit. When nobody said anything, she knew they were all as tired as she was.

The fire was almost out and the cabin was dark when Sarah woke up that night. The square of window where moonlight usually crept in around the shutter was even blacker than the rest of the cabin. Sarah rubbed her eyes. They felt like they were full of sand. She surely had been sleeping hard. . . .

A loud, rumbling roar outside raised the hair on the back of her neck and almost shook the cabin. Hunter was barking furiously inside the barn. Sarah felt, more than saw, Pa grab his gun and head for the door. Luke joined him in the doorway in his night shirt. Pa must have been sleeping with his clothes on, for he was fully dressed. He must have been expecting that bear to show up again.

"If I shoot and miss," she heard him tell Luke as they left the cabin together, "that bear will be gone before I can reload. If I only wounded him, he may attack us. I've got to kill him with my first shot!"

Sarah ran to the doorway. The moon was coming up over the trees, but it was still very dark out there. She could barely make out the shape of the barn and Pa and Luke standing at the corner of the cabin.

"Stay behind me so I won't shoot you by mistake," she heard Pa whisper to Luke. "I can't see much out here."

As they moved away from the cabin, Sarah followed to the corner. She looked back and saw Ma standing in the doorway.

Looking toward the barn, she could see the bear now, standing on his hind legs, a darker shadow among shadows. She could feel her heart begin to pound in her throat.

Pa stooped, picked up something, and threw it at the bear. The bear turned slowly and looked at him. Sarah could see his small, mean-looking eyes glittering red in the moonlight.

"Oh, Lord, guide this bullet!" she heard Pa pray as his gun exploded.

The bear gave an angry roar. He took four or five steps toward Pa, then stopped. Sarah could hear Pa frantically trying to reload the gun. The bear swayed and swiped at his head with one huge paw.

"You hit him, Pa!" Luke shouted.

The bear stood there a moment, then fell to the ground with a heavy thud and lay still.

"Boy, right between the eyes!" Luke yelled.

"His eyes were all I could see, son," Pa answered.

"Praise the Lord!" Sarah heard Ma breathe.

"Well, there's bear steak for supper and a bear skin rug for the floor," Pa said.

"And tallow for candles," Ma added shakily.

"There's one bear that won't hurt my dog again!" Luke said. From inside the barn, Hunter barked, as if to say, "Amen!"

Sarah just stood there, thinking. She knew Pa shot animals for food all the time, but she usually wasn't there to watch. One moment that big bear had been standing there threatening them all, and the next he was lying dead on the ground. Was that the way it was in a war? Did Nate have to shoot other men the way Pa had shot the bear? Then Sarah had a terrible thought. They hadn't heard from Nate for a long, long time. Had some British bullet done to him what Pa's had done to that bear?

All at once, a longing pierced through her as sharply as a bullet, a longing for a time when all of them had been safe by the kitchen fireplace in the brick house, laughing and talking around the table as they ate or worked or played together. She winced at the pain of the memory. Would it ever be that way for them again?

I wish Ma *would hurry up and find something to use for sweetening,* Sarah thought as she reached for the tin box on the mantel to store the new candles she and Ma had made.

Since Ma had not been able to bring the heavy candle molds she used back in Virginia, she had showed Sarah how to dip tightly-rolled strings of cloth into the melted fat from the bear again and again until it hardened into fat yellow candles. Except for the fireplace, those candles would be their only source of light during the long, dark winter evenings, and Sarah was glad Ma had found something to substitute for the sheep's tallow they didn't have here.

Ma almost always knew something to use in place of whatever they ran out of, but it had been two weeks now since the sugar sack was emptied, and so far, she hadn't come up with a substitute. Sarah was so hungry for something sweet that, after her chores were done, she set out to hunt for berries or anything that might satisfy her sweet tooth. She hunted all afternoon, but she came back to the cabin with an empty bucket and an equally empty stomach.

"Hey, Sarah, guess what we found!" Luke yelled excitedly as she started across the clearing. She looked back to see Pa, Luke, and Hunter coming across the meadow.

Hunter was still a good hunting dog, even though he had only one eye now. He could trail deer and rabbits or tree squirrels and raccoons, but that wasn't anything to get so excited about. Wild game was standard fare around here. Anyway, Pa and Luke were carrying nothing but their guns.

"Give up?" Luke asked as they neared the cabin.

"I guess so," Sarah answered crossly. She was in no mood for games.

"How would you like to have some biscuits dripping with sweet, golden honey?" Luke teased.

"Luke, that's not funny," she began. Then she realized what he and Pa must have found. "A bee tree!" she shouted. "You found a bee tree?"

Luke was shaking his head no, ready to tease some more, but Pa said, "Don't be cruel, son. Sary's got a sweet tooth as big as that hollow tree where the bees hid all that sweet, wild honey!" He grinned at her. "The bees don't know it yet, but they're going to share it with us. We'll have hot biscuits and butter and honey for breakfast in the morning, Sary girl."

Sarah danced around the yard with happiness, then ran to tell Ma.

"Won't that taste good!" Ma exclaimed as Pa and Luke came into the cabin. "I'll make us a little cake tomorrow out of flour and eggs and honey. And we can sweeten our coffee, such as it is, and have pancakes and honey. Oh, won't it be nice to have something sweet for a change?"

Sarah laughed. It seemed she wasn't the only one who had been craving something sweet. She didn't think she could wait for Pa and Luke to get back home with it. "Let me help get the honey, please, Pa!" she begged. If she could go with him, she could bite into that syrupy sweetness in its waxy comb as soon as Pa began to cut it from the hollow tree.

"I don't know, Sary," Pa said doubtfully. "The bees get a mite angry when they catch somebody robbing their honeycomb. And I can't say I blame 'em. But I aim to leave enough for the bees to eat on this winter. It's getting too late for them to make another store of honey this year, and I don't want them to starve out. Maybe later I can catch the queen bee and get the swarm to move to a hive I'll build near the cabin. Then we can have honey whenever we want it. They always make plenty for them and us, too."

"That's what God meant for them to do," Ma said.

"You mean God knew we'd run out of sugar?" Sarah asked in surprise. She could feel her face turning red as they all laughed.

"I reckon God made honeybees before Adam and Eve ever learned how to raise sugarcane or tap a sugar tree," Pa said.

That evening, as the sun was sinking in a red glow behind the hills, Sarah dressed in Luke's other breeches and shirt. She tied the legs and sleeves around her ankles and wrists as Pa and Luke were doing to keep the bees out of their clothing. Seeing Pa put on his hat and Luke his 'coonskin cap, she tied a scarf over her head and ears.

Pa carried his gun in one hand and the lantern in the other. Luke had the ax and the big butcher knife. Sarah followed them across the meadow, carrying the extra wooden bucket.

At the edge of the dark woods, she stopped and looked back. Ma stood in the cabin doorway with Jamie in her arms, and, for a moment, Sarah wished she had stayed with them. Over by the creek, the frogs were croaking their evening songs, but here at the edge of the woods, it was still. All she could hear was the whisper of the breeze through the cedars and the far-off, lonesome cry of a whippoorwill.

Pa's lantern bobbed on ahead, and Sarah hurried to catch up before its friendly glow was swallowed by the first big trees. The forest was dark and mysterious, even in the daytime; she certainly didn't want to get lost from Pa and wander around in it alone at night! She wasn't really afraid of the dark, or even of wild animals. But a body never knew when Indians lurked in the woods. That whippoorwill, for instance . . . Sarah shivered as the eerie cry was repeated.

"It's just over this next little rise, beyond that white oak." Pa's voice was just above a whisper.

Sarah couldn't tell a white oak from a sassafras bush in the thick blackness, but Pa's footsteps never faltered, and Luke was right behind him. She followed as closely as she could, doing her best not to stumble over roots and vines.

Suddenly her nostrils picked up a thick, warm, sweet smell that made her mouth water. She could almost feel the smooth sweetness of wild honey spreading over her tongue! She hardly heard the whippoorwill's cry that time, as she stood listening to the roar of the bees.

Pa hung the lantern on a branch several feet away from where they had stopped. When the bees swarmed around the lantern, Pa took his ax and began chopping carefully at a fallen log, lifting the wood chips out and laying them aside. Soon the ax came out dripping golden honey.

"Hand me the bucket, Sary," Pa ordered, not bothering to slap at an angry bee that had landed on his hand. He took the knife and lifted out a sheet of dripping honey-comb. Sarah reached for a piece of waxy comb and sucked on it happily, staying out of the way of the bees. Luke slapped at the bees now buzzing furiously, and got two stings on his hands and one on his neck before Pa had the bucket as full as he could carry it without spilling honey.

"I wish we had more buckets," he said. "We could take several gallons more and still leave plenty for the bees."

The whippoorwill called quietly. Then, not far beyond the circle of light, the call was answered, softly, perfectly. Pa reached quickly for the lantern and blew it out. Sarah felt his hand on her arm, warning her to silence. She could feel the hair rising on the back of her neck.

She sensed, rather than saw, Pa grope for the ax and the gun. He handed her the dark lantern and guided her with one hand through the forest, back the way they had come. At least, she thought it was the way they had come. She couldn't see a foot in front of her face. But maybe that was good for them. Maybe the Indians couldn't see, either.

Sarah clutched the lantern tightly against her chest so it wouldn't rattle. She didn't dare stumble now. The whippoorwills were calling from all directions, softly, but insistently.

At the edge of the black forest, she could see the meadow gleaming silver in the moonlight. How could they make it across the moonlit meadow without being targets for arrows or tomahawks?

"Crawl!" Pa hissed. Sarah dropped to her hands and knees and felt the tall meadow grass close over her head. She was glad she was wearing Luke's breeches and had no long skirt to tangle around her legs. She laid the lantern aside and began to crawl. She could hear a whispering sound and hoped it was Luke or Pa crawling through the grass behind her.

The whippoorwills were at the edge of the forest now. Sarah didn't dare raise up to look, but she could hear them calling to each other.

The cabin clearing stretched ahead of them. Once they reached the clearing, there would be no cover of any kind to hide them. . . . Suddenly Sarah felt something grab her foot, and she almost screamed before she realized it was Pa trying to stop her.

He eased up beside her and breathed his words right into her ear. "Keep still." She felt Luke slide up on the other side of her.

Sarah lay flat on the ground, her heart pounding so loudly she was sure the Indians could hear it. Her mouth was so dry, she couldn't swallow. Her arms and legs ached from crawling.

The whippoorwills hadn't called for several minutes when Pa almost scared her out of her wits by yelling, "Ma! Open the door and keep back!"

Ma must have been waiting for them, for the door swung open. The opening was outlined clearly by the firelight from inside, but Ma was nowhere to be seen.

There was no sound from the forest now. "Run!" Pa whispered. "Zigzag and get inside, quick!"

Luke didn't wait to be told twice. He was up and running, bent over, zigzagging across the open clearing. But Sarah was too scared to move. She was sure that her legs would fold up under her if she tried to run.

"Run, Sary!" Pa hissed.

She jumped up and ran, zigzagging like Luke. Her shoulder blades tingled, expecting an arrow between them at every step, but at last she was through the doorway and diving to safety behind the thick log wall. She sat there a few seconds, panting for breath.

Luke was beside her, and Ma was standing behind the door. Jamie lay sleeping in the corner. Sarah was working up the courage to go see what had happened to Pa, when he came hurtling through the doorway. Ma slammed the door behind him and threw the heavy bar across it.

"Thank the good Lord you're safe!" she sighed, sinking down on the hearthstone.

Pa still had the wooden bucket, Sarah noticed then. It had some twigs and grass in it, but at least half of the honey still was there.

"I left the lantern, Pa," she said. "Weren't you afraid the Indians would catch you if you tried to make it across the meadow with that bucket?"

Pa's laugh was a little shaky. "I feared the Indians," he said, "but I feared more what your ma would do if I came back without that honey!"

Luke and Sarah laughed, but Ma's face was pale and she looked scared. "Hiram Moore, you about scared the living daylights out of me!" she said. "I thought sure the Indians had you all!"

"Never in my life have I heard anything so scary as those whippoorwill calls," Sarah said shivering. "I'll never like whippoorwills again."

"How did you know it was Indians, Pa?" Luke asked. "They sounded just like whippoorwills to me."

"They kept getting closer, son, and there were too many of them. You hardly ever hear more than one or two whippoorwills at a time. Something just told me it was time to go home."

"You think they're gone?" Ma asked. Sarah saw her glance anxiously at Jamie, asleep on his quilt.

"I don't know," Pa answered. "I think so, but I aim to sit up and watch the rest of the night. I don't think it was a war party, though. There were only four or five of them. Most likely a hunting party. They may not think it's worth the risk to attack across the clearing."

"I'll sit up with you," Ma offered.

"Oh, no you won't!" Pa said. "I didn't go to all that trouble and risk my scalp for nothing! You get some sleep so you can get up early and fix hot bread to go with that honey for breakfast!"

"Yum! Yum!" Sarah and Luke said together.

Sarah's heart really wasn't in it, though. When she had run so desperately for the cabin, it had seemed to offer safety. Now, thinking how insecure the small, lonely wooden shelter really was out there in the middle of the vast, untamed wilderness, she wanted to run again—back to civilization, to Miller's Forks, to the brick house so snug behind its trim fences in the midst of its cultivated fields and orchards. And long after the deep, black stillness of night had settled over the cabin, she wet her pillow with silent tears.

W hat are we going to use in place of salt, Ma?" Sarah called, turning the empty salt sack upside down and shaking it.

"Land sakes, Sarah, are we out of salt already?" Ma came over to the corner, drying her hands on her apron. "I knew it was getting low, but . . ." Sarah showed her the empty sack. "Well, then," Ma said quietly, "I reckon we'll do without until your pa can make a trip back over the mountains. Or maybe a peddler will bring some to sell at the forts, and he can get some there. It will cost a pretty penny, though, for it will be scarce. Nothing tastes good without salt, and everybody will be needing it to cure meat for the winter."

"You mean we can't find anything to use for salt?" Sarah asked. This was the first time Ma had given up without a try.

"Nothing on God's green earth can take the place of salt, Sarah," she said sadly.

Luke made a face when he tasted the stew that night at supper. "You forgot to salt this stew, Sarah," he complained.

"I did not!" Sarah snapped. "Anyway, Ma seasoned the stew."

Pa looked up. "Are you out of salt, Della?" he asked.

Ma nodded. She got up from the table and threw another log on the fire, though Sarah thought it already looked hot enough to keep the stew warm.

Pa began to eat. "It's not all that bad, Luke," he said. "Eat up. We're lucky to have it." He looked at Ma's back as she stoked the fire. "The mill's coming right along. We joined the beams to the mill wheel and the cog wheel today," he said. "Soon as Luke finishes carving the funnel, we'll try her out."

Sarah remembered watching Mr. Jason pour wheat or corn through the funnel at his mill. She remembered the sound the stones made as the millstone ground the grain between it and the flat stone beneath it.

"I'll have to send over the mountains for some real millstones the first chance I get," Pa's words broke into her memories. "The two big rocks Bess and Willie helped me haul from the creek are not big enough or smooth enough to grind your flour and meal as fine as you like it, Della. But they'll be a whole lot better than nothing!" He held out his bowl for more stew. "Eat up, young 'uns," he urged. "It'll put meat on your bones."

Sarah had thought nothing could be as bad as being out of sugar, but being without salt was much worse. Nothing tasted right anymore. She had never realized how valuable salt was, but they'd never been out of it before. Now she understood that verse in the Bible that said Christians were the "salt of the earth." Without salt, nothing was any good.

★ Chapter Seventeen ★

And though she tried and tried to find a substitute for it, Ma was right—there just wasn't one.

One evening toward the last of September, Sarah saw another flock of birds settle on the dry cornstalks for a picnic on their way south. Somehow it had become her job to protect the corn they needed so badly to feed their animals and themselves this winter.

"That scarecrow Ma made was a waste of time!" she said aloud as she clapped her hands at the noisy crows and cried, "Shoo! Shoo!"

All at once, the crows flew into the air, cawing excitedly, and Sarah heard a man's voice call, "Halloo there!" Peeking through the cornstalks, she saw two strange men dressed in buckskin, sitting on horses in the yard. The men had tied their bedrolls and cooking utensils behind their saddles. A third, riderless horse carried two big iron kettles and other equipment.

Pa came to the door with Ma, Luke, and Jamie behind him. "Well, howdy!" he said with a wide, welcoming grin. "Get down and come in."

The men hitched their horses to the fence. "Had your supper?" Sarah heard Pa ask as they disappeared inside the cabin. She didn't hear their answer, but she knew Ma would need her help if she had to get a meal for the men. The family had finished their supper awhile ago, and the dishes were washed and put away. Anyway, Sarah was curious about the strangers.

She crept into the cabin and over to where Ma was making coffee from her ground Kentucky coffee tree seeds. The men must have had supper, for Ma wasn't cooking anything. Sarah took down three tin mugs and polished them on her apron. She got out three silver spoons.

"Why don't you come along with us?" one of the men asked Pa.

Sarah saw Pa look at Ma, then at Luke. A frown creased his forehead. "I don't know, Jake. I don't like leaving the family here alone with Indian summer almost upon us."

Indian summer? Sarah thought. *What in the world is Indian summer?*

"There hasn't been a sizable party of Indians seen in Kentucky lately," the tall, thin man said. "There are more people coming in now, and folks are not as isolated as they used to be."

"We're right isolated here, Matt," Pa put in. "You can see that."

"There's a new settlement about six miles up the river," he replied.

The other stranger laughed. "It ain't nothing but a mud hole with a few houses built around it!"

"Still, there are people there, Jake. And there are settlements like it all over the country now. It's just going to keep growing, especially when the war ends."

"Have you heard any news of the war?" Pa asked eagerly. Sarah knew he had Nate on his mind. It had been so long since they had heard from him.

Jake spoke up, "Wal, the British has drove Washington out of New York, but the war ain't over by no means."

Matt broke in, "We've elected George Rogers Clark and John Gabriel Jones delegates to the Virginia Assembly. They're going to ask that Kentucky be made a legal county of Virginia so the laws of the Colony of Virginia will protect us."

"But we're already protected by the laws of England," Pa protested.

★ **Chapter Seventeen** ★

"Man, ain't you heard?" Jake burst out. "We've done throwed off the yoke of England!"

"I know there's a rebellion. My boy's fighting in it somewhere," Pa answered. "But I figured it would all blow over sooner or later."

"It ain't never gonna blow over till we're free!" Jake declared.

"I guess you haven't heard about the Declaration of Independence?" Matt asked. Pa shook his head, and Sarah held her breath to hear as Matt continued. "July the fourth, I think it was. The Colonial Assembly met in Philadelphia and signed a paper that said we want to be free from England, and we want to set up the United States of America as a separate country, ruled by nobody but ourselves."

Nate's words from that long ago April night came back to Sarah, "I believe with all my heart that God is leading these colonies to independence." She reckoned Nate was happy about that Declaration, if he were still alive.

"There's a new wind blowing through this land," Matt went on, "and it won't stop until we're free of all those who would tell us what to do and when to do it!"

Sarah caught her breath. There was that wind again, the one Nate had talked about. Had Matt heard it call his name too?

"We've won this country from the wilderness," Matt was saying, "and nobody less than God is going to tell us what to do with it!"

"Yea!" Luke shouted, jumping up from his place at the table. At Pa's look he sat back down, but Sarah knew just what Pa was going to say next.

"It's time you young 'uns were in bed," Pa said sternly.

135

Someday maybe Luke will learn to keep his big mouth shut, Sarah thought as she crawled under the covers, still in her clothes. She couldn't undress with the strangers in the room.

"Anyhow, we'd sure like for you to come along with us to the salt springs, Hiram," Matt said. "You say you need salt just like all the rest of us, and there's plenty there just for the boiling down."

"I thought only ocean water was salty," Luke said as he headed toward the loft where he slept. "How come these springs have salt in them?"

"Nobody knows," Matt answered. "I heard one fellow talking—a geologist, he called himself, studies rocks and things—he said Kentucky was under the ocean at one time, and when the land came up out of the water, it left salt springs in some of the low places. I don't know about that, but I do know the buffalo and deer come to the springs in big herds to lick the salty banks. And when the water is boiled away, it leaves as good a salt as any I ever tasted."

"And it saves making a trip over the mountains," Jake added. "This time of year, everybody needs salt for curing meat. There's a party of men from Harrodstown gonna meet us there. You come with us."

Pa looked at Ma. She didn't say a word, but Pa seemed to have his answer. "Luke, can you be man of the house for a couple of weeks?"

"Sure, Pa," Luke said eagerly. "I can do anything that needs doing around here. And if an Indian shows up, I'll . . . I'll . . ."

"You'll lock yourself in this cabin with your ma and Sary and the baby and pray like thunder he goes away!" Pa ordered. "Now get to bed!"

The men laughed. "We'd better get to bed too, if we're going to make an early start," Matt said. "All right if we bed down in your barn?"

"You can bed down right here by the fire," Pa said.

Sarah went to sleep that night with the snores of three men for a lullaby.

When she awoke, Ma was frying meat, and the bitter smell of the substitute coffee filled the cabin. Pa was dressed in his buckskin breeches and shirt and was tying a bedroll like Matt's and Jake's.

"I don't know how I'll get along without my kettle. . . ." Ma began.

"We won't need it, ma'am," Matt said quickly. "We've got two big kettles, and we can't all cook salt at the same time. Somebody has to keep the fires hot and the kettles full of water. But Hiram will need something to carry the salt back."

Ma handed Pa the empty salt sack. She hesitated a moment, then handed him the clean sugar sack too. "It may be a long time before we have any sugar to keep in that sack," she said, "and we need all the salt you can bring back, Hi."

Sarah tried to concentrate on how good it would be to have salt in their food again, and not think about how lonely it made her feel watching Pa ride off on old Willie behind Jake and Matt.

It seemed strangely quiet around the cabin after Pa and the men had ridden out of sight. It was scary knowing Pa was gone and they would be alone for at least two weeks. Sarah hoped there were no Indians within miles of Stoney Creek. Suddenly she remembered Pa's words last night. "Ma," she asked, "what is Indian summer?"

"It's that last warm spell in the fall before winter sets in, usually toward the last of October, Sarah. We haven't had any hard frost or real cold weather yet. It's a mite early for Indian summer," Ma answered.

"But why do they call it Indian summer?"

"Because that's when the Indians make their last big raids before bad weather," Luke explained. "Big war parties come across the Ohio River and up from the Cumberlands into Kentucky and kill and burn up a storm!"

"Luke!" Ma scolded.

"It's true," Luke insisted. "I heard them talking about

it at the fort that time. The big attacks come in that warm spell in the fall because the Indians know it's their last chance before winter sets in. They're too busy keeping warm and fed then to do much raiding, so they make the most of that spell of pretty weather. They kill settlers, burn their cabins, then slip back across the rivers to safety."

"Well, children, we'd better get to harvesting the rest of the garden," Ma changed the subject briskly. "We'll have to store everything we can to last us until next year's garden comes on. I'll have to save seed for it too. Luke, you start digging a big hole to bury the sweet potatoes and cabbages so they won't freeze. First thing you know, we'll wake up with a big frost on the ground and everything will be ruined."

Ma put Sarah to picking the rest of the beans and making long strings of them to hang around the cabin walls. At first it was fun to string the bean pods like beads on a necklace, but by the time all the beans had been strung, Sarah knew why Ma called them "leather breeches." Her fingers were sore from pushing the needle through those tough hulls. It would be nice, though, to have a kettle of dried beans now and then this winter when there would be no vegetables growing in the garden.

Ma and Luke were busy burying the other vegetables in the hole Luke had dug and lined with straw. They spread straw over the vegetables to keep them clean, then laid split logs across the top of the hole before covering it all with dirt. It wasn't much like the neat rock cellar they had back in Virginia, but, as Pa always said, "It was better than nothing."

"We'll mark the hole with this stick so we can find it when it's covered with snow," Ma said, driving the end of a long stick into the ground beside their make-do cellar.

It seemed strange, Sarah thought, to be doing all these things without Pa. But the loneliest time that first day was when Ma picked up the Bible, as Pa did every night before bedtime, and began to read Psalm 91.

Sarah felt that scary loneliness creep over her. She wished Pa hadn't gone away. She'd rather do without salt. She wasn't afraid of bears or snakes or even mountain lions, though they had heard one scream the other night. She knew they would be safe from animals in the cabin. But could she, Ma, and Luke fight off Indians?

"Thou shalt not be afraid for the terror by night; nor for the arrow that flieth by day," Ma read. Sarah felt a thrill of wonder run through her. Those words seemed to have been written especially for her.

". . . there shall no evil befall thee, neither shall any plague come nigh thy dwelling." Ma went on, "For he shall give his angels charge over thee, to keep thee in all thy ways."

Ma believed those words. Sarah could tell she did. And Pa believed them too. If he didn't, he wouldn't have left them there alone. And so far, she had to admit something had protected them. Except for that night at the honey tree, they hadn't even heard an Indian. They had been lucky that night too. Or was it luck? No matter how bitter Sarah felt about God letting them come to Kentucky, maybe, like Pa, He wouldn't have let them come if He hadn't "given His angels charge over them." He was their heavenly Father, just like Pa was their earthly father. And fathers take care of their children.

All at once, Sarah was very sleepy. It had been a long, busy day.

In the days that followed, it seemed to Sarah that as soon as she had gone to bed, the rooster was crowing and faint streaks of daylight were showing around the window shutter. There weren't many resting times during the day, either. Sarah looked after Jamie and helped Ma gather and dry herbs and flowers for medicines and seasonings, while Luke stacked the long meadow grass he and Pa had cut for hay.

Sarah found that gathering eggs was easier now. The hens had made nests in the haystacks near the barn, and she didn't have to hunt for their nests all over the meadow.

Pa had not built a hayloft in their barn here like the one she remembered back in Virginia. The barn here was small, and with the sheaves of wheat waiting to be threshed, the corn piled in one corner, and the poles marking off stalls for the horses and the cow and calf, the barn was nearly full.

★ **Chapter Eighteen** ★

"Your pa will be tickled pink to see how much we've gotten done while he's been gone," Ma said as they sat around the fire after supper almost two weeks after Pa had left. They had been so busy, the weeks had gone by before Sarah knew it. She kept listening for sounds of Pa and old Willie as Ma talked. Pa could be home with the salt at any time now.

"About all we've got left to do," Ma went on, "is finish gathering the rest of the corn and kill and cure some meat."

"I know where there's a persimmon tree," Luke said. "As soon as there's a hard frost, we can pick them up. Right now, they're so green they'd pucker your mouth like a drawstring!"

"Don't forget the hickory nuts and walnuts," Sarah reminded them. She loved to sit before a winter fire and crack nuts on the hearthstone, eating the crunchy kernels and throwing the shells into the fire. A person could see mighty pretty pictures in the bright colors of a nut-hull fire.

The hickory logs in the fireplace popped merrily, sending up patterns of blue, red, orange, and yellow that reminded Sarah of the blue October sky and the red oak leaves, the orange maple leaves, and the yellow walnut and willow leaves. Better still, the sweet gum tree had all those colors and more.

"What do the colors in the fire remind you of?" she asked Ma and Luke.

"Patchwork quilts and braided rugs," Ma answered promptly.

"Indian war paint," Luke said.

"Hush, Luke!" Ma ordered.

"But, Ma, that's what they remind me of—war paint."

Sarah shivered. Luke and his big man talk! "I'm going

to bed," she said, yawning. She wished Luke hadn't mentioned Indians. She didn't feel as sleepy now as she had a few minutes ago, but she lay down on the pallet beside Jamie and was relieved to feel sleep creeping over her like mist over the meadow, relaxing her tired bones, carrying her . . .

What is that? Sarah wondered sleepily. It wasn't an animal noise. It wasn't the wind or the creek. . . . Suddenly she was wide awake. It was the mill wheel she had heard. The mill wheel was turning, fast!

Sarah sat up and looked around. Beside her, Jamie slept on his stomach with his little bottom sticking up in the air. It was too dark to see Ma clearly, but her slow, even breathing told Sarah she was asleep. There was no sound from the loft, which meant Luke was asleep too. She must have slept awhile herself, without realizing it, for the last thing she remembered was Ma slipping into her nightgown as Luke disappeared over the top of the ladder into the loft.

The mill wheel was turning furiously. That could mean only one thing—Pa was home! Sarah began pulling on her clothes. They were stiff with cold, but she hardly noticed. How good it would be to have Pa back! She slipped on the buckskin moccasins Ma had made her to replace her outgrown shoes. Moccasins were quieter than shoes, and she was thankful for that as she padded softly across the floor to the door. She didn't want to wake Ma or Luke. She wanted Pa all to herself for a few minutes.

The heavy door squeaked on its leather hinges as she eased it open. She pulled the latchstring through the hole to hang outside, and she pulled the door shut behind her. Sarah paused, holding her breath to listen for sounds of Ma or Luke inside, but apparently the squeaking hinges had not roused them. She let her breath out in a sigh of relief, promising herself she would grease those hinges with bear fat tomorrow.

Outside, it was dark and starry. To the left of the cabin, she could see the black shape of the mill in the moonlight and the high arc of spray the water made as it raced over the wheel. What on earth was Pa doing in the mill at this time of night?

The grass was white and crackly with a light frost. Sarah drew a deep breath of the cold night air that tingled in her nose and chest. Then she became aware of the smell of wood smoke.

The fire in the cabin was banked with ashes for the night. Where was that smoke coming from? Then she saw the thin wisps of smoke hanging over the mill. Pa had never built a fire in the mill. There was no fireplace. . . .

A sick feeling moved into the pit of her stomach. Sarah moved over to stand behind Ma's wash pot, wondering if she should go back and get Luke and the gun.

The wheel groaned, then suddenly stopped with a loud thunk. Sarah's heart sank. Pa would never treat the mill wheel so roughly. It had taken too much hard work to make.

The wheel was quiet, or as quiet as it ever was. It always made little murmuring protests when it was held by the big timber holding bar. Sarah could feel her heart pounding against her ribs.

Suddenly a fierce-looking Indian jumped out the doorway of the mill, looked around, and loped off toward the forest.

"Lord, help us!" Sarah breathed, watching the Indian disappear into the trees. She was shaking so hard her teeth rattled as she ran to the cabin, pulled the latchstring, and slipped inside.

"Ma! Luke!" she called softly. "Come quick! The mill's on fire!"

Sarah sat in the cabin doorway keeping watch while Ma and Luke put out the fire. Then they sat up the rest of the night, just in case the Indian came back. But they saw and heard nothing more of him.

Sarah breathed a sigh of relief when the morning sun peeped into the cabin. Surely they would be safe now, at least for the daylight hours.

Sarah threw a glance over her shoulder at the dark woods as she dipped up fresh water for breakfast. Surely on such a clear, golden morning no danger lurked anywhere around them.

Last night's crisp, light frost lingered on the ground, but both the frost and the hint of a mist hanging over the creek were being burned away by the sun. It promised to be the kind of perfect autumn day that made her glad to be alive, even if it had to be in Kentucky.

Sarah had to admit that Kentucky was especially beautiful in October. She took a deep breath of the mellow scent of fallen leaves. Maybe later she would take Jamie for a walk and they would gather a bouquet of colored leaves. Surely there was no danger now. That Indian had been alone last night, and he was probably many miles from Stoney Creek this glorious morning.

"I believe you're right," Ma agreed as they washed the

breakfast dishes and straightened the cabin. "I think he would have been back by now if he was coming. But don't go out of sight of the cabin, just in case. You never can tell what an Indian might do."

"Hey, Sarah, let's go hickory nut hunting," Luke suggested as he came in the door carrying two squirrels dressed to cook for dinner. "I knocked these out of the grandaddy of all hickory nut trees with my slingshot. There's nuts on that tree as big as my fist, and the hulled ones on the ground are as big as hens' eggs!"

Sarah could feel her mouth begin to water. There wasn't much she liked better than the wild, rich taste of hickory nuts.

"Where is this tree?" Ma asked doubtfully. "I don't want you out of sight of the cabin today."

"It's not, Ma," Luke insisted. "It's right at the edge of the woods out past the barn."

That was the opposite direction from where the Indian had disappeared last night, Sarah thought thankfully. She wasn't really afraid now, but she would rather not take any chances.

Ma handed her one of the hickory bark baskets she had made. The basket was light in Sarah's hand, but Ma had woven the long strips of bark over and under each other so the basket was strong enough to hold several dozen eggs.

"Jamie go, Sadie?" the baby begged. "Jamie go!"

"I don't know, honey. . . ." Ma began doubtfully.

"Aw, let him come, Ma," Sarah said. "I'll watch after him. And he can help pick up hickory nuts, can't you, sweetie?" Sarah picked up Jamie and hugged him. "Why don't you come too, Ma?" she asked. It was such a beautiful day, she wanted everybody to enjoy it.

★ Chapter Nineteen ★

For a moment, Sarah saw a longing in Ma's eyes as she looked out the doorway at the bright colors on the hills surrounding the valley. Then determination spread over her face. "I guess I'd better not go today, Sarah," she answered. "I want to cook off the rest of that wild plum jelly. But you all have a good time and take good care of the baby."

"Ma works too hard," Sarah said as the three of them made their way through the meadow.

"Yeah, I guess so," Luke agreed. "We all work hard."

Luke just doesn't understand, Sarah thought. Being a girl made a difference, and she could see a difference in Ma. Back in Virginia, Ma had worked hard too, but she had always been ready for a walk or a picnic. Now all she did was work, work, work. It was making her look old and worn out. She never wore her best dress or her broach; she just wore that old silver good-luck charm on its rawhide string that the Little Captain had given her.

Luke ran impatiently ahead, leaving Sarah to follow as quickly as she could coax Jamie across the meadow. The baby was walking well now, but his steps were small, and he wanted to stop and examine every bright leaf and every bug. Sarah didn't mind, though. Jamie was such a sweet little thing and he had such a good time throwing hickory nuts into the basket once they got there, she was glad she had brought him along.

In fact, they were all having such a good time that they decided to take their basketful of nuts back home by way of the creek, jumping from stone to stone and stopping to play with crawfish and sycamore-leaf boats along the way.

Sarah didn't see the Indians come out of the woods. She just looked up and there they were in the cabin yard, dressed in buckskin breeches, feathers, and bright-colored war paint. With a loud "whoop," one of the Indians jumped into the cabin and the others all crowded in behind him.

"Indians!" Luke breathed unbelievingly.

"They'll kill Ma!" Sarah cried. "Oh, Luke, what can we do?"

"There's nothing we can do, I reckon, Sarah," Luke answered slowly. "They'll scalp Ma for sure!"

Sarah began to cry.

"Don't cry," Luke warned. "You're scaring Jamie. We've got to hide and keep him quiet. But where? They'll likely search the barn."

All at once Sarah knew where they could go. She didn't even think about not wanting Luke to know about it. "There's a hollow tree up there on the creek bank, and the opening's on this side away from the cabin."

"All right," Luke agreed. "You lead the way, but keep down in the creek till we get there. Then get inside fast!"

By the time they reached the tree, Sarah's heart was pounding. Luke went straight to a hole in the back of the tree trunk through which he could see the cabin. Sarah held Jamie. It was awfully still up there. She hadn't even heard Ma scream.

Jamie reached for one of the new cornshuck dolls Sarah had made. "Sleep little, baby . . ." he sang.

"Shhh!" Sarah warned. How was she ever going to keep him quiet? "God help me!" she breathed. Then she had an idea. "Play mousie, Jamie!" she whispered. "Don't sing! Play mousie!"

Jamie's eyes began to sparkle. He hunched down against the tree trunk and put one finger to his lips. "Shhh!" he warned Sarah solemnly.

"That's right, baby," Sarah said. "Be a little mouse

hiding in his mouse hole." Jamie sat there trying to look like a mouse, his eyes shining with the giggles he was holding back. If only he . . .

Ma's scream went straight to Sarah's heart. She ran to a hole beside Luke and saw Ma come running out of the cabin door behind two Indians who were scattering feathers all over the yard from the feather quilts. Another Indian jumped out the door right behind Ma.

Ma's eyes were glazed with fear and her hair had come down from its neat tuck. Sarah saw an Indian grab her by the hair and whirl her around. The other Indians were whooping and laughing inside the cabin.

Sarah shut her eyes. "God, please don't let him do it!" she prayed silently. "Please don't let him!"

Then she heard a shout—some strange, harsh Indian word. Instantly, it was awfully quiet out there. Sarah put her eye back to the hole. The Indian still had Ma by the hair. He was staring at something he held in his hand. The other Indians stood watching him, the shredded feather quilts forgotten in their hands. The two inside the cabin had come to the doorway and were watching, too.

Then the Indian with Ma raised his hand, and Sarah saw the sun strike the Little Captain's silver disk, which was still around Ma's neck on the rawhide string. The Indian turned the disk from side to side, examining it carefully. He grunted, gave some short, brisk command that Sarah couldn't understand, and all the Indians melted into the woods as quickly and as silently as they had appeared.

Ma sank down in the yard and began to cry. Sarah grabbed Jamie and ran to her, with Luke right behind them.

"Oh, thank God, children!" Ma cried out. "I was sure they had killed and scalped you all!"

"What made 'em leave, Ma?" Luke asked. "That big one was ready to kill you!"

"I know!" Ma answered. "I was so scared! But he saw the Little Captain's necklace, and he made them leave. I don't know. Maybe he thought we were friends of his. I just thank God I had it on!" She got up and picked up Jamie. "Let's see what they tore up inside. I just looked up and there they were! I've never been so scared in my life!"

As she stepped over the doorsill, Sarah felt sick. Everything was ripped or chopped, even the table top and the floor they had worked so hard to smooth. Feathers from the ruined quilts were everywhere, and coals scattered from the fireplace lay smoldering on the floor.

Luke grabbed the empty water bucket and made a dash for the creek.

Sarah stood there looking at the feathers floating in the

squirrel stew that had been dumped onto the floor. Then her glance fell on the wooden silverware holder Pa had made. A dull emptiness was all that was left where Ma's gleaming silver spoons and forks had been.

What kind of a place was this to live, where Indians came screeching out of the forest to kill and rob and burn? Sarah knew there had been Indian raids in Virginia. Only a year or so ago, a whole settlement had been destroyed. But Indians didn't often come around the towns. She had never seen one near Miller's Forks. And as soon as Pa got back, she was going to tell him he just had to take them all home!

The next evening, Sarah was sitting on the cabin doorstep peeling potatoes for supper when she heard a horse whinny. Her heart skipped a beat. Were the Indians back? "God help us!" she breathed. Then she heard Bess answer the whinny from out in the barn, and she saw Pa riding Willie through the meadow toward the cabin.

She jumped up and ran to meet him. "Oh, Pa, I'm so glad to see you! It seems like you've been gone forever! And we've been attacked by Indians! And you've just got to take us back home!" she babbled.

"Whoa, there, Sary girl!" Pa said. "Tell me what happened. Is everybody all right?" He swung down from Willie's back, a worried frown creasing his forehead.

Ma appeared in the doorway. "We're fine, Hi," she assured him, "but it sure is good to have you back! We've had some exciting times!" She told him briefly about their encounters with the Indians.

Pa hugged them both. "Thank God you weren't all killed!" He reached up to untie the two sacks of precious salt he had brought.

Having Pa back made everything seem better, Sarah thought as they sat down to supper. Of course, having salt definitely made the food taste better! Sarah ran her fingers over a tomahawk cut in the table, one of three or four that had been too deep to sand out, along with several like it in the floor. They were constant reminders to her of that dreadful day the Indians had come.

"Pa, can we go back home?" she begged. "Please!"

"You are home, Sary," he said firmly, and her heart sank.

"But, Pa," she began, "the Indians . . ."

"Now, don't you worry about them, Sary," Pa interrupted. "They're not likely to be back, not this winter, anyway. And I told you God would take care of us. Didn't He see to it that Ma had that necklace just when she needed it?"

Sarah hadn't thought about it that way. Had God caused the Little Captain to give Ma that silver disk so it would protect them from other Indians? She surely was glad Ma had been wearing it! She had only to close her eyes to see that Indian's tomahawk above Ma's head!

Whatever the reason Ma had been spared that day, Sarah had to be content with Pa's answer, for he made it plain that they weren't going anywhere. She might as well resign herself to being there until she was old enough to leave on her own. *Someday, though!* she promised herself.

The pretty weather lasted through October and into November. Pa and Luke finished gathering the corn and cut the cornstalks for fodder for the animals. Now they were cutting and stacking firewood near the cabin for the long, cold winter ahead, while Sarah and Ma shelled corn to grind into meal and threshed the plump grains of wheat from the straw by beating it with sticks. Ma made wild grape jelly too, and Sarah stored so many hickory nuts and walnuts in the loft she felt like a squirrel.

"Come help me get that deer meat out of the salt box, Sarah," Ma said one crisp November morning. "Your pa needs to salt down the buffalo he and Luke shot down by the river yesterday."

Carrying Jamie, Sarah followed Ma to the barn. "Has the deer meat got enough salt in it to keep it from spoiling this winter, Ma?" she asked, peering into the huge log Pa had hollowed out for a meat box.

Ma nodded. "It ought to be salty enough by now, and Luke has cut us a stack of green hickory limbs to smoke it."

Sarah's mind went back to hog-killing time in Virginia, remembering the hams, shoulders, and bacons hanging in the hickory smoke until they were partly cooked and had that delicious hickory-smoke flavor. Then all winter, whenever they wanted meat, all they had to do was run out to the smokehouse and lift it down from a peg in the beams overhead.

"Wouldn't you like to have a big old slice of fried ham or some crisp bacon with your eggs in the morning?" Sarah asked wistfully, brushing the salt off a chunk of deer meat before handing it to Ma.

Ma took the meat and hung it over the hickory limbs. "Don't you know it!" she answered. "And I reckon I could eat a whole sack of smoked sausage and a bowl full of fried apples!" Ma stood there a moment, lost in thought. Sarah wondered if she, too, were remembering the smokehouse full of meat and the cellar filled with barrels of apples, pears, and dried peaches, not to mention pickles and . . .

"Hand me another slab of meat, Sarah," Ma said. "Someday we'll have a smokehouse again and hogs to kill, but this winter I reckon we'll be thankful we've got deer and buffalo. And once that buffalo hide is scraped and cured, it'll make a dandy cover for Luke's bed up there in that cold loft."

"We've made covers out of all kinds of hides since those Indians ruined the feather quilts," Sarah said, "and they are warm. But they're nowhere near as soft, and they certainly don't smell as good!"

Ma laughed. "Well, at least they didn't completely ruin both of them," she reminded Sarah. "But I have to admit, the one I patched together from pieces of the two of them is never going to be what it once was!"

"It's kind of lumpy," Sarah pointed out, "like the flour and meal from Pa's mill."

"Sarah, I'm so glad to have flour and meal, I'm not going to say a word about how coarse they are! Anyway, when your pa was at the salt springs, he sent an order for some millstones. They'll likely be here by spring."

Spring, Sarah thought, *is a long way off.* The trees had just lost their leaves. Only a few stray flocks of birds passed over on their way south now. And in the mornings, she sometimes found ice on the water when she went out behind the cabin to wash her face in the log water trough. Winter was on the way, and spring seemed as far away as all the comforts they had left back home in Virginia.

The first snowflakes began falling on Thanksgiving eve. Pa and Luke were feeding and bedding down the animals in the barn, and Sarah was gathering eggs from the hay.

★ Chapter Twenty ★

They made sure Hunter, the chickens, and the geese were inside the barn too, then hurried back to the cabin. There they were greeted by the tantalizing smells of cornbread dressing and wild turkey, and spicy pumpkin bubbling in the kettle to make pies.

Birthdays went by with little notice from Ma, but she had always believed in keeping Thanksgiving. "This year, I really know how those Pilgrims felt when they set aside a time to thank God for their first harvest in the new land," she said.

Sarah tried not to remember how the brick house had looked when they had finished waxing and polishing and decorating for the holiday. She tried not to think of the noisy, happy gathering of family and friends at their house or Aunt Rose's or Grandma's. She busied herself with hanging bright-colored gourds and ears of colored corn over the mantel, and with making a bouquet for the table of red sumac berries and big brown burrs mixed with red and orange bittersweet.

The snow fell all that night, and by morning the cabin was surrounded by a whole new world of sparkling white. Pa and Luke set to work making a path to the barn so they could milk and feed. Ma had to call Sarah twice before she shut the door and went to help with breakfast.

"A body would think you'd never seen snow before!" Ma teased.

"I've never seen Kentucky snow before," Sarah answered. "I like snow. It's so clean and new looking, like a fresh-baked cake with heaps of sugar frosting."

"Everything in Kentucky is fresh and new," Ma said. "That's why your pa was so set on coming here. It meant a fresh, new start. Someday . . ." But she let the thought trail

159

off. "Let's make some snow cream!" she suggested instead.

Snow cream made by mixing snow into a bowl of milk and honey wasn't as good as the snow cream they had made back home with milk and sugar and vanilla. But Sarah decided—as Pa always said—it was better than nothing. And she was glad Ma had let them make it early, for by the time they had eaten their turkey dinner, the snow was melting and leaving bare, brown patches on the hills. The next day the creek was running full, and Sarah was sure she had never seen the mill wheel turn so fast as Pa ran off a batch of meal.

Pa was planning a trip to Harrodstown to trade flour and meal for some sugar. He wanted to buy a sow, too, so they could raise pigs again.

I surely would like to see Ann, Sarah thought, but she knew Ma wasn't going to let her go with Pa, so there was no use asking. Anyway, she was busy making Christmas presents. She was determined to make something for each member of the family.

It was hard to make gifts and keep them secret, living in one room where everybody knew what everybody else was doing. Luke was lucky to have his loft all to himself, and he wouldn't let anyone near it these days without special permission.

Ma was persnickety about her workbasket, too. Sarah had gone to it to get the thimble, and Ma had flown at her like an old setting hen.

The only ones who didn't have secrets these days were Pa and Jamie.

Now that it was too cold to do much outside work, Pa was busy making things, but they weren't secret. He had brought into the cabin some of the wood from a big walnut log he had cut and split back in the summer. After smoothing it, he made a beautiful dark walnut bedstead for him and Ma. Out of that same log he also had made a smaller trundle bed for Sarah and Jamie that could be pushed back under the big bed out of the way during the day.

The big bed, covered with the patched feather quilt, along with the table and benches Pa had made earlier, made the cabin look more like a real house. But, Sarah thought, it's still not home.

The women at Harrodstown had taught Ma how to mix buffalo wool with lint from the nettles that grew everywhere in Kentucky. Once the tangled mess was combed with Ma's carding combs, it could be spun into a light-colored thread. When Pa finished the loom he was making, they could weave the thread into cloth. It wasn't as nice as the sheep's wool they had back home, but it would have to do until they got some sheep.

"Can't linsey-woolsey be dyed anything but that old butternut color?" Sarah asked when she saw Ma making a batch of the yellow-brown dye from walnut hulls.

"Butternut doesn't show dirt much," Ma answered, stirring the dye.

"It's not such a good target for the Indians, either," Pa said.

"It would be nice to have some pretty curtains, rugs, and bed covers, though," Ma said. "I'm plumb out of indigo, and I doubt there's any in Kentucky. It was scarce as hen's teeth back in Virginia. But there's a soft blue-gray that can be made from blue cedar berries, and sumac makes a pretty red. Hickory bark makes yellow, and polk berries make purple. Linsey-woolsey doesn't dye so well, but when my flax is ready, I'll make some linen thread, which dyes real pretty. You hunt the dyes, Sarah," she promised, "and we'll have some pretty colors around here."

"Anything for something besides drab old butternut!" Sarah vowed.

"I could see if there's any indigo when I'm at the fort, Della," Pa said.

"Thank you, Hi, but that won't be necessary. We'll get along just fine with what we have," Ma responded. "Anyway, we need a new pig more than we need pretty colors."

Pa soon left for Harrodstown, but he was back in three days with twenty pounds of sugar, some vanilla flavoring, and a lumpy-looking sack he took to the barn. Pa had brought home secrets. But better than that, he brought news.

"Kentucky has been made a county of Virginy by the Legislature, and they promise to help us against the Indians," he said when he came in from the barn.

"You didn't hear news of the war, I reckon?" Ma asked wistfully.

"Most of the fighting seems to be up north right now," Pa answered. "It's likely that Nate's as snug as a bug in a rug for the winter."

What's Pa up to now? Sarah wondered. She could tell he was fighting a grin from the sparkle in his eyes.

He reached inside his deerskin shirt and handed Ma a crumpled piece of paper. "Anyway, he sent us a letter."

"How did you get it, Pa?" Sarah asked, as Ma took the letter and sank down on the bench. Sarah saw her hands tremble as she smoothed the paper.

"A new settler picked it up at a station on his way in,"

★ Chapter Twenty ★

Pa said. "It was addressed to 'The Hiram Moore Family, Somewhere in Kentucky.' "

Sarah read over Ma's shoulder as she read the letter through and then began reading it aloud. It was dated September first.

Dear Folks,

I hope this finds you well and prosperous. As for me, I am fine as frog hair, except for a small leg wound which is about healed now. If you had been here to doctor it, Ma, I know it would have been well sooner, but I have had good care from a Patriot family here in Virginia. Luke, I wish you had been here to teach me to whittle while I was laid up!

I reckon you heard Patrick Henry is Governor of Virginia now. But I am still with his old troops under the command of General Washington. We haven't seen much action lately, as the general has been getting most of it up north and we have been ordered to guard the home front. There's been some fighting farther south, I hear.

I am sending this by a fellow who is coming west, in hopes it will reach you sometime. Kiss the baby for me. I reckon he will be half grown before I see him again. Pa, don't work too hard. And, Sarah, I hear girls marry young in the backwoods, but don't you get any notions of marrying some country bumpkin before I get to Kentucky. When this war is over, I aim to bring you back to Williamsburg to study with Aunt Charity's girls, if you want to come.

May God richly bless you all. Your humble and obedient son and brother, Nathan.

Ma wiped her eyes on her apron. "I'm just so thankful he's all right," she said, "or was when he wrote this."

Sarah was too excited to cry. Nate was coming for her when the war was over! Marry some country bumpkin? Nate ought to know better! She was only twelve! And she had no intention of getting married for a long, long time. Anyway, who would she marry out here in the wilderness? And "if" she wanted to come! Nate knew she did! Apparently her brother knew her better than God, who had let her be dragged away from her home. Or, Sarah wondered bitterly, did Nate simply care more about how she felt?

I've already had my Christmas, she thought. Just the idea that she would be going home was gift enough.

Almost before she knew it, the spicy scent of cake baking and goose roasting told Sarah it was Christmas Eve.

Sarah fought to keep her thoughts off the memories of Christmases past and added berries and red and orange bittersweet to the blue berries that already decked the fireplace. Smiling, she laid a small speckled gourd in an old bird's nest that was snuggled on the mantel.

Sarah placed a bouquet of cedar and red berries in the center of the table. She stepped back, assessed her handiwork, then let out a sigh of satisfaction.

Ma looked up and smiled at Sarah with the old sparkle in her eyes. "The cabin looks beautiful, Sarah," she said.

Luke and Pa came in from the barn. Luke looked at Sarah's decorations, smiled a secret kind of smile, and went straight to the loft.

Pa went over to stand in front of the fire. He still had not brought in that mysterious lumpy sack he had hidden in the barn after his trip to the fort. Sarah was wondering if she ought to just come right out and ask him about it when Luke came down the ladder. One arm was filled with a bundle wrapped in his other shirt.

"I made something for the whole family to share for Christmas," he explained. "I want to give it to you now."

"Are we finally going to see what you've been working on so long up there?" Sarah teased. But Luke just stood there looking strangely shy.

"Put it on the table there, Luke," Ma encouraged.

He laid the shirt on the table. From its folds, he took a carved figure about four inches tall and stood it on the table. It was a woman, carved out of a scrap of dark wood. Sarah caught her breath at its beauty. Every feature, even to the folds of her clothing, was perfect.

Luke took another figure out of the shirt and stood it beside the first. Then he brought out a tiny box holding a baby lying on hay.

"Mary, Joseph, and the baby Jesus!" Sarah breathed.

"Why, they're just beautiful, son!" Ma exclaimed.

Luke's face turned red, but Sarah could see in his eyes the pleasure Ma's praise brought.

"Walnut's a pretty wood," Pa said. "Makes 'em look almost alive."

Luke was busy setting up other figures—a cow, a calf, and a donkey carved from the dark walnut, and an angel and some sheep made of some smooth, white wood that Pa identified as ash.

"Next year, I'll make shepherds and wise men and their camels," Luke promised. "I ran out of time this year."

Sarah saw Ma blink away tears. "Thank you, son," she said. "It's the nicest gift we ever had."

166

Sarah jumped up. "Let's fix a scene with them on the mantel."

Jamie toddled over to watch. He picked up the donkey. "Hossie!" he said. Then, when everybody laughed, he carried the donkey all over the room, proudly repeating, "Hossie! Hossie!"

This Christmas isn't turning out so bad, even without relatives and friends, Sarah thought as they sang some carols. And there was still Pa's mysterious sack in the barn. She couldn't help feeling there would be something special in that sack.

As they sat around the table listening to Pa read the Christmas story from the second chapter of Luke that night, Sarah couldn't keep her eyes off the scene her brother had made. The story of Jesus' birth seemed so real with Mary, Joseph, and the baby all right there in the room.

Finally Pa closed the Bible and sat stroking its cover

with one work-roughened hand. "It never ceases to amaze me," he said thoughtfully, "that the God who created the earth and all that's in it loved me enough to send His Son to die for my sins!"

"Seems to me it would be easier to send somebody than to do it yourself," Luke sassed. "Wouldn't hurt as much."

Pa studied Luke seriously. "You're wrong there, son," he said. "I'd rather suffer any day than to see one of my children hurt."

Luke looked at Pa. "I'm not being smarty, Pa," he said hastily, "but I just can't . . . I don't . . ."

Ma reached over and patted Luke's hand. "Of course, you don't, son. You won't really understand what your pa's saying until you have children of your own. What amazes me," she went on, "is that Jesus was willing to leave all the glory and splendor of His home in heaven to come to this old earth and live as a man."

Jesus left home and went to a strange place to live, Sarah thought, just like she had. Had He wanted to stay home? Jesus, though, always prayed, "Not my will, but Thine be done." Sarah hadn't been willing to leave home, no matter what God wanted.

Pretend as she would, Sarah still resented being in the crude log cabin in the wilderness, instead of happily celebrating Christmas in the snug brick house back in Virginia. She lulled herself to sleep with thoughts of Nate coming to take her home.

When she opened her eyes, the first thing Sarah saw was Ma moving around in front of the fireplace, just where she'd been last night when Sarah had finally gone to sleep. But it was morning, for she had heard the rooster crowing, and a faint light was showing around the shutter.

★ Chapter Twenty-one ★

There were cloth-wrapped packages beside the hearth that hadn't been there last night, and the mantel held stockings she had never seen before, sagging with the weight of hidden surprises. She was out of bed and dressed to help with breakfast in seconds.

Ma smiled at her. "Merry Christmas!" she whispered. Sarah thought she looked tired, but her eyes were sparkling.

"Merry Christmas, Ma," she answered. "Did you stay up all night?"

"No, I just sat up late and got up early. See about the biscuits, will you, please?"

Sarah lifted the top of the spider and looked at the fluffy, round, white pieces of dough. She put the top back over them. "They're not brown yet, Ma," she said, reaching for the tin plates and the four wooden spoons Luke had carved to replace those the Indians had stolen.

Before she had the table set, Pa and Luke were up, and there was a flurry of "Merry Christmas!" "Merry Christmas!" before they left for the barn. Sarah wondered if Pa would bring the sack when he came back. She could hardly wait!

When the door opened, Sarah looked up quickly from dressing Jamie, but Pa carried only the milk bucket and Luke's hands were full of eggs. No sack. *Oh, well,* she thought, *maybe after breakfast.*

Finally breakfast had been eaten, and the dishes and pans were washed and put away.

"My gifts are there by the hearth," Sarah said, as she hung up the last pan. She ran to get them. She just couldn't wait any longer, though she knew her homemade gifts could not compare with Luke's.

"A handkerchief with my initial on it!" Pa exclaimed. "That's real pretty, Sary." He didn't say a word about the

169

linsey-woolsey being a little rough or the "H" being a little crooked, but Sarah felt sure Luke would have something to say about the funny-shaped "L" on his.

"You keep on, Sarah," Luke said, "and one of these days you'll be able to sew as good as Ma." She wasn't sure that was a compliment, but she let it pass and handed Jamie the little straw-stuffed rag doll she had made for him.

"'Bye, baby," Jamie sang, rocking the doll in his arms. There was no doubt how Jamie felt about his gift!

Ma's present was the one Sarah had worried over most. Finally she had decided to make her a pin cushion out of a scrap of linsey-woolsey stuffed with sand to keep needles and pins sharp. Ma had just one needle left and hardly any pins, though, and Sarah was afraid her gift might remind Ma of things she had to do without.

"Oh, Sarah, this is just what I need!" Ma exclaimed when she saw the pin cushion. "Now I'll have a safe place to keep my needle. I have only one left, and I declare I don't know what I'd do if I lost it!"

Ma began handing out her packages. "I didn't have time to fix much," she apologized.

All of Ma's gifts were practical things. Luke and Pa had new shirts and brown mittens. Jamie had a pair of long pants and a new shirt. And Sarah gasped when she saw what Ma had made her—a beautiful soft red dress.

She held the dress up to her, then ran to the loft to try it on. "It's such a pretty color," she exclaimed as she twirled around to show them all how nicely it fit.

"Sumac dye makes a pretty red, but linsey-woolsey just doesn't take dye like linen does," Ma apologized.

"Oh, Ma, it's beautiful!" Sarah exclaimed. "Could I wear it awhile?"

★ Chapter Twenty-one ★

"Yes, Sarah, you may wear your new dress for Christmas," Ma agreed.

"It's time for stockings!" Pa said. He didn't have to say it twice!

Sarah took her stocking and sat down on the hearth, watching Luke dump everything out of his. Back home, their stockings had usually held some candy, some rolled sweet wafers, and sometimes a small toy. She reckoned Pa was trying to make up for their not having the jolly Christmas they'd had in Virginia, though, for Luke's stocking held homemade candy, a shiny red apple, the mate of the stocking Ma had knitted, and a new knife. He took a piece of red cedar from the firewood and began whittling.

Jamie's stocking held the same kind of candy, an apple, and a small, brightly painted top. He put the top in his mouth, but Pa took it and made it spin. Jamie squealed with delight and chased the top as it spun over the floor. When it hit a rough spot and fell over, he picked it up and held it out to Pa. "Go!" he demanded. Sarah and Luke laughed, and Jamie followed the spinning top, saying, "Go! Go!" and laughing at himself for being so clever.

Now that the time had come, Sarah didn't want to find out what her stocking held. It was more fun wondering. But they were all waiting, so she turned it upside down on the hearth and shook it. Out came the candy and the apple, and with them came a small, shiny silver thimble just like Ma's. Now she wouldn't have to borrow Ma's.

No wonder Pa didn't bring the sack in this morning, Sarah thought. *The things it held were already here!*

There was still a funny-looking lump in the toe of her stocking. It wasn't the mate to the new stocking, for she had taken that out. Sarah reached inside and pulled out a china doll's head with painted black hair, blue eyes, and a smiling red mouth. She ran to Pa and threw her arms around him.

"I didn't know about that doll's head in time to make it a rag body," Ma said, "but we'll do it after Christmas. And we'll make her a pretty red dress to match yours."

Sarah sank down on the hearth, cradling the doll's head in her hands. It was more beautiful than anything she'd ever had, even back in Virginia!

"Whose stocking is that still hanging from the mantel?" Luke asked.

Pa grinned. "That's for your ma."

Sarah recognized the stocking as one of a pair Ma had just knitted for Pa. "I washed it in the creek with lye soap, Della," Pa assured her as she reached for the stocking.

Ma laughed and sat down at the table, holding the stocking carefully between her hands. Finally she reached in and took out—one at a time—a package of needles, a paper of pins, and one of the shiny apples. Then she gasped as she pulled out the first of six silver spoons.

"There was a peddler at the fort," Pa explained, "and he had that doll's head and the spoons. They're not new, exactly, but they're still good. The knife and the top are not new, either," he apologized, "but they're the best I could get right now."

"They're all just perfect, Hiram! Thank you!" was all Ma said, but her face was so happy and young-looking, it made Sarah want to cry.

Looking at all their shining faces, Sarah thought that this first Christmas in Kentucky, which she had expected to be so poor, had been pretty nice after all. She vowed she wouldn't spoil it, as she had last night, by thinking about Christmas back home.

These things are just too pretty to use!" Ma said as she put her silver spoons in the cherry wood cupboard Pa had just finished building. She added the new dough tray and rolling pin Luke had carved from the scraps. "You all will have me putting on airs!"

Pa winked at Sarah, and she smiled back. She could hardly believe how homey the place was looking, with Pa's furniture and the covers and rugs Ma had made. She straightened the thread she was weaving.

It's raining again, she thought, hearing the dismal whispering on the roof. Surely it had rained every day since Christmas! Outside, the mud sucked at her moccasins with each step, but being cooped up in the cabin so much made even getting out to do chores in the mud a treat.

"If there would come a hard freeze, we could have a sugaring off this month," Pa said, pouring the last of a kettle of melted lead into his bullet molds. "I think I'll make some extra tubs and buckets so we'll be ready when the sap starts to rise in the sugar trees." But Pa had the buckets and tubs finished, and he and Luke had started making an extra set of farm tools, and still the weather was soggy and miserable.

Ma set Luke and Sarah to practice reading from the Bible and doing arithmetic, but it wasn't like going to school.

"I'd like to go to school," Sarah said to Luke as they sat doing sums on slabs of wood with sticks blackened in the fire, "even if it was just a small one like they had at the fort." Ma was mending Luke's shirt, and Pa was working off energy by pacing up and down the cabin.

"That's one thing I don't miss the least bit!" Luke answered. "The only things I liked about school were recess and vacation."

"Well, I want to learn everything I can," Sarah responded. "I don't think I'd ever get tired of school."

"People never miss the water till the well runs dry," Pa said with a grin. "We didn't have a school at Miller's Forks when I was a boy," he went on seriously. "My ma taught me to read and figure. Miller's Forks wasn't much different from the way it is around here for quite some time."

"Oh, Hiram," Ma corrected, "there were a dozen or so houses scattered over the countryside when we moved to the farm!"

Pa nodded his head in agreement. "But there was no store until Silas Jason opened his at the mill when Nate was a baby. And remember, Della, how we had worship services in people's homes until the Congregationalists built the church in the center of town?" He turned to Sarah and Luke. "Of course, you young 'uns don't remember that, for

174

you attended that church every Sunday from the time you were born. But what I'm trying to tell you, Sary, is that someday there will be churches and schools and stores here, too."

Oh, someday! Sarah thought. She was sick and tired of hearing about someday. She wished she were back in Miller's Forks where they had all those things right now.

One afternoon in the middle of February, snowflakes began to fall. In less than an hour the ground was covered, and the snow was still coming down. Pa and Luke went to feed the animals and milk the cows early and brought in extra water and firewood. By evening the sun had disappeared completely, and the world outside the cabin was a blinding, whirling mass of white.

Sarah stood in the doorway looking out, but for all she could see, the mill, the barn, the creek, and the woods might never have been there. And the snow was reaching inside the cabin. She shut the door and pushed the bearskin rug against it. With Ma's kettle of bean soup simmering over the fire and herb cornbread baking in the spider, the cabin was warm and cozy. She wanted to keep it that way.

The storm raged all during supper, and when she crawled into bed beside Jamie, the wind still howled around the corners of the cabin. *Thank goodness we're not camping out tonight!* she thought fervently.

A gust of cold wind and snow greeted Pa when he opened the door the next morning. "That snow's forgotten how to stop!" he exclaimed. "A body couldn't see a foot in front of his nose out there." He shut the door. "Luke, we'll eat our breakfast first. Then before we head for the barn, we'll tie ourselves together so we won't get lost and freeze to death."

"Get lost?" Luke echoed. "In our own dooryard? Pa, you're joking!"

"No, I'm not joking, son," Pa answered seriously. "It's easy to lose your bearings in a snowstorm. It's like wandering around with a white quilt over your head."

As soon as they finished breakfast, Pa took a rope and tied one end of it around Luke's waist and the other end around his own. He picked up the milk bucket and the other rope. "If we're not back in a reasonable amount of time, Ma, holler for us so we can follow your voice. If we can hear it over that wind!" he added.

Luke took the egg basket Ma handed him and grabbed some left-over biscuits for Hunter, and Pa opened the door. "We'll tie this other rope to the cabin," Sarah heard him explaining to Luke, "and if we can make it to the barnyard fence, we'll tie the other end to it so we can follow the rope back to . . ." His last words were lost in the wind as Pa plunged into the blinding whiteness, with Luke following like a horse on a lead.

Sarah watched as they were swallowed by the storm, then stood in the doorway listening to the howling of the wind. She shivered.

Suddenly a smothery feeling came over her. She had to get out of that cabin! She glanced at Ma, but Ma had her back to her. Sarah threw a heavy shawl around her shoulders and put on her mittens. "I'm going to get some snow for snow cream," she called, grabbing one of Ma's wooden bowls and plunging into the whirling snow before Ma could forbid her to go. She heard Ma shout something, but her words were swallowed by the wind.

★ Chapter Twenty-two ★

At least I'm out of that cabin, Sarah thought. She took a deep breath, but the air was so cold it hurt her nose. She tried breathing through her mouth, but that sent the aching cold even deeper.

Hard pellets of wind-driven snow stung her face. She covered her mouth and nose with the shawl.

Maybe it wasn't so bad inside the cabin after all, she thought. She scooped up a bowl of snow and turned to go back inside. The cabin was gone! She was alone in the midst of a howling, dancing fury of wind and snow. It was like walking around under a white quilt, only colder and wilder. And she couldn't see a thing.

"Ma!" she called, but her cry was snatched away by the wind. She tried to run, but she didn't know which way to go. A tear slid halfway down her cheek and froze there. Her hands and feet were quickly losing the warmth that had been inside her woolen mittens and padded moccasins.

"S-a-r-a-h!" The name seemed to come right out of the wind. A shiver that had nothing to do with cold traveled down her spine. Was that the wind calling her name? There it was again! "S-a-r-a-h!" it wailed. She turned toward the sound, and there before her was the dark outline of the cabin! And that wasn't the wind calling her name—it was Ma!

"They say the Lord takes care of children and fools," Ma said as she took the forgotten bowl from Sarah's stiff fingers and unwrapped her from the frozen shawl. "I reckon you're a little of both! Whatever made you take such a foolish notion, to wander out in a blizzard?" She took off Sarah's wet things and wrapped her in the feather quilt.

Sarah sat down on the hearth. It felt so good to be safe, out of the wind and the snow, that she didn't even mind Ma's scolding.

Ma made the snow cream with thick cream and real sugar and vanilla, but Sarah just wasn't all that interested in anything made out of snow. She was sure she would never be tired of being shut up in that cozy cabin again.

But before the snow melted off the sunny parts of the hills, Sarah was as restless as a minnow scooped up in a gourd dipper.

"That snow's hanging on for another one," Pa predicted. And he was right. The rest of February and March were snowy enough to make up for all winter, and by the first of March, Pa had his new wooden buckets hanging under the spouts he had driven into the sugar trees. The sweet, sticky tree sap dripped steadily into the buckets.

"We've got enough sap now for a sugaring off," he announced one morning. "It won't be as much fun without neighbors to help, and it will mean a lot more work for all of us, but I reckon we can manage."

Sarah was sure they would. They had managed everything else by themselves for almost a year now. But it was all the four of them could do to keep the fire hot under the big kettle in the yard, keep the syrup stirred, and keep Jamie from dipping his little hands into the boiling sweet syrup.

"I don't think that baby ought to be out here on the damp ground in this cold March wind," Ma said. But Jamie couldn't be left alone in the cabin, and all of them were needed outside.

It took a long time to boil the water out of the sap, but the thick, brown syrup it left would be delicious over pancakes and on biscuits. And when the syrup cooked more, it would make maple cream, then soft sugar, and finally it would harden into cakes of light-brown sugar.

Jamie's hoarse cough made Sarah forget maple syrup. The baby was cross, and she could tell he didn't feel well. She felt his head, but he didn't seem to have a fever. He didn't eat much supper, though, and when Ma put him to bed with a dose of cherry bark cough syrup, he went right to sleep.

Sometime between midnight and dawn, Jamie started coughing. His hoarse crying and gasping for breath wrapped her with cold fear. She got up and went over to the fireplace where Ma was holding the baby. "You want me to hold him, Ma?" she asked.

Ma shook her head. "Just hand me a teaspoon of that calendula mixture, Sarah. He's not hot, but maybe it will calm him down. This crying is making the croup worse."

Sarah handed Ma the spoonful of medicine and watched her pour it into the baby's mouth. She held his mouth shut until he swallowed.

"I just pray this steam will loosen the phlegm blocking his throat and let the little fellow get some air into his lungs," Ma said. She held Jamie as near the boiling kettle as she could without burning him, so he could breathe the steam.

Luke came through the doorway with an armload of wood and dropped it on the hearth. Pa grabbed a couple of logs and added them to the fire under the kettle. Luke went back outside after more wood.

Sarah felt so helpless just standing there watching Jamie fight for breath. "Please, God," she prayed silently, "don't let Jamie die! If You will just let Jamie live," she promised frantically, "I'll never say another word about living in Kentucky!" But the resentment was still there. No matter how she tried, she couldn't forgive God for making her leave her home, and her fear for Jamie's life grew. Sarah paced the cabin floor, incoherent prayers tumbling through her mind.

Finally, the horrible gasping sound stopped, and, for a moment, Sarah's heart stopped with it.

"Praise the Lord!" Ma said, laying the sleeping baby on the bed. "He's breathing easy now. That steam has loosened the phlegm."

"Will it come back, Ma?" Sarah asked anxiously.

"He'll likely be all right now, at least until tomorrow night. I don't know why, but croup always comes in the dark hours. That's one thing that makes it so scary."

"I've heard of many a baby dying with the croup," Pa said, now that Jamie was out of danger.

Ma nodded. "We've been blessed this whole winter not to have had any more illness in the family than a round of head colds and a bout of the croup. At least none of us has had the lung fever, thank the good Lord!"

Sarah lay down beside Jamie and put one arm around him. She'd never actually seen anybody with lung fever, but she thought croup was plenty scary enough. She hoped Jamie would never have it again.

She would be so glad when pretty weather came! If real, honest-to-goodness spring would only come, Sarah vowed, she would never complain about anything again—or at least not until next winter.

A couple of weeks after Jamie's illness, Sarah went out to the water trough early one morning and saw two robins having a tug-of-war over an earthworm. The cardinals, sparrows, juncos, chickadees, and even one red-headed woodpecker had come all winter to eat the crumbs and corn she threw to the chickens. But the robins had gone south for the winter.

"Ma!" she yelled, spilling water in her moccasins as she ran back to the cabin. "The robins are here!"

"The way you were yelling, Sarah," Ma teased, "I thought it was at least General George Washington come to visit!"

"But, Ma, spring . . ."

"I know, child. General Washington wouldn't be half so welcome as spring around here right now. I've never seen a longer winter, but then I've never been cooped up in one room with four people all winter, either. This summer, I hope your pa will build us another room. Wouldn't it be grand to have a sleeping room we didn't have to cook and eat in?"

"I hope we get some neighbors here on Stoney Creek," Sarah said. "Somebody with lots of children and some books I can borrow!"

"Being pioneers is lonesome business," Ma agreed. "We've done pretty well by ourselves this past year, but it would be nice to have neighbors again. What I wouldn't give just to hear another woman's voice!"

Sarah knew exactly how Ma felt. But, at least spring was on the way.

Soon the elms had tender green leaves, and the blue wild hyacinths were blooming in the hollow. Groundhogs stood on their hind legs in the meadow sniffing the air for food or danger, and Pa shot a big gray possum stalking the chickens. Twice, Sarah saw a striped raccoon searching for scraps from the dog's supper, and Hunter came in one night smelling of a big dose of skunk.

The family celebrated Easter on the first Sunday following the first full moon after what Ma figured to be the twenty-first of March.

"For God so loved the world, that he gave his only begotten Son, that whosoever believeth in him should not perish, but have everlasting life,'" Pa began reading just as the sun poured over the dogwood blossoms dotting the surrounding hills and spread across the meadow.

As Pa read on from the Gospel of John about the weeping Mary Magdalene walking through the early morning mist to the garden tomb, where she met the angels and then saw Jesus, alive and victorious over death, Sarah thought how different this Easter was from the ones back in Virginia. There was no gathering of worshipers here on the banks of Stoney Creek as there had been in the Congregational church, and Ma wouldn't even let them color eggs for an egg rolling. She was saving every one she got to hatch chicks to add to her flock.

It was spring planting time again. Before another week had passed, Pa had the cornfield and the garden ready to plant, and he was clearing a new field, saving the logs to build the room Ma wanted.

"If I had a blade, I could run a saw mill off that mill wheel," Pa said one day at dinner. "We could saw some nice planks from that stand of white oaks I'm cutting. Then we could cover these log walls with weatherboarding. Or we just might build us a new frame house on that rise yonder, facing the morning sun." He walked over to the window and looked out. "As soon as I get this field cleared and planted, I think I'll make a little trip to the fort," he said.

Sarah knew better than to ask if she could go. She would have to stay here and help Ma. "Are you going to order a saw blade?" she asked instead.

"Among other things," Pa answered. Sarah knew better than to keep asking questions when Pa was through giving answers, too.

"I'll be back as soon as I can," Pa promised as he left for Harrodstown the next week. "I haven't seen any Indian sign lately, but be careful. They'll likely be on the warpath again now that winter's over," he warned.

"What do you want me to do while you're gone, Pa?" Luke asked glumly. Sarah guessed he wanted to go with Pa too.

"Take some of the small trees we've cut from that new field and start a fence around the garden," Pa said. "I won't be gone long."

Sarah helped Ma plant her herbs and flowers and the seed she had saved from last year's garden. Then they cleaned the cabin from one end to the other.

"It's a good time for spring cleaning with your pa out from underfoot," Ma said.

They were finishing a big spring washing of all the bed covers, rugs, and heavier clothing when they heard the sounds of horses moving through the woods. Sarah's heart jumped, then settled back into place as she heard voices and recognized one of them as Pa's.

"Sarah, I believe your pa's back and has brought company!" Ma said. "I've got greens and cornbread cooking, but I hadn't planned on a big dinner with him away. Run in and put some potatoes in the ashes. I'll fry some meat and stir up another batch of bread. Sounds like several people with him." Then she gasped and grabbed Sarah's arm. "Does that sound like a woman's voice to you?"

Just then, Pa rode out of the woods on old Willie, and he had two men with him. As they drew closer, Sarah realized that one of the men was really a boy, just a little bigger than Luke. They were both leading heavily-loaded pack horses. Another boy was trying to drive hogs in front of his horse. Behind him was a horse carrying a woman with a baby riding in front of her, and—oh, glory!—on the next horse was a girl just about Sarah's size!

"Ma," she breathed, "do you reckon they're just passing through?"

"We'll soon know. Help me get some dinner on the table. They'll be hungry after their long ride."

Sarah laid the spoons on the table and ran to the door to look out. She set the mugs beside the spoons and ran back to the door.

"Mercy, Sarah!" Ma scolded, "do you think you could settle down long enough to dish up the greens?"

Then they were coming through the door, and Sarah felt an unusual shyness creep over her.

"Mr. and Mrs. Larkin," Pa said, "this is my wife, Della, and our other two young 'uns, Sary and Jamie." Luke and the Larkin boys had disappeared.

Mr. Larkin bowed to Ma. "Your obedient servant, ma'am," he said. "My wife, Rowena, and our daughters Betsy and Ruthie."

Little Ruth toddled over, sat down beside Jamie, and began helping him build a corncob fence. Sarah and Betsy exchanged smiles.

"Where are you from?" Sarah asked.

"North Carolina," Betsy answered, taking off her bonnet and shaking out her long blond curls. She had the bluest eyes Sarah had ever seen, and about the friendliest smile.

"Where are you headed?" Sarah asked and held her breath, afraid to hear Betsy's answer.

"Your pa says we can claim good land here on Stoney Creek, so I reckon my pa aims to look around here for a place to settle."

"Oh, I do hope he finds it close by!" Sarah exclaimed. "Is your pa a farmer?"

"Part of the time," Betsy answered. "Back home he ran a store, too. I reckon he'll run one here if enough people come to make it worthwhile. The rest of the store goods will be sent here later."

"You just stay with us until you get your cabin built," Sarah heard Ma offer.

"Oh, please, Ma!" Betsy said. "It's so good to be in a house again!"

Sarah gave Betsy a sympathetic smile. Hadn't she felt the very same way this time last spring?

"Well, the girls and I might stay here, if it's all right with Mark," Mrs. Larkin said. "That is, if we locate close by so I can feed my men, and if it won't put you out too much."

"We'd be proud to have you," Ma assured her, "and your men, too."

Sarah laid awake a long time that night, and it wasn't because there were six extra people in their house. She was praying that Mark Larkin would find such a beautiful spot within walking distance of this cabin that he wouldn't want to go any farther.

Then, just before she fell asleep, she remembered such

a place—a meadow almost as pretty as their own only a mile or so up the creek. If Mr. and Mrs. Larkin could see that meadow early in the morning with the wildflowers and grasses waving in the breeze, with the wild plums abloom on the hills, and with the creek sparkling silver in the sunlight . . .

"Can you go with us?" Betsy asked Sarah as the land-search party prepared to ride out the next morning. Sarah looked quickly at Ma.

"I'll keep an eye on the two little ones," Ma offered. "You all go on. But I'll be expecting you back in time for the noon meal."

Sarah scrambled up on the back of the Larkins' mare behind Betsy. Suddenly Martha flashed across Sarah's memory. She felt a pang of regret but quickly pushed it aside. She wasn't going to let anything destroy her happiness this morning.

Luke and the Larkin boys raced their horses up and down the creek bank and through the water until Pa and Mr. Larkin ordered them to behave. Sarah and Betsy giggled at the sullen looks the scolding brought to the boys' faces. Oh, how good it was to have somebody to giggle with again!

Luke took the boys on up the creek to show them the good swimming and fishing holes, but Sarah didn't mind being left behind today. And either Pa had been reading her thoughts, or he had had that spot in mind all along when he persuaded the Larkins to come to Stoney Creek, for he led them straight to Sarah's meadow.

While the grownups looked over the site, Sarah and Betsy gathered wildflowers. When they came to a big patch of sedge grass, Sarah showed Betsy how to make a sedge broom. Then she told her how to sand a floor and how to chink a cabin.

"You know so much about pioneering, Sarah," Betsy sighed. "I'll never learn it all!"

Sarah smiled. This time last year, she hadn't known any more than Betsy did now, but she didn't say anything. She liked the look of respect Betsy had given her.

"We'll build the cabin on that rise toward the back of the meadow," Sarah heard Mrs. Larkin say. "If that's all right with you, Mark."

"Looks like as good a place as any," he agreed.

Sarah and Betsy clasped hands and danced happily around a clump of bluebells. They were going to be neighbors!

Pa and Luke stayed to help the Larkin men cut logs for their cabin, and Sarah, Betsy, and Mrs. Larkin rode back to help Ma with dinner.

"You've been so good to us, I just don't know how we'll ever repay you," Mrs. Larkin said as she turned the meat Ma had frying over the fire.

"Nonsense!" Ma laughed. "I'm so glad you all are moving in! I never realized how much I've missed having neighbors until you came. I've got plenty of garden seed left over if you need some," she added.

"And I'm going to give you a start off of my pink rose bush," Mrs. Larkin promised. "Mark's going to give you a young sow, too. I'm just so thankful Hiram came to the fort the day after we got there. He said he had an idea there would be new families coming in, wanting to get settled. I know I'm going to like it here. You Kentuckians are so friendly!"

Ma smiled, and Sarah wondered if she, too, were

thinking of how lonely the past year had been, and how it would have helped to have found friendly neighbors living on Stoney Creek when they arrived. Of course, if earlier settlers had named it, it might not be Stoney Creek.

It seemed funny to be called a Kentuckian, but the way Mrs. Larkin said it made it seem special. *Maybe to some people it does mean something special to be a Kentuckian,* Sarah thought, *but to me it just means a lonely, homesick feeling.*

"Didn't you mind leaving North Carolina, Betsy?" she asked as they went to the spring to get a bucket of fresh water for dinner.

Betsy looked off over the hills, as though she could see all the way back home. "Yes, I did," she answered slowly. "I hated it, at first. But now I'm getting excited about our new home. Your cabin looks so homey, and you all seem so happy here."

Sarah stared at her, not knowing what to say. Then she laughed. "Well, I'm happy you're here!" she said finally. She wouldn't tell Betsy how, after a year in their new home, she still longed to be back in the old one. There was no use discouraging her right at the first. Maybe later she would tell Betsy about her plans to go back to Virginia. Right now, they were both Kentuckians, like it or not.

One of these days, though, Sarah told herself hopefully, *Nate will come for me.*

Sarah awoke with a start. A quick glance around the room shattered her dream of being back in Virginia. The thick log walls and the square of rosy light outlining the wooden shutter over the window left no doubt that she was in the bedroom Pa had added to the cabin.

What on earth is the matter with me, sleeping past dawn? She yawned and snuggled back under the feather quilt beside the sleeping Jamie. It must have been because she didn't want to leave her dream of being back in the bedroom under the sloping eaves of the brick house, with the voices of Ma and Pa and Nate coming out of the fireplace from the parlor below.

"I know it may not seem like it right now, Pa, but we're going to win this war. God is on our side. How can we lose?"

"I hope you're right, son," Pa said. "Did you see much Indian sign coming in?"

"Some, but I rode in with some militiamen from over on the Holston River. The Indians don't have much stomach for fighting the famous 'long knives'!"

That's Nate's voice! Sarah thought happily. *He's here!* Careful not to wake Jamie, she eased out of bed, pulled on her dress, and ran barefoot into the kitchen.

The man sitting across the table from Pa had his back toward her, but the shoulders under the homespun shirt looked broader than Nate's, and the hair was shaggier than Nate ever allowed his to get. Sarah's heart sank.

"I heard they made Kentucky a county of the Commonwealth of Virginia, with delegates to the Assembly and everything." The voice was Nate's. There was no mistaking that!

Pa nodded. "And Virginy's supposed to be protecting us, but . . ."

"Nate?" Sarah whispered hesitantly.

He turned toward her. "Hey, Sarah!" He stood up and she ran into his arms. "What a big girl you've grown to be, little sister!" he exclaimed. "And so pretty, too!"

Sarah felt her face turning red. She sat down quickly on the bench across from Nate, reaching up to smooth her sleep-tangled hair.

"Let's see now," Nate calculated, "you're a little over twelve years old?" She nodded. "I turn my back and my little brother's practically a grown man off courting a girl, and . . ."

Sarah giggled. "Luke spends a lot of time 'helping' Mr. Larkin!"

"And my little sister's all grown up over night," Nate finished.

"It's been over a year since you left me at that gate and

192

went off to war, Nate!" Sarah protested. Then she jumped up to hug him again. "Oh, Nate, it's so good to see you!"

He smiled, but Sarah noticed that the smile didn't light up his eyes the way she remembered. Even while they were talking, she had the feeling that Nate's thoughts were miles away. *He's different since he went away,* she thought. *He's leaner and harder and . . .*

"The Indians won't be satisfied until we're all either dead or gone back east," Pa went on with the conversation Sarah had interrupted.

"They're being stirred up by the British, Pa," Nate said.

"Major Clark and Ben Logan want us to turn the tables and make a raid on the Indian villages north of the Ohio River," Pa told him. "He says that's the only way to stop them. It's too easy for them to sashay down into Kentucky to kill and destroy, and run to safety across the river."

"Sounds like a good plan, Pa," Nate agreed.

"But Virginy won't let us do it," Pa continued. "We can only chase them to the river. That's why we sent Major Clark to talk to the Assembly, to try to get them to understand our position."

"George Rogers Clark is a good man, Pa, and a good soldier from all I hear," Nate said. "Any plan of his is likely a sound one." He drew an imaginary map on the table with one finger. "You see, Pa, the Indian villages . . ."

Suddenly Sarah noticed an ugly red scar across Nate's hand. She reached out and touched it gently. "Is it really awful, Nate?" she asked.

"It's just a scratch, Sarah," he answered, "and it's healed up now."

"No, I mean the war, Nate. Is it really horrible?" She couldn't bear to think about him on a battlefield with all those British bullets flying around him.

He patted her hand with the scarred one. "Well, it's not exactly a Sunday afternoon picnic, but it's not as bad as Indian warfare, little sister. At least the British come at you in orderly rows, wearing their bright red coats and beating their drums. There's no doubt about where the enemy is!"

"Do you do that, too, Nate?" she asked. "Do you wear a uniform and march to a drum?"

He smiled, and again Sarah noticed that the smile didn't quite reach his eyes. He shook his head. "We don't have the number of soldiers or the ammunition they do. We have to make every man and every bullet count, so we hide behind rock fences and mounds of dirt and shoot when they least expect it, like the Indians do. As for uniforms . . ." He laughed shortly and stood up to show her the sorry condition of his homespun shirt and breeches, held together in places with pieces of grapevine.

"General Washington's whole army will soon be as naked as a new baby," he said. "There's just no money for uniforms. It all has to go for ammunition and supplies. And even so, we have to depend on help from Patriots around the countryside where we're fighting. This outfit I've got on was made for me by Mrs. Draper and her daughter, Molly—the people who took care of me when I was wounded. My clothes were blown to pieces. If the good Lord hadn't been with me, I certainly wouldn't be here today!"

Sarah heard Ma gasp. The sound of her spoon stirring something in the frying pan stopped, then started again.

Chapter Twenty-four

Sarah turned her mind away from pictures of Nate being "blown to pieces."

"I reckon even the women and girls back home are doing their part to help win the war," Sarah said wistfully.

Nate nodded. "They make us clothes and bandages, send us food and even saltpeter for gunpowder . . ."

"And I've been stuck out here in the backwoods stringing leather breeches!" she interrupted disgustedly.

It made Sarah feel good to hear Nate laugh in the old familiar way, even if he was laughing at her. He reached over and lightly tugged one of her braids. "The backwoods, as you call it, is mighty important in this war, little sister," he said seriously. "If the Indians can clear out all the settlers in Kentucky and Tennessee, the British can slip in behind Virginia. With the British warships and troops on the seacoast, they'd have us between a rock and a hard place!"

He turned to Pa. "Are you thinking on going with Clark if he goes to the Indian villages?"

Sarah glanced at Ma and saw her back stiffen at Nate's words, then she lifted the top of the spider to check on the biscuits. Suddenly Sarah felt guilty for sitting at the table talking while Ma did all the work. She jumped up and went over to the fireplace. "I'll take up the biscuits, Ma," she said. "Why didn't you call me?"

Ma smiled at her and went back to stirring the gravy. "That's all right, child," she said. "I know you are too excited about Nate being here to think. It sure is good to have him home!"

Home? Sarah thought. *This is not home, not for Nate, not for me.* But it was good to have him there.

"Indian warfare is the worst kind, Pa," Nate warned.

Pa laughed. "What do you think we've been doing out here, son?" Then he said seriously, "You thought I came to Kentucky to get out of fighting, didn't you, Nate?"

Sarah held her breath to hear Nate's answer, but he made none.

"I'm no coward," Pa went on. "My heart just wasn't in a revolution against our mother country. My dream is simple: good land for crops and a peaceful, comfortable home for my family. If fighting Indians is a part of what I have to do for that dream, then so be it."

"I understand, Pa," Nate answered. "And I hope you'll forgive my thoughts back then. I have grown up a lot since. But the Revolution still means a lot to me."

"I might feel different about it now, too, son," Pa conceded. "I like being a Kentuckian. I may like being an American, too."

"Well, I'm not a Kentuckian!" Sarah burst out. "I'm a Virginian!"

"And that brings us to one reason I'm here," Nate said. "I want to take Sarah back with me."

Sarah caught her breath. Out of the corner of her eye, she saw Ma look quickly at her, then at Nate. "Sarah's got no business going back to Virginia with a war going on, Nate," she said firmly.

"Oh, Ma!" Sarah gasped. It had never occurred to her that once she got the chance, she wouldn't be allowed to go home. *Oh, God, please!* she begged silently.

Nate laughed. "Ma, there's nothing back east to compare with the dangers you face here every day. There's whole sections of the country that hardly know there's a war going on, at least as far as fighting is concerned. Sarah would be a whole lot safer at Aunt Charity's than she is here with the Indians all around her."

Pa laughed too. "He's right, Della. I don't know what stopped those Indians from coming on up the creek the day they attacked the Johnsons's cabin." The Johnsons had settled just beyond the Larkins, but when a small band of Indians had burned their cabin one day while they were at the fort, they had gone back east.

"You'd be in a lot of danger on the trail, though," Ma insisted.

"We could ride back close behind the militiamen," Nate suggested. "After delivering gun powder to the fort, most of them will be going back to the Holston."

Ma looked from Pa to Nate to Sarah. Then she turned her back and stood staring into the fire. "I reckon I just can't bear the thought of my little girl leaving home," she said so softly that Sarah barely heard, even though she stood right beside her.

Sarah felt a lump rising in her throat. She hadn't thought about leaving Ma and Pa or Luke and Jamie. Always when she thought of the brick house, they were all there, talking and laughing around the big kitchen table as they ate the meals she and Ma prepared together. It certainly wouldn't be the same without them. She would miss Betsy, too, and the rest of the Larkins.

Life's different here now than it was when we first camped in this meadow by the creek, she thought. *But it's never going to be another Miller's Forks, Virginia!* And, in spite of the war and the sadness of leaving her family, she still wanted to go home.

"Ma . . ." she began.

"I'll think on it, Sarah," Ma broke in quickly. "Now help me get this food on the table so I can get started on some new clothes for Nate. It's no telling when he will up and leave again."

Sarah sighed. She would just have to wait and pray that Ma's decision would be the one she wanted. Then she felt a chill of fear. God had not answered her prayers to stay in Virginia. Would He answer her prayers to go back?

I wish Betsy had made up her mind to come with us," Sarah said to Nate's back. "She's been like a sister to me these past few months."

Nate laughed. "She'll be a sister-in-law one of these days, or I miss my guess! Miss Betsy Larkin is not about to leave Stoney Creek as long as Mr. Luke Moore's around. To think that my little brother is nearly sixteen years old and thinking on getting married! And here I am a dyed-in-the-wool bachelor of almost nineteen!"

"You're not fooling me, Nate," Sarah teased. "Likely as not, you've got a girl in every one of the thirteen colonies of America and one or two in the western lands as well!"

"States," Nate corrected. "We're not going to be colonies of anybody anymore! And, no, I don't have a girl in every one of them. But there is one young lady. . . . I told you about Molly, didn't I?"

Sarah sighed. "Only about a hundred times! Pretty little

Molly who helped her ma nurse you when you were wounded."

"That's the one," Nate said, seeming not to notice her sarcasm. "Molly Draper. You'd love her, Sarah."

Sarah had her doubts about that, but she didn't voice them. "This trip has been a sight easier than the one we made into Kentucky," she said instead, nudging her borrowed horse to catch up with her brother's. "Of course, the road is a little better now, and we've found lodging at several stations along the way."

"And we're both on horses, and we don't have much baggage to slow us down. I don't know how you ever made it with all that plunder!"

"The journey was hard, Nate, but it was harder trying to survive out there, with the cold and hunger and sickness and, of course, always the Indians. The Johnsons just gave up and went back home. We've heard that some of the settlers at the forts have gone back too."

"I've heard talk of soldiers receiving land grants for their services in the war, once it's over. Settlers will be coming to Kentucky in droves," Nate predicted.

"Well, they can have it!" Sarah declared. "I'm going back to Virginia where I was born and where I belong!"

"Where we are born is happenstance," Nate said seriously. "We American Patriots are helping a new country to be born. And you Kentucky settlers may have a part in the birthing of a new state as well."

"Kentucky's not a state!"

"I've heard some talk about making it one."

"I don't care what they do with it. I'm going home!" Let Nate look at her with Ma's accusing eyes. Sarah meant what she said. She would never have to see Kentucky again, unless she went for a visit.

Of course, she was going to miss Ma and Pa, Jamie, and Luke terribly. She was going to miss Betsy. But it would be nice to see Martha again, and Tiger, if he were still alive. And wouldn't it be grand studying with Aunt Charity's girls and having new books to read?

When she finished school, she might teach in a little school like the one at Miller's Forks. She knew teachers were supposed to be men, but times were changing. Mrs. Coomes taught the school at Harrodstown. Someday maybe girls would go to school like boys. She certainly wouldn't keep them out of hers if she taught one!

Jamie would be starting to learn to read and write and figure soon. She hoped more people would settle on Stoney Creek, and that the men would build a school. Sarah hoped there would be someone to teach it. If not, she guessed Ma would have to teach him at home, as she had taught her, but she wanted a better education than that for Jamie. She wanted him to learn Latin and Greek and . . .

"The road's rising again," Nate pointed out. "We're heading up the last mountain before Miller's Forks."

Had they come that far already? Sarah recalled that seemingly endless journey to Kentucky, when her thoughts had lagged with every weary step. Of course, as Nate said, they were riding horses this time. *And I'm going somewhere I want to go,* she thought. *That makes all the difference.*

In what seemed like an unbelievably short time, they were riding down the other side of the mountain. And almost before she knew it, they were trotting down the hard-packed road to Miller's Forks, camping out and wayside stations behind them.

As they rode around the last bend, Sarah felt her heart

do a flip-flop. There were the green fields, the orchard, the barn. And there sat the dear brick house, just as she had remembered it—only the grass needed cutting and there was a gap like a missing tooth where a window pane was broken out. One shutter hung crazily from a broken hinge.

The house seemed smaller than she remembered it, though, and somehow strange. *But I was born here!* she reminded herself. *I lived here for eleven years. How can it seem strange?*

"It looks deserted, Nate. What happened to the people Pa sold it to?"

Nate shrugged. "Maybe they fled to England like some of the Tories."

"Were the people who bought our house Loyalists of the king, Nate?"

"I don't know, Sarah. What difference does it make? The house doesn't belong to us anymore."

She guessed Nate was right. And she knew he was in a hurry to get to Williamsburg, but she just had to see inside the house once more.

"I'll only be a minute," she promised, jumping down from the horse's back. She heard Nate groan as she tied the horse to the sagging fence.

Ma's neat flower borders were nothing but weed patches now, Sarah noticed as she picked her way along the grass-grown stepping stones to the front door. She pushed the rusty door latch, and the door creaked open. She hesitated, then stepped inside.

The house smelled musty and damp and too long shut up without air and sunlight. Spiders' webs were thick in the corners and swung from the ceiling. She held her skirts carefully off the floor as she crossed the hallway into the dusty parlor where the sunlight peeked timidly through long unwashed window panes.

Sarah made her way back to the kitchen, remembering happy hours spent there helping Ma, or doing lessons, or playing games around the table. Ma's china cupboard held only dust and the memory of flower-sprigged china. The floor was gritty with dirt.

When she had pictured the house in her mind these past months, it had been with sunlight spilling through polished windows onto polished floors, or with candlelight shining softly on gleaming furniture, with a mother humming over her cooking, with a father whistling at his chores, and with laughing children around the hearth.

Sarah had expected to find again the warm, safe, happy feeling she had known when she and Ma and Pa and her brothers had lived here. She had expected the house to welcome her back. Instead, she had a flat, lonely feeling and a lump in her throat. The house was as cold and dead as a body without a spirit.

She hurried back outside, pulled the door shut behind her, and stood shivering in the sunlight. Where had all the laughter gone, the love?

All at once, Sarah pictured a warm, cozy log room where firelight played over rough wooden furniture and sand-polished floors. She saw laughter and love in the dear, familiar faces. And the truth hit her so hard it all but knocked the breath out of her. Ma and Pa, Luke, Jamie, Nate, and even she had been the spirit of the brick home. Without them, it simply was a sad, lonely, empty house.

"God did answer my prayers," she whispered. "All this time I've thought He made me leave home when we moved to Kentucky. But I never left home at all! I took it with me!"

Had Ma known that all along? Was that why she could be content even in a one-room cabin as long as they were all there?

Tears of regret for the wasted hours of bitterness stung her eyes. *Lord, please forgive me!* she prayed silently.

It was then that she finally heard it. "Sarah!" it called softly. Then more insistently, "Sarah!"

Most people would have said it was Nate telling her to hurry, but she knew better. That voice had come from farther away than Miller's Forks, Virginia.

Someday, the Stoney Creek school would need a teacher who knew more than the pupils, and she planned to get a good education. Then . . .

"I'm coming!" she promised both Nate and that far-off, soft Kentucky wind.

Echoes from the Past

The Indians had two names for Kentucky. Because of its natural beauty and abundance of game, they called it "happy hunting ground," their name for heaven. Sometimes, because of the terrible wars fought over it and the many who died there, they called it "dark and bloody ground."

Settlers like Sarah's family found both Indian names to be true. The land was wild and beautiful, filled with game, flowers, and fruit. Its soil was rich enough to grow crops like they had never seen. It had lakes and rivers and fresh, clear streams in abundance. It did appear to be a paradise on earth.

As they struggled to survive in it, however, the settlers often found their new land to be a dark and bloody place of sorrow and hardship. Illness and accidents claimed many lives. Thunderstorms and floods, icy wind and blizzards took their toll. One terrible winter, game froze to death in the forests and cattle in their pens. And, always, there was the threat of Indian attack.

★ Home on Stoney Creek ★

Still, the settlers came—the rich and the poor, the well-educated and the ignorant, the godly and the wicked. Some came seeking fortune. Some, like Sarah's pa, came seeking new, rich land for farming. Some sought a place to hide from justice for crimes they had committed. And some came seeking freedom from the growing oppression of the British government upon the eastern colonies.

The Indians did not want settlers coming into their "happy hunting ground," even though they did not live there. And like the Little Captain, they believed the land was haunted by the Allegewi, "a very long-ago, pale-faced people" who farmed the pleasant land along the rivers and lakes of Kentucky long before white settlers from Europe followed Columbus to America.

Where did these people come from in a land supposedly inhabited only by Indians? Where did they learn to build permanent stone buildings instead of portable teepees made of animal skins? Where did they learn to use a written language, and to embalm their dead like the highly civilized peoples of Egypt and other lands?

Some say they walked into America by way of a land bridge that may once have joined Alaska and Siberia, and wandered down into Kentucky. Others say they came by boat from the Middle East when God destroyed the Tower of Babel and scattered its builders. Some speculate that they fled to the American continent when the legendary island called Atlantis sank into the ocean. The truth is: No one really knows.

We do know where they went, though. When the Leni Lenape Indians came from the "sunset," seeking an easy passage through Kentucky to the "sunrise," they found their way blocked by the strong stone forts of the Allegewi. Joined

206

by the fierce Iroquois from the far West, the Indians drove the Allegewi to an island in the Ohio River. There they killed the Allegewi, leaving their bones to be discovered many years later by a new generation of Kentuckians.

The new settlers who came to this wild land and stayed to tame it had courage, determination, and a strong faith in God that enabled them to cope with unbelievable hardships until they could build a new and better life for themselves and their families. Those settlers who lacked these strengths soon gave up and went back east, leaving a tough breed of ancestors to produce future Kentuckians after their kind.

There was an old saying in Kentucky that "you can lead a Kentuckian a long way, if he's of a mind to go, but you can't push him very far!" This meant that Kentuckians—both men and women—were willing to listen to new ideas and to go along with them, if they could be persuaded the ideas were good. But try to force them to do anything against their will, and their stubborn independence refused to budge.

This may explain why Colonel Richard Henderson and Colonel John Luttrell, with a group of men from North Carolina and Virginia, were soon told to forget their dreams of setting up their own little kingdom in Kentucky. The Henderson Company hired Daniel Boone as their interpreter to negotiate with the Cherokee Indians, offering them 10,000 pounds (British money) in exchange for their "happy hunting ground." Convinced that they would be unable to stop the tide of white settlers pouring into Kentucky, the Cherokees agreed, although they were not the only Indians who claimed the land.

Henderson set up headquarters at Boonesborough and began to sell land in what he called his own kingdom. But the pioneers who had crossed the forest ahead of Henderson to establish Harrodstown, Saint Asaph, and numerous other individual stations throughout Kentucky, refused to surrender their new-found freedoms to any self-appointed king. They had risked too much to gain them.

The settlers sent messengers to Williamsburg to plead their cause with the General Assembly of Virginia, and soon won their case. The government of Virginia, which claimed Kentucky as part of its territory, gave Henderson and his partners 200,000 acres of land along the Green and Ohio rivers and ended their claims to the rest of the area.

So the people settled in this wild place and put their mark upon it. Just as Sarah's pa had predicted, the tangled forests gave way to farms, busy towns, and cities. The game shared its meadows with cattle and horses. The tumbling creeks and mighty rivers were spanned by bridges. The rough trails became winding country roads and broad highways. Churches and schools dotted the countryside. And, in 1792, sixteen years after Sarah's family settled on the banks of Stoney Creek and Sarah was an "old lady" of twenty-seven, Virginia's County of Kentucky became the fifteenth state of the United States of America.

The "land of tomorrow," however, also put its mark upon its settlers. It produced a friendly, hospitable people with a vision for the future, but with their roots sunk deep into the rich heritage of their past. And to this day, the old adage holds true: "You can lead a Kentuckian a long way, if he's of a mind to go, but you can't push him very far!"

In her next adventure, Sarah finds that she is more Kentuckian than she thought. *Stranger in Williamsburg* is on sale at your local Christian bookstore now.

Stranger in Williamsburg

"A spy? Gabrielle can't be a spy!"

The American Revolution is in full swing, and Sarah Moore is caught right in the middle of it. When she returned to Virginia to live with her aunt's family and learn from their tutor, she certainly had no plans to get involved with a possible spy.

With a war going on, her family back in Kentucky, and people choosing sides all around her, Sarah has begun to wonder if she can trust anyone—even God.

Wanda Luttrell was raised and still lives on the banks of Stoney Creek, Sarah's Kentucky home. Wanda and her husband have shared their home on Stoney Creek with their five children.

Be sure to read all the books in Sarah's Journey:

Home on Stoney Creek
Stranger in Williamsburg
Reunion in Kentucky

Also available as an audio book:
Home on Stoney Creek

Reunion in Kentucky

"Sarah, I need your help."

Whenever trouble came her way, Sarah knew Marcus would be there to help her. Now that she's leaving Williamsburg to return to Kentucky, she's determined to help him.

Years ago, Marcus lost his wife and son to slave traders, and he has reason to believe his family is now in Kentucky. If they are there, Sarah vows she'll find them. What she doesn't plan on finding, however, are sickness, non-stop Indian raids, and extremely harsh living conditions. Through it all, however, Sarah comes to a new understanding of what it means to be a child of God.

Wanda Luttrell was raised and still lives on the banks of Stoney Creek, Sarah's Kentucky home. Wanda and her husband have shared their home on Stoney Creek with their five children.

Be sure to read all the books in Sarah's Journey:

Home on Stoney Creek
Stranger in Williamsburg
Reunion in Kentucky

Also available as an audio book:
Home on Stoney Creek

Grandma's Attic Series

Pieces of Magic

Remember when you were a child—when all the
world was new, and the smallest object a thing of
wonder? Arleta Richardson remembers: the funny
wearable wire contraption hidden in the dusty attic, the
century-old schoolchild's slate which belonged to
Grandma, an ancient trunk filled with quilt pieces—each
with its own special story—and the button basket, a
miracle of mysteries. And best of all was the remarkable
grandmother who made magic of all she touched,
bringing the past alive as only a born storyteller could.

Here are those marvelous tales—faithfully recalled for
the delight of young and old alike, a touchstone to
another day when life was simpler, perhaps richer; when
the treasures of family life and love were passed from
generation to generation by a child's questions . . . and
the legends that followed enlarged our faith.

Arleta Richardson has written the beloved Grandma's
Attic series as well as the Orphans' Journey series. She
lives in California where she continues writing and
public speaking.

Be sure to read all the books from
Grandma's Attic:

In Grandma's Attic
More Stories from Grandma's Attic
Still More Stories from Grandma's Attic
Treasure from Grandma

The Grandma's Attic Novels

At home in North Branch—what could be better?

The Grandma's Attic Novels bring you the story of Mabel O'Dell's young adult years as she becomes a teacher, wife, and mother. Join Mabel and her best friend, Sarah Jane, as they live, laugh, and learn together. They rise to each occasion they meet with their usual measure of hilarity, anguish, and newfound insights, all the while learning more of what it means to live a life of faith.

Arleta Richardson has written the beloved Grandma's Attic series as well as the Orphans' Journey series. She lives in California where she continues writing and public speaking.

Be sure to read all the Grandma's Attic novels:

Away from Home
A School of Her Own
Wedding Bells Ahead
At Home in North Branch
New Faces, New Friends
Stories from the Growing Years

6 What is one area of your life in which you feel you have a good and healthy grip?

What is contributing to this area being so positive?

7 What area do you need to get a grip on as soon as possible?

What is standing in the way of you getting a grip on this area of your life?

What needs to change if you are going to finally get a grip on it?

Read Snapshot "It's Time to Get a Grip"

IT'S TIME TO GET A GRIP

We live in a day and age of delayed responsibility. We hear the ads say, "Buy today and don't pay for one full year!" Credit card use is at an all-time high. We plan to start dieting and exercising "tomorrow"—but we have had these plans every day for the last year! We forget that our actions have consequences, and that *lack* of action can have just as severe consequences. Waiting, delaying, and procrastinating make change only more difficult.

It is time for us to get a grip and face reality. Postponing the battle, delaying the inevitable, and waiting until tomorrow will never make things any easier. If we are going to experience order in our chaotic lives, we need to acknowledge the disorder. We need to admit that things are spinning out of control. It's time to get a grip.

8 In the coming five sessions we will look very closely at five specific areas in which you may need to get a grip on your life. Take a moment and assess your life. On the continuum below, mark where you are right now in each area:

My Schedule

Spinning out of control	I have a loose grip on this area	I have a good grip on this area

1   2   3   4   5   6   7   8   9   10

My Physical Health

Spinning out of control	I have a loose grip on this area	I have a good grip on this area

1   2   3   4   5   6   7   8   9   10

My Personal Finances

Spinning out of control	I have a loose grip on this area	I have a good grip on this area

1   2   3   4   5   6   7   8   9   10

My Spiritual Growth

Spinning out of control		I have a loose grip on this area				I have a good grip on this area			
1	2	3	4	5	6	7	8	9	10

My Relationships

Spinning out of control		I have a loose grip on this area				I have a good grip on this area			
1	2	3	4	5	6	7	8	9	10

Identify one area of your life that your small group members can begin praying for you to grow and get a grip on in the coming weeks.

9 What is your strongest area right now?

How can your small group members help you celebrate the strength you are experiencing in this area of your life?

PUTTING YOURSELF IN THE PICTURE

TIME INVENTORY

Take time in the coming week to take an honest assessment of how much time you spend doing the following things:

Item:	Amount of time in a week:
• Work and work-related activities	_____
• Hobbies and recreational activities	_____
• Watching TV	_____
• Exercising and developing physical health	_____
• Being with friends	_____
• Time with your spouse (if married)	_____
• Time with children (if you have them)	_____
• Time reading the Bible and praying	_____
• Time in worship and with other followers of Christ	_____
• Other things you do:	
_____	_____
_____	_____

PERSONAL "GETTING A GRIP" LIST

When we slow down enough to really look at our lives, the chaos can feel overwhelming. So many things are out of control that we just don't know where to begin. Take time in the coming week to identify two—three at the most—areas in your life where you really desire to get a grip. Write them down below.

Areas in which I want to get a grip:

- _____
- _____
- _____

Begin praying for God to help you look honestly at each of these areas, and for strength to begin reclaiming control in each area.

GETTING A GRIP ON YOUR SCHEDULE

REFLECTIONS FROM SESSION 1

1. If you did a time inventory for yourself, what was one insight you gained about yourself and how you order your life?
2. If you formed a "Getting a Grip" list and related goals, what are you doing to get a grip on one area of your life on this list?

THE BIG PICTURE

Over the years there have been numerous "one-minute" books written. Books such as *The One Minute Manager* started it all by providing some helpful principles on managing a business. In a busy, schedule-crazed world, the book just flew off the shelves. Who wouldn't want to learn how to manage their life in just one minute?

Books to follow have been *The One Minute Lover*—I didn't bother to read that one. I have some suspicions about anyone who thinks love can be attained in sixty seconds. There is also *The One Minute Father* and *The One Minute Mother*. Can you believe it, just one minute to excellence in parenting? Seems pretty unbelievable, doesn't it?

Some years ago, when these books were really hot, I read an article called *The One Minute Christian*. The author, Greg Contelmo, with tongue in cheek, wrote about what a "one minute" book on the Christian life would look like. There could be a chapter called "The One Minute Sin." From now on, all sin, whether in word or action, should never take longer than sixty seconds. The next chapter could be "The Thirty Second Confession." If your sin only took one minute, the confession should take only half a minute. Then the next chapter could be "One Minute Repentance." Can you see how nice and neat this would be? If you have sinned the one-minute sin, you could take a minute to evaluate what you've done, how it has affected God, others, and yourself. Then, use a few seconds to ponder the temporal and eternal consequences. Finally, you could strategize how to take realistic steps to prevent your one-minute sin from occurring again.

Do you see the beauty of this? The whole process takes less than three minutes. By following these simple steps, within 180 seconds you will have experienced the agony of depravity, the cleansing of confession, and the joy of restoration. Wouldn't it be wonderful?

If people enjoyed the simplicity and convenience of these chapters, they could read on and learn about "One Minute Devotions," "One Minute Praying," "One Minute Fellowship," "One Minute Patience," and the list of chapters could go on and on. By using the dynamic new principals set forth in this book, it would take only ten minutes a day to live the Christian life.

A WIDE ANGLE VIEW

1 "One minute" books have been very popular. Why do you think so many people are attracted to this approach to life?

What is wrong with the "one-minute" approach to the Christian life described above?

A BIBLICAL PORTRAIT

Read Ecclesiastes 3:1–13 and Ephesians 5:15–20

2 What do you learn about time and scheduling from Ecclesiastes 3:1–13?

3 The apostle Paul gives great wisdom in Ephesians 5:15–20 about how we use our precious resource of time. How should we use our time?

How should we not use our time?

Summarize Paul's message in this passage in your own words. In one sentence, what is he trying to communicate?

SHARPENING THE FOCUS

Read Snapshot "A Life Out of Balance"

A LIFE OUT OF BALANCE

Many people need to be honest and admit that there are some segments of their life that are way out of balance. They are spending too much time on things that don't matter and too little time on the things that matter most! In the community where I minister, a large number of people have way too much of their lives devoted to vocational pursuits. Some people invest excessive time in recreational pursuits. Others are so consumed with personal advancement that they have no time for family, friendship, and their spiritual life. Still others get so overcommitted at church that they are out of balance and need to step back from some of their service commitments. If your life is out of balance, it is time to be honest and begin to get a grip on your schedule.

4 To what area of your life are you devoting too much time? (You may want to refer back to session one, question five.)

What needs to happen for you to cut back in this area?

5 What is one area you are neglecting?

What needs to happen for you to develop this area?

Read Snapshot "A Life in Balance"

A LIFE IN BALANCE

Then there are those people who have been moving from being out of control to getting a grip on their schedules and coming into balance. They are tired of being out of control. They have sensed the Holy Spirit's power of self-control being infused into their life and they have been working diligently on balancing their life over a period of time.

These people have discovered that God is very concerned about every area of their lives. God designed humans to be creatures of labor. He is concerned that people are committed to excellence in the marketplace, but He meant for it to be a profession and not an obsession. God is also concerned about recreational life. Even Jesus left the sick and the hurting to go up on a mountain to rest, to be refreshed and refueled. And God is concerned about relationships too. In both family and friendships we need to invest the needed time to develop deep and healthy relationships. Along with all of this, God is concerned for our spiritual lives, with having us commit to corporate worship as well as carve out time every day to be with Him.

6 See pie chart above for an example of a life with balance in relational, physical, vocational, and spiritual areas. What are some of the advantages of living with a life in balance?

7 The picture painted above looks pretty balanced and positive. Can you see any problems with it?

Read Snapshot "A Life Beyond Balance"

A LIFE BEYOND BALANCE

Picture a pie chart with its different sections, only this pie has a cross at its center. This picture captures a very significant step in the life of a follower of Christ. Instead of the spiritual dimension of life being just another activity to be balanced with work, family, and recreation, it becomes the core of every area of life.

The Bible teaches that our relationship with Jesus Christ needs to be at the very center of our life. Jesus is the all-important, ultimate priority. When this happens, you find yourself thinking about Him throughout your day. You find yourself praying and talking to Him at your lunch hour, between conversations with other people, and while driving down the road. You spontaneously begin thinking of ways you can please Him and honor Him. You sense His presence throughout the day, and when you go for periods of time when you don't sense His presence, you say, "Oh, Lord, I'm sorry. I just went through a large portion of my day and never gave You a thought. Let's pick up from here and help me tune in to Your presence more closely." When Christ moves from just being a part of your life to become the center of it, then He will begin to influence every thought, every conversation, every decision, and every activity of your life.

8

How do you feel during those moments when you are in communication with God right in the middle of all of life's busyness?

What helps you stay tuned in to God's presence through the daily grind of life?

9 What is one thing you do to keep God in the center of *one* of these areas of your life:

- Your family life
- Your friendships
- Your vocation
- Your free time
- Some other area

10 What is one thing you need to begin doing to help you keep God in the center of *one* of these areas of your life:

- Your family life
- Your friendships
- Your vocation
- Your free time
- Some other area

PUTTING YOURSELF IN THE PICTURE

CHRIST IN THE CENTER

If you have identified an area of your life where Christ needs to be placed in the center, commit yourself to do all you can to make room for Him in this part of your life. First, pray for God to open this part of your life to His presence, and for God's Holy Spirit to break down any resistance you may have in surrendering this area to His control. Second, set some specific goals that will position God in the center of this area of your life (the more specific, the better). Finally, find a friend who is committed to following Christ. Ask this person to pray for you and keep you accountable. Invite that person to ask you how you are doing in this area on a weekly basis.

MAKING THE MOST OF YOUR TIME

Take time to memorize Ephesians 5:15–16:

> Be very careful, then, how you live—not as unwise but as
> wise, making the most of every opportunity, because the days
> are evil.

Pray for God to give you a deepening sense of how to use
your time wisely. Pray also for eyes to see when you are using
your time for things that don't have a kingdom impact.

GETTING A GRIP ON YOUR BODY

REFLECTIONS FROM SESSION 2

1. If you have been working at placing Christ at the center of a specific area of your schedule, how are you experiencing a greater sense of His presence in this area of your life?

2. If you took time to memorize Ephesians 5:15–16, would you be willing to recite it for your group? What is one way the truth of this passage has motivated you to make better use of your time?

THE BIG PICTURE

Most of us occasionally take time to set personal goals. The beginning of a new year is a natural time to set personal resolutions, but any time is a good time to honestly evaluate our lives and set goals. When we make a list of personal goals, they almost always include some mention of action to be taken with regard to our bodies.

- Take a night class toward my degree
- Work at not raising my voice with the kids
- Exercise at least three days a week
- Drop ten pounds
- Begin reading the Bible on a regular basis
- Volunteer in a ministry at church
- Take my wife out for a date on a weekly basis
- Read at least one book each month
- Stop smoking
- Run four times a week
- Start getting to bed by 11:00 P.M.

Most of us really do care about our bodies. We are concerned about how they look, how they function, and how they are maintained. However, I would guess that few of us understand how much *God* cares about our bodies. It seems we often hear about the value God puts on our souls and we forget how much He cares about our physical selves as well.

A WIDE ANGLE VIEW

1 Name one goal you have set concerning your physical health that you have kept. How has this commitment improved your quality of life?

What is one you have not kept, and how have you regretted this?

A BIBLICAL PORTRAIT

Read Romans 12:1–2; 1 Corinthians 6:19–20

2 What does it mean to "offer our bodies as living sacrifices"?

How is this an expression of worship?

3 1 Corinthians 6:19–20 says the Holy Spirit of God
actually lives within each follower of Christ. The apostle Paul reminds us of the price God paid for us (the
blood of Jesus). With this in mind, we are told to
"honor God with your body." What are examples of
honoring God with your body?

What are examples of dishonoring God with your body?

SHARPENING THE FOCUS

Read Snapshot "God Cares About Your Body"

GOD CARES ABOUT YOUR BODY

God cares more about our physical health and condition than we do. Our physical bodies matter to Him! God has proved this concern for our physical bodies time and time again throughout the Bible.

1. In Genesis, God molds and shapes our bodies from the dust of the earth and breathes life into them. All the rest of creation was made through His spoken word, but we were made by His hands! (Gen. 2:7)

2. Jesus taught that God provides for our physical needs. God feeds the birds and clothes the flowers. How much more will He provide for us? (Matt. 6:25–30).

3. Jesus proved the value of human bodies by taking one on Himself. He felt cold; He knew hunger; He knew pain. He also felt the embrace of a friend, the sunshine against His face, and the taste of a good meal. God chose to have His only Son come to us in a human body (Phil. 2:6–8).

4. The Holy Spirit of God dwells within each follower of Christ. In what greater way could God give dignity to our physical bodies? (1 Cor. 3:16–17).

5. God proves His concern over our bodies by promising to raise them from the dead at the end of time (1 Cor. 15:42–44; Rev. 20:5–6).

God shows us the depth of His concern for our physical bodies from Genesis to Revelation. Don't you think we should share His concern?

4 One way God shows His concern for your body is through providing for your needs. Finish this statement: "God has provided for my physical well-being by ..."

5 If your body is the temple (dwelling place) of the Holy Spirit, then God is always with you! If God was physically walking with you through this next week, what is one thing you would change?

In reality, God will be with you through every moment of the coming week (His Spirit lives in every one of His followers). Why doesn't this motivate us in the same way that His physical presence would?

Read Snapshot "What You Put in Your Body"

WHAT YOU PUT IN YOUR BODY

Some years ago I used to race motorcycles with some of the guys on our church staff. We went to the track every Saturday. It was an amazing thing to watch as all the guys arrived in their beat-up vans and rickety trailers. When it came time to put fuel in the tanks of those motorcycles, these backyard grease monkeys would turn into chemists. They would take out a little jug of very high-performance fuel and then take some of the best synthetic oil on the market and would mix it together just right.

Then they would take out a hankie, put it over the top of the tank, and mix it in carefully. They were meticulous about what they put in that tank; they wanted their bike at its peak performance. All this care was put into the upkeep of a thousand-dollar motorcycle.

Now think about the "fuel" we put into the priceless bodies God has given us. Look what we put into the tank of our body. We have been handmade by God, sustained by His providing hand, filled by the Holy Spirit, and given the promise of a bodily resurrection. Knowing all of this, how can we continue to put all kinds of trash into our bodies and naively assume our performance won't be affected?

---

6 If you compared your body to a high-power performance engine, how would you describe the fuel you are putting into it?

What needs to happen in your life and eating habits to upgrade the quality of fuel you are putting into your body?

Read Snapshot "How You Condition Your Body"

HOW YOU CONDITION YOUR BODY

The benefits of being in shape are almost too many to list. Higher energy levels, higher self-esteem, higher resistance to colds, and a controlled appetite are just a few. Doctors, and many others, praise the effects of regular exercise on the human body. I read an article some years ago by Dr. Malcom Cruthers entitled *The Emotional Healing of Running*. In this article, Cruthers communicates his belief that most people could ban the blues and fight depression with a simple, ten-minute exercise session three times a week. He continues on to say that exercise *doubles* the body's level of a particular hormone that has a long-term effect of destroying depression. With all the reports, studies, and advice that come to this same conclusion, why is it that we still struggle to condition our bodies on a regular basis?

7

What stands in the way of you developing habits of regular physical conditioning?

What can your group members do to help you develop good habits in this area?

Read Snapshot "How You Use Your Body"

HOW YOU USE YOUR BODY

You can glorify God with your body by how you use it. If Mr. Universe is not willing to be a tool in the hands of God, he becomes a tragic waste of the human body. All the years of conditioning, good eating habits, and muscle toning profit nothing if his body is not available to be used for God's purposes. You see, if all you want to be is sexier, if all you want is to be more macho, if all you want is to attract attention to yourself, you are missing the point. You need to watch what you put into your body and work at conditioning it so that you can become a tool in the hands of God. When you are in good shape—well-rested, eating good food, and taking care not to put toxic substances in your body—you can become a more energetic servant for God. You will have the strength and health to serve Him more fully.

8 What is one way you are using your physical abilities to serve God?

How would better health and a higher energy level help you in this area of service?

9 What is one goal you will set in response to the message of this session?

Who will you ask to pray for you and hold you accountable to this new goal?

PUTTING YOURSELF IN THE PICTURE

A PRAYER OF CONFESSION

If you have struggled to keep a grip on your body and your physical condition, take time to pray this prayer:

Father, forgive me. Forgive me for all the "garbage" I put in my "tank." Forgive me for how I have complained about my health problems, lack of energy, and aches and pains, when often these things are a direct result of what I choose to put into my body. Forgive me for not conditioning my body the way it ought to be conditioned. My body is the temple of Your Spirit; I should treat it with dignity. Forgive me for not having the right motivation. Forgive me for not offering my body as a living sacrifice to You.

You say if I confess my sins, You are faithful to forgive and cleanse me. Today is a new day. May I experience a fresh start as I dedicate myself to glorify You with my body. I belong to You, inside and out. I matter to You, my spirit and my body. Teach me to live in a way that gives glory to You. Amen.

MY BODY, THE TEMPLE OF GOD

Take time to memorize these two passages from 1 Corinthians:

Don't you know that you yourselves are God's temple and that God's Spirit lives in you? If anyone destroys God's temple, God will destroy him; for God's temple is sacred, and you are that temple.

1 CORINTHIANS 3:16–17

Do you not know that your body is a temple of the Holy Spirit, who is in you, whom you have received from God? You are not your own; you were bought at a price. Therefore honor God with your body.

1 CORINTHIANS 6:19–20

GETTING A GRIP ON YOUR FINANCES

REFLECTIONS FROM SESSION 3

1. If you have spent time this past week confessing to God that you have put bad fuel in your physical tank or neglected conditioning your body, how has this confession empowered you to begin changing some of these habits?
2. If you have memorized 1 Corinthians 3:16–17 or 1 Corinthians 6:19–20, would you recite one of these for your group? How has the truth and conviction of these passages impacted the way you care for your body?

THE BIG PICTURE

We go to school to learn how to earn it. We work forty to sixty hours a week acquiring it. We commit Friday and Saturday evenings to creatively spending it. We get caught up for countless hours worrying if we have enough of it. We daydream about how to get even more of it. We wonder what we could do if we stumbled into a lot of it. Arguments over handling it are one of the leading causes of divorce. Despair over mishandling it has contributed significantly to the suicide rate. Love of it causes many of society's crimes. The absence of it creates some of society's greatest nightmares. Call it a root of all kinds of evil. Call it the means for supreme good. But one thing you can't do, you can't ignore it. What is it? The answer is obvious! MONEY!

Money is a very sensitive subject for many people. When the topic of personal finances comes up, tensions rise. No matter what outward appearances might indicate, this is a hot spot for many people. Some who read these words are barely making ends meet. They are working very hard but seem to be slowly sinking into a sea of debt. This creates tremendous loads of anxiety. Others have experienced the pain of financial ruin. Just talking about money and finances is like pouring salt on an open wound. Others might have a healthy income, but are still overextended and feeling the financial pinch. And there may be some who have it all together in this area and earn more income than they need. These people have most likely come to the realization that money does not guarantee happiness. The truth is, across the whole spectrum, money can be an area of real tension and struggle.

A WIDE ANGLE VIEW

1 How have you experienced tension in your life because of money?

What is one joy you have experienced because of money?

A BIBLICAL PORTRAIT

Read 1 Timothy 6:6–10; Proverbs 30:8–9; Hebrews 13:5

2 What are some of the possible consequences for the person who becomes consumed with a love of money?

3 How should a follower of Christ view money and personal finances?

SHARPENING THE FOCUS

Read Snapshot "Beware of the 'Permissible Lie'!"

BEWARE OF THE "PERMISSIBLE LIE"!

One deadly threat to our personal finances is deceitful advertising. Just think about it, there are thousands of brilliant, well-trained, highly paid professionals who are trying to find a way to motivate you to purchase their products. These professionals are competing against other advertisers who want you to purchase their products. The competition is fierce, the stakes sky-high. As the years go by, the battle seems to get dirtier and dirtier, the tactics and techniques lower and lower. There is an all-out war going on to get your dollars out of your pocket and into someone else's bank account!

In his book entitled *The Permissible Lie,* Sam Baker, who worked in the advertising industry for thirty years before choosing to leave the profession, exposes the deceptive advertising produced by the inner circles of some of the nation's largest ad agencies. He says, "To increase sales, almost anything goes: misrepresentation, deception, and lies. The goal is to produce the hardest-selling campaign without perpetrating recognizable fraud."

To illustrate, he tells a story of a meeting of advertisers for a specific company. One of the corporate leaders said, "Our top canned goods item is slipping. We need some new excitement in the advertising. We are going to redesign the label to give it a new look, so come up with a new, improved campaign. Lots of big promises. Show us layouts in a week so we can move fast." Someone asked, "Will there be anything new or improved inside the can?" The client blared, "What the %#?+@ kind of question is that? I would have told you if we had made any changes other than the label. The label will be redesigned and the product will look new and improved. Whose side are you on, anyhow?" The questioner wasn't on any side for very long. He was fired from the agency.

4 Take time as a group to evaluate the message and the level of honesty in this advertisement.

5 What are some of the common deceptions in advertisements?

How can you learn to become sensitive to these lies and resist their magnetic appeal?

Read Snapshot "'I Want It All, and I Want It Now'"

"I WANT IT ALL, AND I WANT IT NOW"

The second major threat to financial freedom is the availability of easy credit. I saw a bumper sticker once that said "I want it all, and I want it now." Doesn't that say it all? This little saying summarizes the worldview of so many people today. Never before has there been a society more committed to a "Live for the day" philosophy. Yesterday is gone, tomorrow may never come. I want it all, and I want it now.

We want fast food, fast service, mail-order diplomas, a comfortable standard of living, quicker computers, and high-speed everything. Almost every product you can think of is promoted with the phrase, "easy monthly payments." The question is, easy for whom?

In the past people actually had to qualify for credit cards. Now anyone can get a steady stream of them in the mail. Companies are begging people to use their credit cards. These plastic man-eaters can devour you before you realize they are coming. I once talked with a gentleman who said, "I am in deep financial trouble. Can you meet with me?" He was an old friend. I sat down with him and after hearing about his financial trouble I had to respond honestly, "You are in serious trouble. I don't know what you are going to do." He had all his credit cards up to the max. He couldn't make his minimum monthly payments. We talked about some ideas for reducing debt, but then he called me a couple weeks later and said, "I solved the problem." "You solved the problem already?" He said, "Yeah, Visa just sent me another card and now I am borrowing on that to make my minimum monthly payments to my other cards." He thought he was smart, but in reality he was sinking in a sea of debt.

6

What are some of the dangers of the credit game?

How have you experienced the seductive lure of easy credit?

7

What are some practical strategies for getting out of credit trouble?

*If you struggle in this area, how can your group members
keep you accountable to avoid further credit trouble?*

Read Snapshot "When Spending Spins Out of Control"

WHEN SPENDING SPINS OUT OF CONTROL

We all need to watch out for the lure of deceitful advertising and the black hole of easy credit. If we
avoid these two pitfalls, we will be so much better off. A third area in which people stumble is in
undisciplined budgeting practices. Most people groan when they hear the word "budgeting." Men-
tioning budgeting is about as popular as encouraging people to diet!

But let's try to look at budgeting from another perspective. What if someone disconnected your fuel
gauge without telling you? Within a very short time most people would have it fixed. Why? Because you want to know
how much gas you still have in your tank. You don't want to be driving around and all of a sudden run out of fuel! A fuel
gauge is a lot like a budget; it helps you know how much is coming in and how much is going out. A budget tells you if
you are going to run out or if you have plenty.

What do many of us do? We operate our personal finances just like a person who drives a car without a fuel gauge. We
go from day to day with no sense of how much we have spent, and then, in the middle of the month, we say, "Oops. I
am out of money. I guess now I have to borrow."

8

Finish *one* of the statements below:

- I have never lived with a budget, but I wish I knew
  how to . . .

- I have budgeted in the past, but can't seem to stay
  on my budget. I wish someone could explain . . .

- I live with a clear budget and have learned . . .

PUTTING YOURSELF IN THE PICTURE

The Freedom of Budgeting

Believe me, a budget is one of the best friends a person can have. You should set a new budget every year. First, assess what your income will be. Next, decide what portion will go to God's work. The biblical model is to give the first ten percent to God, but some will be led to give more than ten percent because they have experienced provision well beyond what they need. Third, determine how much is going to go into savings. Even when you don't have a large income, the discipline and habit of saving is critical.

Next, it is important to lay out your regular monthly expenses. Be specific and realistic about all your regular bills. Go right down the list, set an amount of money for each, and then say, "That's it. That is our budget for this year." Commit yourself to hold to those amounts. This approach will help lead you to financial freedom. Whether you make $20,000 or $200,000, you can be freer than you are today if you watch out for deceitful advertising and easy credit, and commit yourself to a budget.

Take time in the coming week to lay out a basic budget. First, specify what you will give to God. Next, decide what you will put into savings on a weekly or monthly basis. Third, make a detailed list of each area of monthly spending and how much you will allow yourself to spend. Finally, struggle to stay within this budget. It may seem confining, but it is truly freeing.

Ready for True Riches?

Over the years I have been deeply challenged by Luke 16:10–12. It says:

> Whoever can be trusted with very little can also be trusted with much, and whoever is dishonest with very little will also be dishonest with much. So if you have not been trustworthy in handling worldly wealth, who will trust you with true riches? And if you have not been trustworthy with someone else's property, who will give you property of your own?

You see, financial freedom is *not* the final goal. You should not leave this small group study saying, "The goal in life is to be financially free." Attaining financial freedom should just serve to liberate you to pursue the more important endeavors of life. We are called to love the Lord our God with all our heart, soul, mind, and strength, and serve and love our neighbors as ourselves.

Take time in the coming week to pray for God to lead you to financial freedom. Pray for your motivation to be right. Pray that discovering this new freedom will release you to love God more and to love and serve others.

GETTING A GRIP ON YOUR SPIRITUAL LIFE

REFLECTIONS FROM SESSION 4

1. If you have begun budgeting for the first time, describe one way this new practice is impacting your life.
2. If you have been reflecting on the ultimate goals of financial freedom, how has this been leading you toward a deeper love for God and others?

THE BIG PICTURE

Every church has people who go to church out of habit. They have been churchgoing people all their lives, and it is almost as automatic as breathing. Every Sunday they go to a church service that feels right to them—one that is comfortable, painless, beautiful, entertaining, or inspirational. They don't really tune in to what is happening. They don't apply what they hear. But they are in church like clockwork.

There are also those who attend church and perform their "religious duties" to silence a spouse, child, or parent. In other words, the conflict is so great when they don't go, they figure the best way to avoid the weekly battle is to acquiesce. These people endure church simply to keep peace in the family. They can't wait until it is over.

Some people attend worship services because they are paying some form of penance. They keep track of their unethical decisions, harsh words, dishonest transactions, immoral acts, and other sins, and by the end of the week they say, "I had better go to church. I have to pay for what I have done this week." For these people, church is a punishment. After enduring an hour of church, they leave with a clean slate, all ready to get muddied up again the next week.

Others go to church to meet people. They find a popular singles' ministry, a hot youth group, or a good social setting and jump right in. Some come to build relationships for business purposes. They see church as another place to network and develop their clientele base. Used right, church can be one of their most profitable hours of the week. They might even be able to write off their offering as a business expense!

Still others attend church because they are just flat-out bored. Who wants to go to work on a Sunday morning, after all? And television programs on Sunday morning aren't all that hot. Getting out for church is just a way to kill a few hours on a slow morning.

Certainly, many people attend church because they are hoping that something during the service—the Scripture reading, the music ministry, the singing, the drama, or some part of the sermon—will trigger something new in their heart. They hunger for a spiritual discovery that will help them understand more about God. They want to learn how they can love Him more, how to feel inspired to live for Him, or how to change the course of some behavior. They want to go the next step in their Christian life.

A WIDE ANGLE VIEW

1 How would you describe your attitude and motivation when you first started attending church?

What moves you to attend church today?

A BIBLICAL PORTRAIT

Read Hebrews 4:14–16; 10:19–25

2 Some followers of Christ struggle with feeling that God is angry with them and does not want them entering His presence. How do these passages destroy that false mind-set?

3 What has God done so that we can approach His throne any time, any place, with boldness and confidence?

Why would God go to such lengths just to be in relationship with us?

SHARPENING THE FOCUS

Read Snapshot "The Militaristic Approach"

THE MILITARISTIC APPROACH

One approach to improving your companionship, relationship, and dialogue with God is what I will call the "militaristic" approach. You may already know what I am talking about. Most of us have heard Christian leaders say, "If you are ever going to improve your relationship with God, you need to get up every morning at 6 A.M. and spend at least thirty minutes with God—fifteen minutes reading the Bible and fifteen minutes in prayer. If you do this on a daily basis, you are all set. Get up early, do the devotional thing, and you have covered your spiritual bases for the day!"

4 What are some advantages to this approach to your relationship with Christ?

What are some disadvantages?

5 Respond to *one* of these statements:

- If a follower of Christ does not spend fifteen to thirty minutes in the Word every day, they just don't measure up to God's standard.
- If I don't spend the first fifteen minutes of my day on my knees in prayer, I just can't go on. This is the only way to start a day! By the way . . . what do *you* do first thing in the morning?

- The key to a real and deep Christian faith is having a daily, consistent, and in-depth devotional time of Bible study and prayer. There is no other way to spiritual growth.
- I like to get my devotional time over first thing in the morning so I can move on with my day.

Read Snapshot "The Libertarian Approach"

THE LIBERTARIAN APPROACH

On the opposite extreme of the devotional spectrum you find what I will call the "libertarian" approach to building a relationship with God. Libertarians are those people who seek spiritual growth when it feels right. They attend church when they happen to wake up on time. They read their Bible when they feel like it. They pray when there is an urgent and pressing need. They like to say things like, "I don't usually go to church. I get more out of sitting alone in a forest preserve for an hour." Any set form, discipline, schedule, or established time pattern seems to offend their free-flowing spirit. They say, "I will build my relationship with God as the Spirit moves me and when the Spirit moves me."

6 What are some of the pitfalls of this approach to growing as a follower of Christ?

What are some signs that a person is approaching their faith with a libertarian mind-set?

7 Where do you see this mind-set in *one* of these areas:
- In the church at large
- In your local church
- In your own life

Read Snapshot "The Creative-Relational Approach"

THE CREATIVE-RELATIONAL APPROACH

God doesn't want a half-hour of your time; He wants to be a part of every single moment of every single day. He wants you to be aware of His presence as you wake up, as you go through your day, and as you put your head on the pillow at night. He wants to be in the center of your life in the family room, the boardroom, the classroom, and the laundry room. He wants your devotional life to permeate the totality of your life. And He wants it to be real, not mechanical.

Think about it in terms of a human relationship. Imagine if you took a week off from work and spent each day with this person. You show up at his house at seven o'clock in the morning and have breakfast with his family. You ride in his car to work, watch him fight his way through traffic and find a parking place, sit in his office, listen to his conversations, meet his coworkers, and watch him handle all his daily tasks. You ride home with him at night, share dinner, and then go for a run in the evening. Imagine what could happen to a relationship if you creatively spent each day together!

Now imagine what could happen in your relationship with God if you invited Him to be part of every aspect of your life. Of course Bible study is important. Do it regularly and God will teach you great things. Of course prayer is essential, but don't limit your conversation with God to fifteen minutes in the morning and a few quick prayers before meals. Instead, talk with Him all day long. Let praise pour out of your mouth in the car as you drive, in the shower, around your house. Read Christian books and listen to Christian music. Connect with other followers of Christ on a regular basis to encourage, sharpen, and inspire each other. Let your relationship with God be creative, dynamic, and fill every aspect of your life.

8 How have you experienced an open relationship and communication with God through the course of your daily activities?

9 What tends to keep you from experiencing this creative and dynamic interaction with God in *one* of these spheres of life:

- In the workplace
- In your home
- In church settings
- In your recreational pursuits
- In any other areas of your life

PUTTING YOURSELF IN THE PICTURE

RECEIVING FROM GOD

One essential ingredient in the "creative-relational" approach to growth is spending time reading and learning from the Bible. Start with a small New Testament book, like James, Philippians, or Colossians. Then go to a Christian bookstore and buy a little commentary. A commentary is a tool that helps you understand the difficult parts of what you are reading. Read a section of verses, read what the commentary has to say about those verses, and pray about how you can apply the passage to your life. You may want to tell a friend what you have learned and how you plan to live out this truth. Keep reading, section by section, until you finish the whole book.

Then, before you dive headlong into another book of the Bible, take a few days off. Put the Bible on the shelf, find a couple of highly recommended Christian books, and spend a few days reading them. Or ask your pastor to recommend a good book for where you are in your spiritual growth curve.

You can also mix in some Bible memorization. Pick a passage that really impacts you and commit it to memory. This might be your time of focus on God's Word for a few days. You might even want to get some sermons on tape and listen to them with your Bible open in front of you.

Think about the coming two weeks and lay out a plan for at least three different ways to learn from Scripture. Ask a friend to pray for you and keep you accountable as you learn to get creative in your relationship with God.

In the coming two weeks I will grow in God's Word through:

_____

_____

_____

_____

A PLACE FOR PRAYER

Have you ever tried to pray for fifteen minutes each morning and found your mind wandering? People tell you to pray, so you sit down with your list of names and needs and begin cranking through them. After a few days, this can become dry and routine. But the Bible never says that longer prayers are better prayers. The Bible simply calls us to pour out our hearts to our heavenly Father. We are not called to lift up mindless and repetitive prayers and praises. Instead, just talk openly with God. Improve your dialogue with him.

As you talk you will discover that there are several different kinds of prayers. *Closet prayers* are those where you go away to a quiet place and spend focused time in prayer for needs and burdens you carry as well as lifting up your praises. *Catch prayers* happen throughout the day where you find yourself saying, "Lord, help me, give me wisdom, help that person in need, watch over my children, thanks for Your presence," and whatever else comes to heart.

There are also *written prayers*. Put a blank piece of paper in front of you and write "Yesterday" on the top, "Today" in the middle, and "Tomorrow" near the bottom. Once you have that, begin pouring out your heart to God through writing. Or maybe you'll find yourself driving along, lifting your voice in a praise chorus or hymn. Let these words become your prayer. The key is to communicate with God. He cares about you and wants to hear your joys and sorrows.

In your prayer life this week, try to note the different ways you communicate with God. Write down a few of your observations in the space below:

Where were you when you prayed?

- _____
- _____
- _____
- _____

What moved you to pray?

- _____
- _____
- _____
- _____

What kind of prayers did you lift to God? If you don't have an official name for a specific kind of prayer, make one up:

- _____
- _____
- _____
- _____

GETTING A GRIP ON YOUR RELATIONSHIPS

REFLECTIONS FROM SESSION 5

1. If you have been experiencing creativity in your study of the Bible, how has this breathed vitality into your spiritual life?

2. If you have been taking note of your prayer life over the past week, tell your group what you have discovered. What kinds of prayer have you been moved to lift up to God?

THE BIG PICTURE

As you begin this session, you will be taking a fill-in-the-blank quiz. There are no right or wrong answers; you will not be graded. All you need to do is write in the name of a person (or persons) after each scenario. Some of these scenarios might not apply to where you are in life right now. Still, try to imagine if you were in this circumstance, whose name would come to mind.

1. After missing your original connecting flight, you have finally arrived at the airport at midnight. Who would you call to come pick you up and take you home?

   Name: _____

2. You have been working like crazy to get a shot at an exciting promotion at work. The promotion means

increased responsibility and opportunities, and much more pay. You really don't think you are going to get it, but one day your supervisor comes in and says, "The position is yours." Apart from a spouse or an immediate family member, who would you call to tell the good news and invite to share your joy?

Name: _____

3. You and your spouse have been trying to conceive a child for more than three years. Finally you get the test back. You are going to have a baby! Who do you call first to tell the good news?

    Name: _____

4. Things have not been going well at home. Tensions are high both at work and in your marriage. Your spiritual life is as dry as the Sahara Desert. You need to talk with somebody; to confide in someone who cares and who will keep things confidential. Who could you call who will be straight with you and who will be able to provide you with some decent counsel?

    Name: _____

5. You are bored stiff. You want to call someone to go out to a show or to go out to dinner with. Who do you call?

    Name: _____

6. You have just won a two-week, all expenses paid Hawaii vacation. If you are a married couple you get to invite another married couple to come with you. If you are single, you get to invite a friend. Who would you invite?

    Name: _____

A WIDE ANGLE VIEW

1
Identify one person you named on your quiz and tell why you chose to call that person.

How would your life be changed if you were no longer in relationship with this person?

A BIBLICAL PORTRAIT

Read Genesis 2:15–23; Psalm 133:1

2 What does Genesis 2:15–23 tell you about our need for human relationships?

3 What are some outward indications that people are experiencing unity in a relationship?

What are some of the indications that they are experiencing disunity?

SHARPENING THE FOCUS

Read Snapshot "Putting an End to Aloneness"

PUTTING AN END TO ALONENESS

One reason for pursuing strong, meaningful relationships is to put an end to aloneness. In Genesis 2:18 God said it is not good for man to be alone. Another way of saying this is that human beings were created for community. We are not living up to our God-given potential as human beings if we try to lead Lone Ranger lives. God, in His grace, provided a way to end our aloneness. He designed us to lead deep, authentic relationships—in community—with other people. We were intended to communicate, to give and take, to love and be loved, to serve and be served.

4 Describe a time you have experienced loneliness.

How have meaningful relationships helped you through a lonely time?

Read Snapshot "Meaningful Relationships Multiply Our Joy"

MEANINGFUL RELATIONSHIPS MULTIPLY OUR JOY

A second reason for pursuing strong interpersonal relationships is that developing relationships allows us to multiply our joys. In the gospel of Luke, chapter 15, we find stories about a lost sheep, a lost coin, and a lost son who wanders away from home. In each of these cases, when that which is lost is found, there is great rejoicing! When the lost treasure is finally discovered, it's time to call friends together to come and celebrate. "That which was lost is now found. Let's party!"

It is almost impossible to experience joy and not share it. What happens when a young woman gets engaged? She can't contain the joy she feels. She wants to share that joy with other people. Similarly, we feel like we are going to explode if we don't let others know the joys we may be experiencing.

5 What is one joy you are experiencing in your life right now?

Read Snapshot "Meaningful Relationships Divide Our Sorrows"

MEANINGFUL RELATIONSHIPS DIVIDE OUR SORROWS

The third reason for pursuing significant relationships is that relationships divide our sorrows. Ecclesiastes 4:10 says, "If one falls down, his friend can help him up. But pity [woe to] the man who falls and has no one to help him up!" In the Old Testament the word "woe" points to ultimate tragedy. It was about the worst thing that could happen. In other words, having friends to help bear our sorrows and pick us up when we fall is God's desire and plan. Facing the struggles of life with no one to help us is tragic in God's sight.

Some of life's struggles are bearable only because the burden is divided and shared by friends. Yet, many Christians don't understand their need for close relationships. They say, "Community is for weak people. Relationships are crutches for those who can't handle their own problems." Or "I don't want to bother anyone." They struggle under the burdens of life trying to handle everything in their own power. These people still have not learned how to share the burdens of life with others.

6 Describe a time others came alongside you and helped carry a burden you were facing.

What is one load you are carrying right now that your small group members could help carry?

Read Snapshot "Meaningful Relationships Afford Us Counsel"

MEANINGFUL RELATIONSHIPS AFFORD US COUNSEL

A fourth reason for pursuing strong relationships is that they offer us counsel and perspective. Proverbs 11:14 says, "For lack of guidance a nation falls, but many advisers make victory sure." Even the wisest of people needs counsel and wisdom from others. I often wonder how many bumps, bruises, heartaches, and sorrows could be avoided if we would only learn to seek counsel before we make decisions.

Presidents, rulers, prime ministers, and world leaders surround themselves with counselors because they know their decisions have grave consequences. They are committed to getting perspective from peers they respect. The decisions we make may not have implications on the direction of nations, but they are still very important. We need to learn the importance of seeking the counsel of others when making major life decisions, and even when making decisions that don't seem so critical! Seeking counsel almost always helps and is rarely regretted.

7 Tell your group members about a life situation you are facing right now in *one* of the areas listed below. Invite them to offer counsel and perspective.

- In the workplace
- In a family relationship
- In a friendship
- In a ministry situation
- In your neighborhood
- In some other area of life

Read Snapshot "Meaningful Relationships Create a Place for Accountability"

MEANINGFUL RELATIONSHIPS CREATE A PLACE FOR ACCOUNTABILITY

A fifth reason for developing strong relationships is to create a place for intentional accountability. I had spoken to a group of Christian leaders about the importance of community and relationships. After I finished speaking, one of the men in attendance broke into the conversation and said, "I want to affirm that what we have just heard about community and relationships is God's Word." But then he went on to say, "But I want to announce to all of you that I have enough truth about this topic. What I need now is a few brothers to help me apply these truths for the rest of my life." He declared, "I don't have to *learn* more in this area, I need to *conform* more. I need people to hold me accountable and help me practice the truth I just heard."

What a refreshing and honest response! We need to commit ourselves to one another and say, "Hold me to the truth." We must invite others into our lives and say, "Cheer me on. Encourage me. Challenge me. Redirect me. Correct me. Do whatever you have to do because I want to live out God's truth . . . not just know it." This rare and powerful practice is called accountability, and it should be a central part of our relationships.

8

Describe someone who keeps you accountable
and how this relationship has helped you grow as
a follower of Christ.

9

What is one area in which your small group members
can pray for you, encourage you, and keep you
accountable?

PUTTING YOURSELF IN THE PICTURE

ENDING LONELINESS

In this lesson we discussed that relationships help put an end
to our loneliness. Who is one person in your life that you sus-
pect may be facing some kind of loneliness today? Maybe he
or she has lost a loved one, gone through a time of illness, or is
simply dealing with some tough times in life. Give that person a call and set a date to get together. Plan to take a walk,
have a meal together, or visit for an evening. Be intentional
about helping put an end to the loneliness of others.

BURDEN ASSESSMENT

Take a blank sheet of paper and write down three burdens
you are carrying right now. They can be emotional, relational,
professional, physical . . . any kind of burden. After you have

written down these burdens, make a list of the people you have asked to help you bear them. If you have never asked anyone to help you bear a burden, think of some people in your life who could help you with these burdens. Commit yourself to contacting these people within twenty-four hours. Tell them about what you are facing and ask them for their prayers and support. You will be amazed at how many people are excited and willing to help you bear your burdens. In some cases, they have been waiting for you to ask!

LEADER'S NOTES

Leading a Bible discussion—especially for the first time—can make you feel both nervous and excited. If you are nervous, realize that you are in good company. Many biblical leaders, such as Moses, Joshua, and the apostle Paul, felt nervous and inadequate to lead others (see, for example, 1 Cor. 2:3). Yet God's grace was sufficient for them, just as it will be for you.

Some excitement is also natural. Your leadership is a gift to the others in the group. Keep in mind, however, that other group members also share responsibility for the group. Your role is simply to stimulate discussion by asking questions and encouraging people to respond. The suggestions listed below can help you to be an effective leader.

PREPARING TO LEAD

1. Ask God to help you understand and apply the passage to your own life. Unless that happens, you will not be prepared to lead others.
2. Carefully work through each question in the study guide. Meditate and reflect on the passage as you formulate your answers.
3. Familiarize yourself with the Leader's Notes for each session. These will help you understand the purpose of the session and will provide valuable information about the questions in the session. The Leader's Notes are not intended to be read to the group. These notes are primarily for your use as a group leader and for your preparation. However, when you find a section that relates well to your group, you may want to read a brief portion or encourage them to read this section at another time.
4. Pray for the various members of the group. Ask God to use these sessions to make you better disciples of Jesus Christ.
5. Before the first session, make sure each person has a study guide. Encourage them to prepare beforehand for each session.

LEADING THE SESSION

1. Begin the session on time. If people realize that the session begins on schedule, they will work harder to arrive on time.

2. At the beginning of your first time together, explain that these sessions are designed to be discussions, not lectures. Encourage everyone to participate, but realize some may be hesitant to speak during the first few sessions.

3. Don't be afraid of silence. People in the group may need time to think before responding.

4. Avoid answering your own questions. If necessary, rephrase a question until it is clearly understood. Even an eager group will quickly become passive and silent if they think the leader will do most of the talking.

5. Encourage more than one answer to each question. Ask, "What do the rest of you think?" or "Anyone else?" until several people have had a chance to respond.

6. Try to be affirming whenever possible. Let people know you appreciate their insights into the passage.

7. Never reject an answer. If it is clearly wrong, ask, "Which verse led you to that conclusion?" Or let the group handle the problem by asking them what they think about the question.

8. Avoid going off on tangents. If people wander off course, gently bring them back to the passage being considered.

9. Conclude your time together with conversational prayer. Ask God to help you apply those things that you learned in the session.

10. End on time. This will be easier if you control the pace of the discussion by not spending too much time on some questions or too little on others.

We encourage all small group leaders to use *Leading Life-Changing Small Groups* (Zondervan) by Bill Donahue and the Willow Creek Small Group Team while leading their group. Developed and used by Willow Creek Community Church, this guide is an excellent resource for training and equipping followers of Christ to effectively lead small groups. It includes valuable information on how to utilize fun and creative relationship-building exercises for your group; how to plan your meeting; how to share the leadership load by identifying, developing, and working with an "apprentice leader"; and how to find creative ways to do group prayer. In addition, the book includes material and tips on handling potential conflicts and difficult personalities, forming group covenants, inviting new members, improving listening skills, studying the Bible, and much more. Using *Leading Life-Changing Small Groups* will help you create a group that members love to be a part of.

Now let's discuss the different elements of this small group study guide and how to use them for the session portion of your group meeting.

THE BIG PICTURE

Each session will begin with a short story or overview of the lesson theme. This is called "The Big Picture" because it introduces the central theme of the session. You will need to read this section as a group or have group members read it on their own before discussion begins. Here are three ways you can approach this section of the small group session:

- As the group leader, read this section out loud for the whole group and then move into the questions in the next section, "A Wide Angle View." (You might read the first week, but then use the other two options below to encourage group involvement.)

- Ask a group member to volunteer to read this section for the group. This allows another group member to participate. It is best to ask someone in advance to give them time to read over the section before reading it to the group. It is also good to ask someone to volunteer, and not to assign this task. Some people do not feel comfortable reading in front of a group. After a group member has read this section out loud, move into the discussion questions.

- Allow time at the beginning of the session for each person to read this section silently. If you do this, be sure to allow enough time for everyone to finish reading so they can think about what they've read and be ready for meaningful discussion.

A WIDE ANGLE VIEW

This section includes one or more questions that move the group into a general discussion of the session topic. These questions are designed to help group members begin discussing the topic in an open and honest manner. Once the topic of the lesson has been established, move on to the Bible passage for the session.

A BIBLICAL PORTRAIT

This portion of the session includes a Scripture reading and one or more questions that help group members see how the theme of the session is rooted and based in biblical teaching. The Scripture reading can be handled just like "The Big Picture" section: You can read it for the group, have a group member read it, or allow time for silent reading. Make sure everyone has a Bible or that you have Bibles available for those who need them. Once you have read the passage, ask the question(s) in this section so that group members can dig into the truth of the Bible.

SHARPENING THE FOCUS

The majority of the discussion questions for the session are in this section. These questions are practical and help group members apply biblical teaching to their daily lives.

SNAPSHOTS

The "Snapshots" in each session help prepare group members for discussion. These anecdotes give additional insight to the topic being discussed. Each "Snapshot" should be read at a designated point in the session. This is clearly marked in the session as well as in the Leader's Notes. Again, follow the same format as you do with "The Big Picture" section and the "Biblical Portrait" section: Either you read the anecdote, have a group member volunteer to read, or provide time for silent reading. However you approach this section, you will find these anecdotes very helpful in triggering lively dialogue and moving discussion in a meaningful direction.

PUTTING YOURSELF IN THE PICTURE

Here's where you roll up your sleeves and put the truth into action. This portion is very practical and action-oriented. At the end of each session there will be suggestions for one or two ways group members can put what they've just learned into practice. Review the action goals at the end of each session and challenge group members to work on one or more of them in the coming week.

You will find follow-up questions for the "Putting Yourself in the Picture" section at the beginning of the next week's session. Starting with the second week, there will be time set aside at the beginning of the session to look back and talk about how you have tried to apply God's Word in your life since your last time together.

PRAYER

You will want to open and close your small group with a time of prayer. Occasionally, there will be specific direction within a session for how you can do this. Most of the time, however, you will need to decide the best place to stop and pray. You may want to pray or have a group member volunteer to begin the lesson with a prayer. Or you might want to read "The Big Picture" and discuss the "Wide Angle View" questions before opening in prayer. In some cases, it might be best to open in prayer after you have read the Bible passage. You need to decide where you feel an opening prayer best fits for your group.

When opening in prayer, think in terms of the session theme and pray for group members (including yourself) to be responsive to the truth of Scripture and the working of the Holy Spirit. If you have seekers in your group (people investigating Christianity but not yet believers), be sensitive to your expectations for group prayer. Seekers may not yet be ready to take part in group prayer.

Be sure to close your group with a time of prayer as well. One option is for you to pray for the entire group. Or you might allow time for group members to offer audible prayers that others can agree with in their hearts. Another approach would be to allow a time of silence for one-on-one prayers with God and then to close this time with a simple "Amen."

GETTING A GRIP ON YOUR LIFE

GENESIS 1:1—27

INTRODUCTION

No one likes being out of control. We all have a built-in desire and need for order in our lives. All of us desire to have a grip on our lives. The question is, how?

Most of us have tried the regular list of New Year's resolutions and have thrown in the towel before the end of January. We have been moved, motivated, and manipulated to make the big commitments, only to watch our lives continue spinning out of control.

Yet, we keep trying. We go on one more diet and commit to a new exercise program. We buy a new planner and declare that this year we will master our schedule rather than have our schedule master us. We get out our Bible, buy a blank journal, and say, "This is the year I'm going to get face-to-face with God." We mean business! We are serious! But we still struggle.

This series of studies will help you walk through some critical areas of life that we all want to have under control. But the first and essential step is to take an honest and rigorous look at your life. If you can't be honest with yourself and the members of your small group, it will be tough to get a grip on these areas. Open your heart to what God wants to do, be painfully honest, and anticipate great things in the weeks to come. God wants to see you get a grip on your life even more than you do!

THE BIG PICTURE

Take time to read this introduction with the group. There are suggestions for how this can be done in the beginning of the leader's section.

A WIDE ANGLE VIEW

Question One We all have stories to tell. Some will be humorous and others very serious. Inviting group members to tell their stories will be a great way to learn some of their personal history as well as hear about how they have responded to times when they were out of control.

A Biblical Portrait

Read Genesis 1:1–27

Question Two Genesis teaches that God created the beauty of this world out of shapeless, chaotic nothingness. Not only did He bring order to chaos, the order He established is extraordinary. Just look at the world around you: the colors, the animal life, the ecosystems, the planets in orbit—all of this was put in place by the hand of a powerful and orderly Creator.

Even the succession of days in Genesis and the progression of what God made shows purpose and order. The very nature and character of God is seen in creation. He made it all and grips it firmly in His hand. We are not set adrift in a sea of space, but are safely under the control of a loving and powerful Creator.

Question Three I suppose part of the reason we feel such discomfort when something in our own lives is out of control is because we have been made in the image of an orderly Creator. Just look at creation, the sequence of the seasons, the regularity of the sunrise, the symmetry of the human body, and the movement of the celestial bodies. There is no denying that God is an orderly Creator.

We are made in the image of an orderly Creator, and have been called to live well-ordered lives. God has given us guidelines and laws to help order our lives. He never intended for us to live in chaos. He knew we could never enjoy life if we were spinning out of control.

He didn't ordain straightjacket living and legalistically regimented lives. But He does want us to live with some form of balance and order. If God's character is one of order, and we have been made in His image, then we will find the greatest level of fulfillment in life when we reflect the character of an orderly Creator.

Sharpening the Focus

Read Snapshot "An Honest Look at Your Life" before Question 4

Question Four Three pie graphs are given as examples. Each one gives a window into what a person's life might look like.

Take time as a group to unpack some of the implications of each life represented.

Question Five Now we are moving from the abstract to the concrete. Let's stop talking about some hypothetical person on a pie graph and take a good look into a mirror at ourselves. This is a tender topic. Many people spend a great deal of time and energy to be sure no one ever sees the picture they are about to draw (including themselves).

As you enter this portion of the study, do so prayerfully and with great sensitivity. For some, this kind of self-examination and self-disclosure may come easily. For others, there may be resistance and fear. You may want to pause as a group for a brief time of prayer. Ask for God to grant courage to each group member as they reflect on their life.

Questions Six & Seven Begin with the positive. Celebrate the areas where group members are experiencing control. Rejoice that they have a grip on these areas of life. Next, reflect on those areas where there is a desire to get a grip. Don't talk about these as areas of failure, but lift them up as areas where there is a deep desire to see the particular area come under control.

**Read Snapshot "It's Time to Get a Grip"
before Question 8**

Questions Eight & Nine Now we are going to get very specific. There will be five primary areas of focus in the rest of this study. Take time for personal reflection on each area. Give a few minutes for group members to quietly pray, think about, and mark where they see themselves in each of the five areas. When you pull back together, the focus will not be an all-out disclosure of every area; simply invite group members to communicate one area in which they desire prayer from the other group members. This could form a great prayer list for the coming weeks as well as direction for prayer as you close your group.

Also encourage group members to celebrate one area where there is strength. One person's story of having a grip in a particular area might just give another group member the inspiration they need to believe God can help them gain control of this area in their life.

PUTTING YOURSELF IN THE PICTURE

Tell group members that you will be providing time at the beginning of the next meeting for them to discuss how they have put their faith into action. Let them tell their stories; however, don't limit their interaction to the two options provided. They may have put themselves into the picture in some other way as a result of your study. Allow for honest and open communication.

Also, be clear that there will not be any kind of a "test" or forced reporting. All you are going to do is allow time for people to volunteer to talk about how they have applied what they learned in your last study. Some group members will feel pressured if they think you are going to make everyone provide a "report." You don't want anyone to skip the next group because they are afraid of having to say they did not follow up on what they learned from the prior session. The key is to provide a place for honest communication without creating pressure and fear of being embarrassed.

Every session from this point on will open with a look back at the "Putting Yourself in the Picture" section of the previous session.

GETTING A GRIP ON YOUR SCHEDULE

ECCLESIASTES 3:1—13; EPHESIANS 5:15—20

INTRODUCTION

Trying to tame a schedule in our insanely busy world may seem impossible. It seems the pressure to move faster, produce more, and accomplish greater things never lets up. On the freeway of life, if you don't keep up the pace, you get run over!

In the midst of our pathologically fast-paced society, God calls us to get a grip on our schedule. We are called to move from imbalance to a place where God has control of every aspect of our lives. This is not only possible, it is what God expects of His followers.

THE BIG PICTURE

Take time to read this introduction with the group. There are suggestions for how this can be done in the beginning of the leader's section.

A WIDE ANGLE VIEW

Question One Contelmo writes his article with tongue in cheek. We will never build a relationship with God on ten minutes a day. It can't be done. We would like to think we can build a relationship with God in the same way we pick up a burger in the drive-thru lane at McDonald's. But a deep relationship with God requires energy, concentration, devotion, regular church attendance, Bible study, small groups, prayer, confession, and a lifetime of growth. There is no such thing as microwave Christianity.

A BIBLICAL PORTRAIT

Read Ecclesiastes 3:1–13; Ephesians 5:15–20

Question Two There is a time for everything, says Ecclesiastes. This means we are given the awesome task of discerning and deciding what needs to be done today. Every day we face countless options; we simply can't do everything. Part of growing as a follower of Christ is knowing what we need to do today, what can wait until tomorrow, and what does not need to be done at all!

Think of the words of Jesus in Matthew 6:34: "Therefore do not worry about tomorrow, for tomorrow will worry about itself. Each day has enough trouble of its own." With all the things we could do, we need to learn to ask the question, "What does God want me to do today?" God will never call us to do more than we can handle. When we get overextended and burned-out, that is our own doing.

Question Three This passage gives some general insights on how to use and not use our time. Encourage group members to draw these insights from the text. Finish your reflection on this biblical text by inviting group members to summarize the meaning of Paul's teaching in their own words. You may want to give a minute or two for group members to reflect on this and maybe even have them write down a clear sentence putting this message in their own words.

SHARPENING THE FOCUS

Read Snapshot "A Life Out of Balance" before Question 4

Questions Four & Five You may want to encourage group members to look back at the pie graph they drew in session one, question five. This may help prime the pump for discussion. All of us have areas to which we are devoting too much time and other areas that require greater focus and energy. Honest discussion about this will free each person to face areas in which they need to grow.

One area that will probably come up for many people is an overemphasis on work. Some are *addicted* to work, while others simply allocate large segments of their pie to work. When a large portion of our pie is taken up with vocational pursuits, the rest of the dimensions get crowded out and neglected. When this happens, you don't have time or energy to be the type of spouse, parent, or friend you need to be.

A Cornell University professor did a study to determine the average amount of time fathers spend with their small children on a daily basis. The professor actually put microphones on fathers and little children and recorded the direct interaction between them. They gathered the data, analyzed the results, and announced that the average amount of time the middle-class father spends with his small child is 37.7 seconds *per day*. Put that data on one side of the spectrum and then consider this: The average amount of time the middle-class child spends watching television per week in the preschool years is 54 hours. The next question is obvious: Who is raising that child? Who is influencing that little life? If our schedule is out of balance, the damage could be worse than we imagine.

Read Snapshot "A Life in Balance" before Question 6

Questions Six & Seven The picture of a life in balance has the illusion of being the best of all possible scenarios. Isn't balance the best thing? Well, if you look closely, you will see that, although there are some advantages, the place of faith is only one segment of the pie. This approach compartmentalizes faith as one part of life, removed from the rest. The problem with this picture of "balance" is that it is a facade. Keeping Christ in a box, in a compartment, in one little section of life will never work for the person who wants to become a fully devoted follower of Christ. As you will see in "A Life Beyond Balance," Christ should be in the center of every area of life, not just another aspect of life.

Read Snapshot "A Life Beyond Balance" before Question 8

Questions Eight & Nine Christ deserves to be at the center of our life. God doesn't seem to mightily use people who are committed to Him casually. Anything less than radical devotion makes a mockery out of what Christ has done for you.

What happens when Christ is at the center of your life? Think about the pie graph with the cross in the center. Imagine that cross being able to spin around like the pointer on a table game. The Bible says that if Christ is at the center of your life, He will be your guide. He will show the way. That means He will point to which area in your life needs to be emphasized at any given time.

It's rather simplistic to think that we are going to be able to keep all pieces of the pie equal for the rest of our lives. Our life ebbs and flows, and there are times when certain parts of our life will demand more attention. Those who work with distinct seasons understand this concept well. For CPAs, bookkeepers, and accountants, January 15 to April 15 means work up to their ears. During those months, things will feel out of balance. If Christ is at the center of your life and the freedom of the Holy Spirit leads you, the cross will point to your vocational life for that season. When that season is over, the Lord will move you over so you can make it up to your family, make it up recreationally, make it up spiritually.

Mothers with small children face this as well. Theirs is a season of radical focus on family. It may feel out of balance, but it is a time when service in the church and even personal pursuits may need to be put on the back burner. In the middle of it all, though, mothers need to be sure Christ is in the center of their life.

Having Christ in the middle of your life is the best way to handle the calendar monster. It is the most effective way to bring discipline to your schedule. He is the only One who can give you the assurance that your emphasis is right at that time in your life. He is alive, living and dynamic. He can move with the ebb and flow of your life. This is called "walking by the Spirit." There is great freedom in Christ. You can enjoy the confidence of knowing that your schedule is under God's control.

PUTTING YOURSELF IN THE PICTURE

Challenge group members to take time in the coming week to use part or all of this application section as an opportunity for continued growth.

GETTING A GRIP ON YOUR BODY

ROMANS 12:1—2; 1 CORINTHIANS 6:19—20

INTRODUCTION

Historically, Christians have emphasized the importance of the soul. Regretfully, we have emphasized the soul or spirit to the near exclusion of all the clear teaching in Scripture pertaining to the importance of the body. God certainly cares for souls, but He also cares for our bodies. God sees us as total beings, our body, soul, and spirit bound inextricably together. Dichotomization (splitting ourselves into body and soul) should be avoided at all costs. In short, God is concerned about you and all that makes you who you are. Your personality, your emotional makeup, your temperament, your body, your soul, and your spirit all matter to God. This session highlights what has been so grossly ignored in the church, the importance of our bodies.

THE BIG PICTURE

Take time to read this introduction with the group. There are suggestions for how this can be done in the beginning of the leader's section.

A WIDE ANGLE VIEW

Question One We all have stories to tell about victories and struggles on the battlefield of personal health. Start with the positive. Affirm the victories and steps of growth group members have taken. Then, allow group members to tell a few war stories. By putting this on the table up front, it will ease the tension about being honest about our struggles.

A BIBLICAL PORTRAIT

Read Romans 12:1–2; 1 Corinthians 6:19–20

Questions Two & Three God demonstrated His concern for our bodies in that He chose, by the power of His Holy

Spirit, to dwell in human bodies. In the Old Testament we read that God, at one point in time, decided to focus His presence among His people. In order to do that, He called them to build a tabernacle and, later, a temple. In those places God would periodically focus His presence. When He commanded the people to build the tabernacle and the temple, God was very specific about how they should be constructed. He demanded they be built with elaborate materials and decorations. They were ornate, surrounded by precious items, and impeccably maintained. These buildings were held in awe because God, from time to time, focused His presence there.

In the New Testament, the writers unfold a startling truth. God, they announced, had decided He was going to move. He would have a new address. He was not going to focus His presence in buildings anymore. The apostle Paul and others announced that God would take up residency in the bodies of individual believers.

God thinks so much of human bodies that when people become believers He lives inside each of them in the presence of His Holy Spirit. With this in mind, God has issued a comprehensive command concerning how we should treat our bodies. We are His temples and we should offer ourselves as living sacrifices.

SHARPENING THE FOCUS

Read Snapshot "God Cares About Your Body" before Question 4

Question Four God has richly provided for each of us. Take time as a group to openly celebrate what God has done to prove His concern for you through filling your needs.

Question Five What would change this week if God was physically walking with you through every moment? Could you imagine it? The God who loves you, who gave His Son for you, walking with you each step of the way? What would be different in your week? How would your speech change? How would you use your free time? How would you treat your family, friends, neighbors, colleagues at work? What would change?

In reality, God is with you each moment of every day. He sees what you do, hears what you say, even knows the intentions of your heart. Through the Holy Spirit, God is in and with you at all times.

Read Snapshot "What You Put In Your Body" before Question 6

Question Six This is where the proverbial rubber hits the road. If we are putting junk fuel into our bodies, we can expect poor performance. If we put top-grade fuel in the tanks of our lives, we can expect much better performance.

When we put junk in our systems for years and years and then experience physical deterioration and serious medical problems, we have no right to look angrily at heaven and demand an explanation of God. We wonder why He has arbitrarily chosen to afflict a person as righteous and pious as we are. In reality, we have been abusing our bodies for years, filling them with poisons. It is not God's fault at all.

A ten-year study was done on the effects of a high-cholesterol diet. It was no surprise to discover that a high-cholesterol diet increases blood pressure and produces higher rates of heart attack. A leading nutrition expert asks, "Does the U.S. have a health problem?" Look at it this way: Heart disease was unknown in 1900, but it is a major killer today. Most of the food in America today will support life, but it won't sustain health.

Most health problems underlying the leading causes of death in the U.S. could be modified by improvements in the diet. We buy food for taste, convenience, and according to habit, not according to nutritional needs. Processed foods have increased from ten percent of the American diet in 1940 to over sixty percent today. Forty percent of all Americans are overweight.

In addition, increasing numbers of our children are influenced by advertising, and those children are growing up overweight. Breakfast cereals, cookies, candy, gum, snacks, tarts, and frozen waffles make up about two-thirds of the televised food advertising directed at children. These advertisements have subtle ways of leading children to believe that the product is not only delicious and fun to eat, but even good for them. The foods children are allowed to consume during the first years of life usually become their favorites. We need to begin with ourselves, but also teach the next generation to fill their bodies with fuel that will lead to a high-performance life that will honor God.

Read Snapshot "How You Condition Your Body" before Question 7

Question Seven We can all come up with plenty of reasons why it is hard to exercise and establish a pattern of regular physical conditioning. Be honest about these roadblocks to health and also discuss how you can remove them. Invite other group members to encourage you, pray for you, and keep you accountable. You might even find a commitment to walk, run, or exercise together. Partnering up is one great way to create regular accountability in this area of life.

Read Snapshot "How You Use Your Body" before Question 8

Questions Eight & Nine Finish your session by expressing practical goals for growth in getting a grip on your personal health. The goals will vary: running on a regular basis, changing eating habits, quitting smoking, getting more sleep, or some other practical sign of desired growth in this area. Be sure to close the group by praying for those who have committed to a specific growth goal toward getting a grip on their body.

PUTTING YOURSELF IN THE PICTURE

Challenge group members to take some time in the coming week to use part or all of this application section as an opportunity for continued growth.

GETTING A GRIP ON YOUR FINANCES

1 TIMOTHY 6:6–10; PROVERBS 30:8–9; HEBREWS 13:5

INTRODUCTION

The goal of this session is to instruct and inspire you to get a grip on your money. The money monster is a hard character to pin down—after all, we live in a culture obsessed with earning, saving, and spending it! We have all been drawn into the maze of confusion surrounding money. What we need to do is learn how to get a grip on our finances so that we will not fall prey to the patterns that will cause the fear, anxiety, frustration, and friction so often associated with personal finances. In this session we will focus on the three greatest threats to your personal financial freedom: the effect of deceitful advertising; the availability of easy credit; and the absence of disciplined budgeting practices. The goal will be to become free from the magnetic pull of finances so we can turn the attention of our lives to loving others and God with all our heart, soul, mind, and strength.

THE BIG PICTURE

Take time to read this introduction with the group. There are suggestions for how this can be done in the beginning of the leader's section.

A WIDE ANGLE VIEW

Question One Money can bring great joy and freedom. It can also cause despair and pain beyond description. Begin your group by describing how you have experienced both extremes of this spectrum.

A BIBLICAL PORTRAIT

Read 1 Timothy 6:6–10; Proverbs 30:8–9; Hebrews 13:5

Questions Two & Three The Bible is filled with teaching on how to deal with personal finances. I once heard it said that two-thirds of Jesus' parables have something to do with money. Jesus' teachings on money inform us that there is a lot more to life than the almighty dollar and what it can buy. Jesus says some pretty strong stuff about people who are obsessed with a desire to acquire more money; without apology He calls them fools. It is foolish men and women who pursue money and material things as a life goal.

The Bible says that money in the hands of the right people, if it is handled the right way, can accomplish wonderful works for God and others. Money can be used to feed the hungry, clothe the naked, help the sick, support families, educate children, allow for travel, and expand opportunities, among other good things. Money can be used to support widows and orphans and advance the spreading of God's love through kingdom activity.

But the Bible says that money in the hands of the wrong people, people who mismanage money, can end up wreaking havoc in our society. That type of money can stir up sins of greed, oppression, envy, self-centeredness, inequity, and injustice. That is why the Bible teaches that the love of money is the starting point of all kinds of evil.

I've seen both sides of this, and so have you! I've seen people who have their money in the proper perspective. They have decided how much energy to invest in earning money and are not addicted to earning it. I've seen followers of Christ learn how to control money so that it doesn't control them. I've seen them invest it wisely and share it generously. These people seem to handle money and they live with freedom. They have confidence and satisfaction with all of their financial affairs. They have a grip on their money, and this should be the goal for each of our lives.

SHARPENING THE FOCUS

Read Snapshot "Beware of the 'Permissible Lie'!" before Question 4

Questions Four & Five When it comes to advertising, almost anything goes. Whole truths become half-truths. Reality becomes fantasy. Persuasion becomes manipulation. The problem is that we are bombarded from all sides by these campaigns. Every newspaper, magazine, billboard, neon sign, radio, television program, and airport concourse we go down blares out a message. Buy this, try this, travel here, believe our slogan, trust our promise. The sheer volume wears down our defenses.

Beyond the volume of this avalanche of advertisements is the effectiveness of some of them. They make us feel like *we have to buy*. I come home from a long day at work, sit down on one edge of the couch, and flip on the evening news. All of a sudden, I see a familiar restaurant ad. In living color I see a plate right in front of my face. I am already hungry when I see it . . . the green lettuce, yellow corn, a huge sizzling steak. Next to the luscious steak are crab legs, swimming in melted butter. A hand comes into the picture squeezing a lemon and the camera captures every crystal of lemon juice spurting all over the place. Without even thinking, I begin drooling. I find myself calling out to my wife, Lynne, "What's for dinner?" She says casually from the kitchen, "Lentil burgers and trail mix." Or at least that is the way it sounds as my eyes are still transfixed on the plate of food on the television. How can she compete with this carefully crafted image? Everything inside of me wants to say, "Let's go out tonight!" Have you ever been there?

I think the beer ads top them all. After watching a professional football game you end up feeling like a freak of nature if you don't drink beer. The advertisements hammer you, one after another. You start thinking, *I want to sit around the red-checked tablecloths and slap people on the back and share in the joy, laughter, and camaraderie that seems to always accompany throwing back a few cold ones*—at least in the commercials. If you watch enough beer ads, you end up thinking that real fellowship happens best in bars.

I was watching a football game with a recovering alcoholic once and after a big beer ad he muttered something to the effect, "They make hell look like heaven." I knew exactly what he meant. I would love to demand equal time from the beer companies. I would like them to show a family going through an intervention because Dad has just lost his job and beat up Mom again. Maybe we could hear a brief story told by a little girl who is growing up without a daddy because someone got drunk and decided they could drive themselves home. This is the part of the story we never see in slick advertisements.

Read Snapshot "I Want It All, and I Want It Now" before Question 6

Questions Six & Seven Proverbs 22:7 warns us about the lure of easy credit. It tells us that the borrower becomes the lender's slave. The concept of slavery can create vivid pictures in our minds. We think of those who are bound, trapped, and despairing, sensing they would never be free. That is exactly what it feels like when you get involved in easy credit and have to deal with large monthly payments. You are a slave. You feel trapped and bound. Suddenly you realize that even if you keep making the monthly payments, you will probably never get out of the trap.

You should never borrow on a depreciating item. This rules out almost everything, with the exception, perhaps, of real estate or a home. If you borrow for furniture, appliances, clothing, or anything that drops in value quickly, the minute you walk out of the store you have taken a beating. Now you are paying on something that is worth less and less. Above all else, beware of credit cards. Use them for identification purposes only. Pay everything in cash. Learn how to say no. You will never get a grip on your finances until you learn how to say no to easy credit.

Read Snapshot "When Spending Spins Out of Control" before Question 8

Question Eight Close your group with a time of truth-telling. Have group members finish one of the question's statements. Encourage other group members to respond if they have some perspective or wisdom to communicate.

PUTTING YOURSELF IN THE PICTURE

Challenge group members to take time in the coming week to use part or all of this application section as an opportunity for continued growth.

GETTING A GRIP ON YOUR SPIRITUAL LIFE

HEBREWS 4:14—16; 10:19—25

INTRODUCTION

There are many motivating factors when it comes to attending church. There are also many motivations for growing in our spiritual lives. In this session, we will not focus primarily on church attendance, though this is certainly a key part of growing as followers of Christ. Instead, we will focus on how we approach the topic of spiritual growth. We will identify some of the pitfalls of the militaristic and libertarian approaches, and we will then focus on the value of a creative and dynamic approach to our spiritual lives that invites freedom and room for the Holy Spirit to work within us every moment of every day.

THE BIG PICTURE

Take time to read this introduction with the group. There are suggestions for how this can be done in the beginning of the leader's section.

A WIDE ANGLE VIEW

Question One Each person has their own set of reasons for attending worship. Although spiritual growth through corporate worship is not the primary focus of this session, this discussion will help group members get a pulse on what has motivated them toward spiritual growth in the past and what is motivating them now.

A BIBLICAL PORTRAIT

Read Hebrews 4:14–16; 10:19–25

Questions Two & Three It is human nature to feel unworthy in the presence of a perfect and holy God. Too many followers of Christ avoid intimacy with God because they feel unworthy. The good news of God is that He loves us even though we don't deserve it. Through Christ and His shed blood on the cross, the way to relationship with our heavenly Father has been opened.

We can draw near to the Father with boldness and confidence. Just think about it. The Maker of heaven and earth has thrown open His door and said, "Drop in any time!" When God extends an invitation, He means it. He wants us to connect with Him all through the day. He has opened the way so that we can experience the joy of a day-by-day, moment-by-moment relationship with Him.

SHARPENING THE FOCUS

Read Snapshot "The Militaristic Approach" before Question 4

Questions Four & Five When someone encourages a follower of Christ to adopt a militaristic approach to devotions, they are not giving an entirely bad idea. What they are suggesting is really a good thing. What can be wrong with reading the Bible and praying in a regular and disciplined way? As a matter of fact, biblical illiteracy is rampant throughout all Christendom. Some people have only a thimbleful of God's truth. They have never really learned the truth of God's Word. Reading your Bible expands your vistas of understanding of who God is and how faithful He has been throughout history. This is essential and imperative.

However, although this approach can be valuable, it is not the best approach. Even though there are some advantages to a rigorous, regimented, militaristic style of devotions, there are certainly some shortcomings. The first is that it has a tendency to compartmentalize your relationship with Christ. It's as though He intensely impacts about thirty minutes a day. After you have had your devotion, you get up from the table, put your Bible away, and go on with your day . . . business as usual.

Another concern about this approach is that it has a tendency to become mechanical, repetitious, and meaningless. The same old, same old can often lead to boredom.

This approach can also produce enormous amounts of guilt. If you don't keep up the regimen, you feel terrible. You have let down God and yourself! If this time feels dry or you miss a few days, you can feel like a real failure.

Now imagine keeping the regimen faithfully, day in and day out, so that you have it down to a pat routine. This can breed a poisonous form of spiritual pride. A group of Christians is sitting around the breakfast table and one guy says, "Well, this morning at 4:30, while I was having my devotional time . . ." and everyone around the table cringes. They feel bad that they are not as spiritual as him, and he feels great because of his disciplined spiritual exploits. Everyone looks at him and thinks, *Four-thirty, Wow! I barely made this meeting today, and this spiritual giant was up at four-thirty spending time with God!* The problem is, this is probably the exact reaction he was looking for. Pride has taken over.

Read Snapshot "The Libertarian Approach" before Question 6

Questions Six & Seven If I had to choose which extreme I would counsel people to take, I would encourage them to go on the militaristic side—at least it would help them develop consistent habits of Bible study and prayer. I have yet to meet a person with a libertarian attitude toward building a relationship with God who ever amounted to much spiritually. These folks rarely help others, they are sporadic in growth, and they almost never have a fire burning in their life. I don't see libertarians with a real zeal for God. They don't tend to experience great strides in building their relationship with Christ.

They have a tendency to let their relationship with Christ slide and watch their Bibles grow dusty. Their hearts get cold as they wait for the "feeling" to move them. Sadly, many of these people eventually fall away from the Lord.

Read Snapshot "The Creative-Relational Approach" before Question 8

Question Eight Most of us have had those wonderful times of feeling connected to God. In the middle of a busy schedule, we sense God's presence and love. Communication flows freely and the relationship is sweet. Tell some stories of these moments and celebrate how God reveals His presence in our lives.

Question Nine We all face things that act as roadblocks to intimacy with God. Identify where these exist in various areas of life. Identify the roadblocks and communicate ways you can remove these from your spiritual lives.

PUTTING YOURSELF IN THE PICTURE

Challenge group members to take time in the coming week to use part or all of this application section as an opportunity for continued growth.

GETTING A GRIP ON YOUR RELATIONSHIPS

GENESIS 2:15—23; PSALM 133:1

INTRODUCTION

In this final session we will focus on the significance of relationships. It is critical that we establish strong ties with people who will positively influence our life. To a highly relational person who has many close friends, the richness of community is something they already experience. This session will be an affirmation and encouragement to go even deeper in their relationships. To the Lone Ranger types, the significance of relationships is still not clear. In this session we will focus on five reasons for pursuing strong, meaningful relationships. God made us to be in relationship, and we need to commit ourselves to get a grip on this essential element of a healthy life.

THE BIG PICTURE

Take time to read this introduction with the group. There are suggestions for how this can be done in the beginning of the leader's section.

A WIDE ANGLE VIEW

Question One Open your small group with a celebration of those people who mean a great deal to you. What do they add to your life, and what would you miss if they were gone?

When I think about the rich relationships I have, many memories flood my mind. I remember a time I went with some men from our church staff to Camp Paradise (our church camp). We spent a couple days shoveling snow off cabin roofs because we were concerned they might come crashing in due to the snow load. One night, as we sat exhausted around a fire in one of the cabins, we spent the evening counting our blessings. One of the guys said, sort of out of the blue, "I count this moment as one of my greatest blessings. Being with friends and experiencing rich relationships, that's real joy!" He said, "It is staggering for me to think that if I really needed transportation for two or three weeks, there are four or five people who would give me their car. If I needed a loan, I can think of four or five people who would give me a loan. If I needed help around my house for something, I could think of four or five people who would be there just at a phone call." He meant every word of it, and we all sat there with a deep sense that he was absolutely right.

A BIBLICAL PORTRAIT

Read Genesis 2:15–23; Psalm 133:1

Question Two God made us to be in relationship. When Adam was alone, God looked at the situation and said, "This is just not right. Something is missing from this picture." Until Adam was in relationship, things were not right. Once Adam and Eve were in relationship, things were "Very good!" From the very start, God's plan was community.

Question Three God's design for us is not simply relationships, but good, healthy relationships marked by unity. Take time as a group and reflect on what a relationship looks like when two people are experiencing unity. Paint a picture of what a relationship can look like when unity pervades the life of each person. Next, turn that coin over and discuss what marks a relationship that is filled with disunity. God's desire is for us to live together in unity. To know what this means, we need to have a picture of what unity and disunity look like.

SHARPENING THE FOCUS

Read Snapshot "Putting an End to Aloneness" before Question 4

Question Four We have all faced lonely times. Sometimes we can feel the deepest loneliness when we are surrounded by people! Allow time for group members to tell their stories. Also reflect on how deep and real relationships helped you through the lonely times.

Read Snapshot "Meaningful Relationships Multiply Our Joy" before Question 5

Question Five Joy is contagious. Just as we have all faced times of loneliness, we have also experienced the heights of joy. If relationships really do multiply joy, do some multiplication as a group and tell your stories of joy.

Read Snapshot "Meaningful Relationships Divide Our Sorrows" before Question 6

Question Six Some years ago my wife and I were leading a discipleship group. For the first six or eight months I had felt like I had to sell the idea of community to our group. We would do the lessons, pray together, do our memory work together, and study the Bible, but somehow it just felt like we were not connecting on a deep level. Then, a strange thing happened. One of the members of our group found out he had to have a serious surgery. The night before he had surgery our whole group got together and went to the hospital. We asked the nurse if we could have a little conference room and she gave permission. The ten of us sat around a little conference table and began to pray. Through this process, I could feel ten strangers becoming family. After everyone had prayed, the brother we were praying for wanted to pray, but he struggled. His struggle was not a fear of praying, but that he had been touched by community. Here were people he didn't really even know eight months before, yet who were all there, holding him up in prayer. This is dividing your sorrows. This is the joy of community.

Read Snapshot "Meaningful Relationships Afford Us Counsel" before Question 7

Question Seven The best way to experience the reality of how valuable counsel can be is to open the door to receive counsel. Take time as a group to communicate a specific area of life where you need the counsel of other Christ followers. Listen as other group members give you their perspective and wisdom.

Read Snapshot "Meaningful Relationships Create a Place for Accountability" before Question 8

Questions Eight & Nine Proverbs 27:17 says, "As iron sharpens iron, so one man sharpens another." We are called to sharpen the lives of our brothers and sisters. Do you know what would happen to your spiritual life, your business life, your financial life, or your physical life if you would give others full access? Dramatic change would be inevitable! You could not stop it.

It is time to say, "I want to be a godly man. I want to be a godly woman. I invite you into my life and I want you to hold me to the truth. I want you to coach me. I want you to confront me. I want you to cheer me on. I want you to tell me what I am doing right and what I am doing wrong. Show me how I could do it better. You pray for me and love me and I will do the same thing for you." If you would do that with just one brother or sister, there would be a radical transformation in your life.

PUTTING YOURSELF IN THE PICTURE

Challenge group members to take time in the coming week to use part or all of this application section as an opportunity for continued growth.

ADDITIONAL WILLOW CREEK RESOURCES

Small Group Resources

Coaching Life-Changing Small Group Leaders, by Bill Donahue and Greg Bowman
The Complete Book of Questions, by Garry Poole
The Connecting Church, by Randy Frazee
Leading Life-Changing Small Groups, by Bill Donahue and the Willow Creek Team
The Seven Deadly Sins of Small Group Ministry, by Bill Donahue and Russ Robinson
Walking the Small Group Tightrope, by Bill Donahue and Russ Robinson

Evangelism Resources

Becoming a Contagious Christian (book), by Bill Hybels and Mark Mittelberg
The Case for a Creator, by Lee Strobel
The Case for Christ, by Lee Strobel
The Case for Faith, by Lee Strobel
Seeker Small Groups, by Garry Poole
The Three Habits of Highly Contagious Christians, by Garry Poole

Spiritual Gifts and Ministry

Network Revised (training course), by Bruce Bugbee and Don Cousins
The Volunteer Revolution, by Bill Hybels
What You Do Best in the Body of Christ—Revised, by Bruce Bugbee

Marriage and Parenting

Fit to Be Tied, by Bill and Lynne Hybels
Surviving a Spiritual Mismatch in Marriage, by Lee and Leslie Strobel

Ministry Resources

An Hour on Sunday, by Nancy Beach
Building a Church of Small Groups, by Bill Donahue and Russ Robinson
The Heart of the Artist, by Rory Noland
Making Your Children's Ministry the Best Hour of Every Kid's Week, by Sue Miller and David Staal
Thriving as an Artist in the Church, by Rory Noland

Curriculum

An Ordinary Day with Jesus, by John Ortberg and Ruth Haley Barton
Becoming a Contagious Christian (kit), by Mark Mittelberg, Lee Strobel, and Bill Hybels
Good Sense Budget Course, by Dick Towner, John Tofilon, and the Willow Creek Team
If You Want to Walk on Water, You've Got to Get Out of the Boat, by John Ortberg with Stephen and Amanda Sorenson
The Life You've Always Wanted, by John Ortberg with Stephen and Amanda Sorenson
The Old Testament Challenge, by John Ortberg with Kevin and Sherry Harney, Mindy Caliguire, and Judson Poling

WILLOW
Willow Creek Association

Willow Creek Association
Vision, Training, Resources for Prevailing Churches

This resource was created to serve you and to help you build a local church that prevails. It is just one of many ministry tools that are part of the Willow Creek Resources® line, published by the Willow Creek Association together with Zondervan.

The Willow Creek Association (WCA) was created in 1992 to serve a rapidly growing number of churches from across the denominational spectrum that are committed to helping unchurched people become fully devoted followers of Christ. Membership in the WCA now numbers over 12,000 Member Churches worldwide from more than ninety denominations.

The Willow Creek Association links like-minded Christian leaders with each other and with strategic vision, training, and resources in order to help them build prevailing churches designed to reach their redemptive potential. Here are some of the ways the WCA does that.

- **The Leadership Summit**—a once a year, two-and-a-half-day conference to envision and equip Christians with leadership gifts and responsibilities. Presented live at Willow Creek as well as via satellite broadcast to over 130 locations across North America, this event is designed to increase the leadership effectiveness of pastors, ministry staff, volunteer church leaders, and Christians in the marketplace.

- **Ministry-Specific Conferences**—throughout each year the WCA hosts a variety of conferences and training events—both at Willow Creek's main campus and offsite, across the U.S., and around the world—targeting church leaders and volunteers in ministry-specific areas such as: small groups, preaching and teaching, the arts, children, students, volunteers, stewardship, etc.

- **Willow Creek Resources®**—provides churches with trusted and field-tested ministry resources in such areas as leadership, evangelism, spiritual formation, spiritual gifts, small groups, stewardship, student ministry, children's ministry, the use of the arts—drama, media, contemporary music—and more.

- **WCA Member Benefits**—includes substantial discounts to WCA training events, a 20 percent discount on all Willow Creek Resources®, *Defining Moments* monthly audio journal for leaders, quarterly *Willow* magazine, access to a Members-Only section on WillowNet, monthly communications, and more. Member Churches also receive special discounts and premier services through WCA's growing number of ministry partners—Select Service Providers—and save an average of $500 annually depending on the level of engagement.

For specific information about WCA conferences, resources, membership, and other ministry services contact:

Willow Creek Association
P.O. Box 3188
Barrington, IL 60011-3188
Phone: 847-570-9812
Fax: 847-765-5046
www.willowcreek.com

TOUGH QUESTIONS
Garry Poole and Judson Poling

Softcover

REALITY CHECK SERIES
by Mark Ashton

We want to hear from you. Please send your comments about this book
to us in care of zreview@zondervan.com. Thank you.